THEY ALL
FALL THE
SAME

THEY ALL
FALL THE
SAME

THEY ALL FALL THE SAME

A NOVEL

WES BROWNE

CROOKED LANE

NEW YORK

Copyright © 2025 by Wesley Browne

Published in the United States by Crooked Lane Books, an imprint of The Quick Brown Fox & Company LLC.

Crooked Lane Books and its logo are trademarks of The Quick Brown Fox & Company LLC.

Library of Congress Catalog-in-Publication data available upon request.

ISBN (hardcover): 978-1-63910-910-4
ISBN (ebook): 978-1-63910-911-1

Cover design by Lynn Andreozzi

Printed in the United States.

www.crookedlanebooks.com

Crooked Lane Books
34 West 27th St., 10th Floor
New York, NY 10001

First Edition: January 2025

10 9 8 7 6 5 4 3 2 1

For Mom and Dad

For Mom and Dad

Part 1

CHAPTER

1

Burl Spoon never lingered long over sex or a cigarette. Whitney knew she had to act fast. He'd already burned one and was sitting at the edge of her couch, pulling on his boots, when she came out of the bedroom, wearing a new summer dress.

"You leaving already? I was fixing to model some clothes for you." She hooked a finger under his chin, trying to get his eyes on her, but he didn't lift his head. He'd been distant like that since he got there. His daughter, DeeDee, was a no-call, no-show for her shift at his check-cashing store that morning. He'd showed up real agitated about it and kept checking his phone for a message, which wasn't like him.

Once he had both boots on, he stood up in his finest Western wear, beheld her, and finally acknowledged the wardrobe change. He whistled. "You're a sight, girl."

She pouted. "That's it? I got this one thinking you'd like it."

He jutted his lower lip. "It's real nice. I like them birds." He patted the wallet in his back pocket. "I got to be getting up the road, though. You good on money?"

She creased her nose. "Yeah. I'm fine."

He went into his wallet and pinched out an indeterminate number of bills. He dropped the knot of doubled-over cash on her coffee table. "Well, here's some more for you anyway. Why don't you get you some new shoes to go with that pretty dress."

Whitney knew well that money was Burl's cure-all. She looked at her bare feet and freshly painted toes. "You don't wear shoes with a dress like this; you wear boots. I just didn't put none on because *I ain't* the one running out the door."

She let the bills lie while Burl was at the mirror, shaping up his carefully kept pompadour. She still had hopes of coaxing him to get someone else to pick up his granddaughter from school. She'd thought modeling would do the trick. She'd put on a fashion show for him once before and back-loaded it with some real seductive stuff. It had gotten him all revved up, and she got her way, but the last time she'd commenced the show before they'd gotten intimate. Her current effort was looking bleak. She was beginning to grasp just how hard it was to reignite a man Burl's age. He was a spent shell.

Even in the face of it, Whitney had never been one to give in easily. She wasn't tall, but she was lithe, and at five feet four inches not much shorter than Burl, though he stood close to five seven atop his bootheels. She went to him and stood on her tiptoes, kissed him firmly on the mouth, and pressed herself against the pearl snaps on his ornately stitched shirt.

"You really can't send someone else? Why don't you stay here with me, cowboy? We'll have us a big time." She was awash in the smell of black raspberries and vanilla. That was the body spray she'd worn the first time they got together, and he'd gone on about it. Leaving nothing to chance, she'd added the lotion to her arsenal.

He patted her back. "You know I'd like to, but I got a lot pressing on me. I got to get to the school, I got me a goat kidding, and I got to sort out DeeDee. I'll be by again soon, though."

She scrunched her nose, let her hand trail down to his waistband and rest behind his belt buckle. "There isn't anything that would change your mind?"

"It ain't a question of that. I got to be where I got to be."

She flipped her hair. "What about later?"

"You mean tonight?"

"Yeah. I was thinking we could go over to Red Lobster. I been craving that shrimp scampi, and you could get you some of them Cheddar Bay Biscuits you like."

He smiled at her, took her by the wrist, withdrew her hand, and stepped back. "I'm afraid that ain't in the cards tonight. Why don't you go on over there? You could get you them boots you was talking about, and next time I come by, you could model the whole outfit for me. How'd that be?"

"Red Lobster don't taste as good alone."

Burl pulled in a deep breath and sighed it out just as long. "No, I know it don't, but it can't be helped." He tugged at the seams at the edges of his jeans and smoothed them down his thighs. "What about your little girlfriend Marci? I bet she'd eat some shrimp with you."

"You mean Mandy?"

"Yeah. Her."

Whitney crossed her arms. "We ain't talking."

Burl stepped toward the door leading out. "Well, that's too bad. Why's that?"

"Duh. Why you think?"

Burl pointed at his own chest.

"I done told you," she said.

"Well, shit. I'm sorry about that. Some people just ain't reasonable." He put one finger to his forehead on the way out, then extended it her way in a sort of hatless hat tip. "I do got to go, though. I'll be getting up with you directly."

When Burl opened the door, Mrs. Nelson, from across the breezeway, who always wore those Velcro-strapped diabetic shoes, was out there with a yellow plastic Dollar General bag dangling from her fingers. As many times as Whitney had told Burl who she was, he could never remember. Whitney had noticed he didn't really register people who couldn't advance his interests. Mrs. Nelson's eyes got stinky when she saw who it was leaving.

Burl said, "Afternoon, ma'am."

Her demeanor didn't change. "Burl Spoon, you got you a wife at home. It's a shameful thing you're doing. Shameful."

Burl took her in silently as his shoulders rose. Whitney knew she only had a moment to act before he took the old lady's head off. She laid her hand on his back. "Hey, Mrs. Nelson. I know we never talk, but I went to school with your grandson, John David. We ain't talked in ages, but I've known him since forever." She gestured at Mrs. Nelson's door. "The thing about that is, once a month I see you go in there with a Walgreen's bag. Then, not fifteen minutes later, John David turns up, and he packs that same bag out. Happens every month. Now, I know he sells pills, and I don't care about that. And I know where he gets them pills, and I don't care about that neither." Whitney shook her head. "But what I'm saying is, people ain't perfect. And if you ain't perfect, then you oughtn't go on about how other people ain't perfect. It ain't Christian."

Whitney squeezed Burl's shoulder while she waited to see if Mrs. Nelson had anything else to say, and hoped she didn't. She hoped the same of Burl. Mrs. Nelson's mouth trembled just a hair, but nothing came out. After the silence had drawn on a bit, Whitney pointed at a box protruding from Mrs. Nelson's shopping bag. "Oh, I like them Swiss Rolls too. Ain't they good?" Mrs. Nelson just stood there. Like if she was still enough, she'd disappear into the scenery, but her yellow bag swung gently.

CHAPTER

2

Burl sat behind the wheel of his black Cadillac in Whitney's parking lot and let it idle while he lit a cigarette and checked his phone. His satellite radio bumped the twang of the boy from Lawrence County who'd gotten so big. Burl was hoping for a text back from DeeDee. He wasn't much on texting, but when it came to DeeDee and her sporadic communication, he'd been conditioned to take what he could get. What he could get from her more often than answered calls was text messages. On this occasion, he got nothing.

DeeDee was always late to work—and pretty much anything else—but most of the time she showed up eventually, or at least she called in some lame excuse. That she hadn't had set him to worrying. DeeDee had a history, and her history had a bad way of repeating itself. It concerned Burl enough that he'd sent one of his boys by her house to look for her. Her car was there, but she wasn't.

As if that wasn't enough, Burl had gotten word that one of his pregnant goats was showing signs of kidding soon, and acting distressed. The two boys back at his farm, Clarence and Toby, were panicked because neither one was much of a hand when it came to livestock. Their talents fell more on the horticulture side, and the shooting at anyone who turned up on Burl's property side. They wanted no part of delivering a baby goat.

He knew he'd disappointed Whitney by thwarting her plans, but he was overbooked and out of sorts. If he'd given in to her, he wouldn't have enjoyed it. She was one of the few distractions from business he allowed himself. Ordinarily, seeing her was a way to get his mind off things, but he'd had a hard time clearing his thoughts. The world wasn't sitting right. He wasn't too concerned how Whitney felt about any of it because he knew she'd be right there waiting for him when he came back around.

Burl kept Whitney in spending money. He also took care of the rent on her apartment and her student loans. He gave her a car to drive. When he'd first gotten her number while she was serving him his dinner at Opal's Restaurant, she had a wide, dark stripe down the middle of her blonde hair the width of a dollar bill, and her nails looked like a mouse had chewed them. Now she never showed roots, kept her nails lacquered like a new Mustang, had real sharp eyebrows, and teeth that were impossibly white. Whitney, more than anyone before her, had absolutely risen to the task of being his diversion.

Throughout his marriage, Burl had been known to consort with women who were not his wife. He barely hid it. The dalliances usually sputtered out within a few weeks. After three decades of extramarital prowling, his longevity with Whitney was an outlier.

Anymore, most of the women in Jackson County willing to run around with someone like Burl had one problem or another. His money didn't fix those problems—it fed them. And even though he always went in suspecting it, he lost interest once he confirmed it.

As far as he could tell, Whitney didn't have any sort of drug issue. Add to that, she was going on thirty with no kids and no ex, a bona fide rarity. What she had was ambition. She'd studied accounting at a for-profit college in Richmond that had closed down. She'd gotten stuck with loans she couldn't pay and no degree. Sometimes she mentioned going back to school, like she was taking Burl's temperature about paying for it. She was trying to make a life. That was more than Burl could say for most of the women he'd trifled with. Most of their goals didn't extend past the next week or the next fix.

What really kept Burl's interest in Whitney was her interest in him. Like her proposing that they eat Red Lobster. It seemed like nobody else much cared if he was around after they'd gotten in his pockets, which usually suited him because he didn't want to stick around after he'd been in their beds. Whitney was the only one whose eyes stayed on him after the money came out. That charmed him. He didn't even care if the whole thing was an act, because even if it was, he admired her guile. He didn't have time to run off to Richmond for scampi and biscuits at the drop of a hat, but he was flattered she wanted to.

Burl's phone vibrated, giving him hope that DeeDee had turned up. Instead, it was a text message from Greek, who was second in command in his operations. Greek typically texted rather than called when he thought Burl was with Whitney. Greek wanted Burl to come by the body shop to check out their new wrecker. Burl had been in the auto body business for years but was just now dipping into towing. But he had a stop to make before he could head that way.

He dropped the car into gear and headed out. He rolled down his window a few inches and flicked the still smoldering filter of his already spent smoke onto the scarred and crumbling concrete. He was after another almost before the butt was on the ground. He turned left and got on the gas real heavy. He didn't like being too far back in the pickup line at the school.

There was a common sentiment that went around Jackson County. The first person to say it to Burl's face was one of his old middle school teachers. They were standing near the casket during a visitation at Lakes Funeral Home. Mrs. Hayes was ahead of him in line. "You're not all bad, Burl. You're just mostly bad." His teacher laughed as she said it, but there was no mistaking she'd meant it. He didn't smile, but he didn't argue with her either. In truth, he kind of liked for people to believe it. His purposes were best served by a healthy ration of fear. And at least it allowed him a small niche for goodness. That was twenty years ago. Mrs. Hayes was dead now too. Burl hadn't bothered going to her services.

At one time Burl felt like being a dad was the biggest part of him that fell into that niche of goodness. His son, Darron, was everything he could have asked for right up until he wasn't. Now they didn't speak. DeeDee had charmed him from the moment he laid eyes on her, and he spoiled her like you'd expect. Unfortunately, spoiled things tend to rot.

He'd gotten another chance at raising a child with DeeDee's daughter, Chelsea. Burl and his wife, Colleen, were Chelsea's de facto parents, and DeeDee really didn't seem to mind too much. It suited her situation, really.

Burl's days were busy: he ran one of the largest marijuana cultivation operations in Kentucky—where it still wasn't legal—as well as more than half a dozen other mostly legitimate businesses. After Chelsea came along, he carved out part of his routine to look after her. One of his responsibilities was dropping her off and picking her up from first grade at McKee Elementary. It was no chore for him. In fact, those were two of his favorite parts of the day. It was a week before summer break, and he already knew he'd miss their routine once school let out. Heading that way pulled him out of his funk a little bit.

* * *

Burl flicked another newly lit Marlboro Red into the school parking lot just as a teacher opened his rear passenger door and Chelsea climbed in. He never smoked when she was in the car. Not ever. And woe be to anyone else who lit up around her.

He greeted Chelsea, "How's Papaw's girl?" as she pushed her backpack into the back seat. She followed it in, and the teacher helped her buckle into her booster seat without either saying a word.

Burl tried again to strike up a conversation, asking after Chelsea's day, but she rode with her arms crossed for nearly a mile before finally speaking. "I got in trouble because of you, Papaw."

"Because of me? That ain't good. What'd I do?"

"Kaden Thatcher was aggravating me. He wouldn't quit. So, I said, 'Why don't you leave me alone, Kaden?'"

"That don't sound like nothing bad. Did you hit him or something?"

"Naw, I didn't hit him. I told him he was a fucking half-wit. Then I got in trouble. Mrs. McCoy made me sit in the time-out chair all recess."

Burl howled out laughing and slapped the steering wheel. He went a quarter mile before composing himself. "Now, no. You can't be saying that."

"But you say it all the time."

"I'm grown, darling. And I say it about grown people. You can't be saying that to ol' Kaden, even if it's true. He's just a little kid."

"Can I say it about grown people?"

"Hmm." Burl kneaded his chin. "You can say it to Papaw. How's that? That best be all. If your nana hears it, she won't like it too good."

"Okay." Chelsea met her Papaw's eyes in the rearview mirror. "Mrs. McCoy's a fucking half-wit."

Burl like to have beat the steering wheel right off the column.

3

"WE IN THE goddamn wrecker business now, boys," a twenty-something kid they called Pot Roast said, while running his hand along the side of the used Hino Rollback Burl had bought cheap out of Pennsylvania. Sheriff Horne, a deputy, and a few other of Burl's men milled around the shiny rig. Greek had set Chelsea in the driver's seat, and she pretended to steer.

"It's a real nice truck, Burl," Pot Roast said, beaming. "It didn't give us no trouble all the way back. Runs like a top."

Burl eyed it. "We got to get us some new wraps on the thing, but other than that, we're ready to go, ain't we?"

"Yeah. It being under twenty-six hundred, we ain't got to do nothing else," Pot Roast said, tugging at the neck of his Country Boy Brewing T-shirt, which bore their pickup truck logo. "I don't even need my CDL for it. I let Jared drive some, and he's doing pretty good with it."

"All right then. You done good, Pot Roast." Burl turned his attention to Sheriff Horne. "Make sure all the boys know to send all their tow calls our way." Burl glanced at his wristwatch. "I need to talk to you right quick, but then I got to go. One of my mama goats is about to pop."

"All right, Burl." The sheriff held his brown campaign hat in both hands in front of him. His tan uniform had dark brown pockets to match the hat. He had the physique of a squat trash can, and his blunt mustache had begun to gray. He didn't cut a real impressive figure, but he was who Burl wanted to be sheriff, so that meant he got it.

The men stepped aside, and Burl's voice dropped. "I need your boys to keep an eye out for DeeDee, all right? She didn't show up to work this morning, and her car's home but she ain't there."

"Shit, Burl." The sheriff winced. "I was fixing to talk to you about her."

Burl glowered. "What now?"

"One of the boys said he heard she's been going out of county a lot. That there's rumors coming back."

"Like what?"

"Like using again. Not sure what all. I hope it ain't true, but you might want to get up with your state boy in Richmond to look about her."

Burl pinched the sheriff's sleeve and brought him closer. "Why ain't you tell me sooner? I could've put Greek on it."

"This is my first opportunity since finding out. You know I don't keep nothing from you, Burl. We do the best we can, but unless you want one of my boys riding with her everywhere she goes, I can only do so much."

Burl turned loose of him, but his brow was tight knit. "Goddamn. I's hoping like hell rehab had took this time. Like trying to babysit a cricket in a cow field." He slapped his own pant leg. "Greek's got him a way he can track her. We'll run her down. I got to get."

Burl put his fingers to his lips and whistled to get Greek's attention. Greek cut a hulking figure and was pale as could be wherever he wasn't darkly tattooed, which was most everywhere up to the top of his neck. The stark variation in coloring between his skin and his tats made his arms look something like the limbs of a paper birch. The many bats on his forearms represented kills he'd made, mostly overseas but a few close to home. Greek would do anything Burl asked him. And Burl asked a lot.

Chelsea held Greek's hand and skipped Burl's way, but her head was swiveled back at the tow truck. "I want to honk the horn, Greek."

"Next time, Peanut," Burl said. "Go get in Papaw's car, and I'll be there to strap you in."

Chelsea went on, but she was still fixated on the truck. Burl rapped Greek on the arm with the back of his hand. "I need you to find DeeDee and bring her to me. She may be into something she hadn't ought to be into, and we got to get that lined out."

"Where's she at?"

"Not sure. If she still ain't home, she may be in Richmond. Horny says she's sneaking over there and using again. I've still not heard from her."

"Fuck."

"Well, get up with her, and we'll figure out what's what."

"What if she don't answer me either?"

"You can still track her phone, right?"

"I can."

"Get her that way, then. I don't care how you get her, just get her, and bring her home. We'll figure it out then."

"I'll find her."

Burl put a hard pack of Marlboro Reds to his mouth and plucked one out with his lips. He drew a matte black Zippo toward it, and just as the flame licked the end orange, he flicked it closed. "Goddamn it." He'd forgotten he was driving Chelsea. He broke the smoke in half between his fingers and threw it over his shoulder.

CHAPTER

4

B URL OWNED A lot of guns, but he mostly carried the same
three .38s, two at a time, one in his waistband and a
second on his ankle. The gun at his ankle never changed, but
he carried a snake gun at his waist whenever he was in the
woods or out on his farm. Pearl-handled, so he could tell the
difference, and loaded with shot shells. That's what he had
tucked to him as he and Chelsea rode through the hills of his
farm out to his goat pasture in a four-seat RZR, the air thick
with pollen and the smell of it.

Seeing the goats was Chelsea's favorite part of their routine. She always ran among the new kids, giggling her curly
head off at their antics. Burl's men had let him know the
expectant mother was showing signs of kidding real soon,
and Chelsea was excited to see the new baby born.

Burl knew before he got out to get the gate unlatched
that this would be no giggling trip. The boys had put the
mother in a large enclosure by herself, thinking that'd be better, but it was a mistake. Burl found the chain and got his key
in the lock, but his eyes were up. His herd of goats stood
huddled near the fence line shared with the next enclosure
over, agitated and grumbling at a wake of black vultures and
one turkey vulture feeding.

Chelsea stood in the RZR, trying to get a look. "What're them birds doing up there, Papaw?"

Burl held the gate in one hand and his chin in the other. "I ain't sure, honey." He was sure, though. "Why don't you wait here and let Papaw go on up and have him a look?"

Burl closed the gate behind him and left Chelsea looking uncertain. He made his way slowly until he was roughly twenty yards away, and the birds began to take some notice. He could see what was left of the mother goat's carcass at their feet. Black vultures weren't shy about taking live animals when the opportunity arose. Anything vulnerable. Nothing was more vulnerable than a laboring mother left all by herself. Turkey vultures joined in once an animal was down.

He crouched as their eyes found him, and he unholstered the .38 at his ankle. He raised it just as the half dozen birds took wing. He unloaded when they rose as one, but a piece of the whole broke off. A single black vulture contorted and plunged back to the ground in a grotesque heap and commenced a disordered hopping, one wing flapping uselessly. Burl rose and replaced the weapon as he strode up the hill, exchanging it for the pearl-handled snake gun. The vulture flapped and spun about a car length from the nearly stripped goat's carcass. Burl drew near and spit at the bird. "Sack of shit." He plastered the vulture's gnarly head with number six shot, making it no more than formless spray. All flapping ceased. He'd committed a federal offense. Black vultures were protected by the Migratory Bird Act and could only be killed with a permit. Something Burl never would have bothered to get.

When Burl got back to the RZR, Chelsea was still standing, peering up the hill. "Was that a bad bird, Papaw? You killed it."

"Your Papaw wouldn't kill a good bird, would he?" Burl locked the gate back. He climbed into the driver's seat.

"Them dogs is probably ready for a run. What say we go see Waylon and Johnny?"

"We ain't gonna see the goats?"

"Your Papaw's got to get one of the boys up here and take care of that bird first. Maybe we can come out and see them goats later."

"What was them birds doing?"

"They was taking what wasn't theirs to take." Burl cranked the engine and turned away. "I reckon we'll have to hang that old boy Papaw done in to make sure his friends know what happens when you take what ain't yours."

"Was that old bird a fucking half-wit, Papaw?"

Burl frowned. "Less of a half-wit and more just a thieving bastard."

5

ARRON WAS THE first child who altered Burl's view of himself as a parent. He'd made good enough grades at Jackson County High School to get an academic scholarship to Transylvania University in Lexington, where he was also recruited to play on the basketball team. Even though Burl and Darron didn't share the closest father–son bond, as far as Burl was concerned, his parenting had been tip-top. He fully expected Darron to come home after college and assume a role in the family business. That's not what happened.

Darron's sophomore year, he came out. Colleen had never verbalized anything before then, but she said she'd suspected for some time. She'd more or less accepted it before Darron confirmed it, and nothing changed for her. Burl was another story. He'd not seen it coming and made no attempt to stifle his displeasure. He could scarcely look at Darron, would hardly speak to him except for a stray dig, and hadn't done so much as pat his back in over ten years. Darron had stopped coming back to Jackson County at all. He'd moved to Louisville after graduation, and although Colleen visited him often, Burl wouldn't go.

About the time Darron revealed himself, DeeDee was a junior in high school. She was barely passing, came and went from home any hours she pleased, and only managed to stay out of juvenile court by virtue of her father's stranglehold on law enforcement and the Jackson County courts. During what would have been her senior year, she went to inpatient rehab for the first time. While she was there, she got her GED.

Burl thought she might be the type who liked work better than school, but putting her on as a clerk at any one of his convenience stores guaranteed two things: a short drawer and her friends loitering about the place. The dumber ones skimmed merchandise. Getting caught on camera meant a visit from one of Burl's men, and what those fools didn't pay for, they paid for.

The criminal justice system in Jackson County was slow and unreliable, largely by design. Burl's justice system was quite the opposite. It was fast and efficient. One young man named Daniel, who worked for Burl, decided to push the envelope more than the rest. As any pilot could have warned him, it ended in flames. It ended with Greek.

He might have survived if not for one big mistake. Daniel took up with DeeDee. Being with her meant feeding her habit, and feeding her habit led to stealing from Burl. In Burl's eyes, either of the two was a killing offense. All Daniel left DeeDee with was a stash of pills and a baby in her belly. That baby, Chelsea, was where Burl turned his efforts to make good where he thought he'd failed his own kids. To Burl's way of thinking, Daniel's absence only increased his chances. On Chelsea's birth certificate, no father was listed, and her last name was recorded as Spoon.

6

G REEK INSISTED ON riding out to Burl's house to update him on his hunt for DeeDee. When he arrived, Chelsea was out front with Burl's pair of black lab brothers, Waylon and Johnny. She had a rope toy she threw for the dogs to chase, and after tussling over it, one of them would eventually bring it back. Burl sat in one of the many rockers on the hanging-basket-decked wraparound porch with a smoke in one hand and a short glass of brown liquid and cubes in the other. The front door had a small metal sign hanging on it with a pineapple cut out of it. The symbol of welcome, although, in fact, very few people were.

As Greek ascended the porch, Burl asked, "What is it you got to report that you had to come all the way out here for?"

Greek stood at the rail and drummed his fingers against it. "She ain't home. Her car's there, but she's not. I banged on her neighbors' doors, but they ain't seen her in a day or two. Said there's always some vehicle or another coming to pick her up, but couldn't describe any. I asked."

"She never did want to drive herself. Too much fucking effort."

"I can't reach her on her phone either. No answer, no texts back, nothing."

Burl pushed back in his chair. "Unsurprising."

"So, I brought her location up on the app. It says she was last in Richmond, like you was saying. Out Greens Crossing. I called our boy at post over there to see what's at the address. He says she's probably at the Begley place."

"The fucking sod people?"

"That's what he said."

Burl stubbed out his cigarette in an ashtray at his feet and left it there smoldering. "Christ almighty. Worst fucking dopers in Madison County. Clovis's been dealing thirty years. I hear one of his boys is running with the Detroit boys now, slinging heroin."

"That'd be Micah."

"And that's who she's goddamn took up with? The fucking sod junkies. Why ain't you gone after her yet?"

Greek's fingers stilled. He went in his pocket for his phone and worked the screen. "When I track y'all's phones, it tracks all y'all's phones. Everyone on the account."

"So?"

"You mentioned Mrs. Spoon went to see Darron this weekend."

"Left this morning."

"For Louisville?"

Burl took a long pull from his drink and kept one cube in his mouth. He crunched on it as he spoke. "Yeah."

Greek turned his screen so Burl could see it, and Burl leaned in. "That's not where her phone went."

CHAPTER

7

BURL'S CADDY CORNERED hard over and again, but
Greek's black Challenger stayed glued to its tail all the
way to Boone's Trace, a development that sat at the crest of
the Kentucky River Palisades. There was a good bit of traffic
on I-75 North, but they hit one hundred more than once on
their way to exit 97 at the northern tip of Madison County.
If he'd thought about the fact that Chelsea was in Greek's
car, he may have slowed down, but Burl's mind was not there.

A fat man in thick glasses, wearing a gray security uniform, worked the entry gate at the head of the subdivision. He
came out of the booth with a clipboard. "Where you headed?"

Burl looked straight ahead. "This is a golf course,
ain't it?"

"You're going golfing?"

Burl wore jeans and a heavily stitched red Western shirt.
"That's right."

The guard looked him over before he handed him the
clipboard. "Let me get your name."

Burl wrote *Dave Bob* and handed it right back.

The guard went behind Burl's car and took down his license
plate number. While he did, Burl texted Greek: *Were golfing*

As soon as the arm went up, Burl went on, not waiting for Greek and Chelsea. He held his phone atop his steering wheel, watching the green circle with the picture of his wife's phone in the middle. Greek had added the app to Burl's before they lit out.

It was true that Boone's Trace had a golf course, but the vast majority of the development was houses, many of them on big, wooded lots. Avawam Drive ringed the entire community and was roughly five rolling miles all the way around. Burl took the left fork.

In tighter quarters it may have been more difficult to tell which driveway led to Colleen's phone, but given the spacing of the houses in Boone's Trace, it was easy. Burl turned left up a bending drive hugged by ripe green trees. His tires crackled over nuts and sticks that littered the blacktop. About a hundred yards in, he came to the house, an imposing brick number with two ostentatious turrets and a slate roof. Although the house had a three-car garage, Colleen's silver Mercedes sedan sat in a circular section of the drive out front. Burl pulled in opposite it.

He was out of his car, up the many steps to the elevated front porch, and ringing the bell before Greek's car came into sight. He kept it well back from where Burl and Colleen were parked, blocking the way out.

The doorbell was one of those deals with the camera in it, and a man's voice came out of it. "Can I help you?"

Burl bent at the waist and looked into the doorbell camera from six inches away. "Burl Spoon. I'm here to collect my wife."

The doorbell didn't have anything else to say. Burl pushed it again, but there was no response. After that didn't work, he started hammer-fisting the frame of the ornate double door beside the textured glass. The longer he pounded, the harder he hit.

Minutes passed before the door opened, and Colleen emerged with a small rolling suitcase, not looking at Burl. She tried to close the door behind her just as fast. He stuck his foot in it.

"Burl, don't." She grabbed him by the sleeve and pulled. "I'm leaving and you don't have any other business here."

He jerked his arm away. "Get your granddaughter and go on home."

For the first time she looked him in the face. Her eyes were blazing. "You brought the baby here? What the hell is wrong with you? My god."

"You goddamn right."

She grabbed his arm and pulled harder. "Let's go, Burl. Chelsea doesn't need to see this."

He pulled away again and took two steps back. "Get the hell on, then. Our goddamn daughter's missing and I got to come out here hunting you? Don't you try telling me shit."

Colleen stilled. She looked Burl up and down, like the sight of him made her want to retch. "The only reason I'm leaving is to get the baby out of here, but this is beyond the pale, even for you. So help me god, don't you hurt him. You have no right."

"Look here. I just want to talk to the man. Come to an understanding. I ain't gonna hurt him."

"Don't you dare." She locked eyes with him ten seconds before she went down the steps. Burl motioned and Greek got out of his car and let Chelsea climb from the back seat. She ambled up the drive toward Colleen.

Burl called to Chelsea, "Darling, your nana's going to take you on home. Papaw'll be there directly. You ask her nice, and I bet you she'd get you some Wendy's."

When Chelsea reached her grandmother, Colleen took her by the hand and chirped her key fob with the other. "Come on, Sweet Pea." Colleen helped Chelsea in and got her strapped in her booster before coming around to her driver door, getting in, and starting the engine. She stared hard at Burl. As she pulled out of the drive, Greek backed out in front of her, and she was gone. Shortly after, Greek's car returned to its previous location, impeding the exit.

Burl opened the door all the way, drew his fingers to his lips and whistled. "Hey now. It's time to come out. We need to talk." He looked around the grand entrance—at the travertine tile, the molding stacked on molding around the ceiling of the entryway, the massive chandelier.

"Mister, I'm gonna stand here, and I'm gonna smoke until you come talk to me. That's all I want." Burl fired up a Red. "And if you ain't out here pretty goddamn soon, I'll find me something else to light. How'd that be?"

Burl had the fingers of his left hand tucked in his waistband while he smoked with his right. He was nearly to the filter of his second when a man appeared in the doorway in front of him with a shiny silver pistol trained on Burl's head. He looked to be about Burl's age, late fifties, with a slightly paunchy build. His receding hair was graying. He had on flat-front chinos and brown shoes with a subtly shiny golf shirt that looked to be pricey.

Burl shook his head. "You ain't supposed to point your gun at nothing you don't intend to shoot." He dropped his cigarette on the tile as casual as could be and ground it out with his toe right beside the previous one. "That ain't no way to greet a guest. I bet you treated Colleen better."

The man's hand holding the gun shook ever so slightly. The large silver watch on his wrist gave it away. "Other people might be afraid of you, but I'm not."

Burl said, "That so?" He darted right as he drew the gun from his waistband, dropped to one knee, and fired a snake round at the man's right leg near his groin, shredding his chinos. The man's gun went off twice as he bleated something that wasn't words, the shots both going high and left. Burl laid on his right side and fired again, this time spraying

the man's left shin with shot. The man cried something piti-
ful and splayed gracelessly to the floor, where he whimpered
the Lord's name and writhed.

Burl replaced his gun at his waist as he got up. He
approached the man, who lay on his back wriggling, both his
hands on his upper leg, smearing the tile with his blood like
it was finger paint. Burl noted his bloodied wedding band.
He kicked the man's gun away, then stood over him.

"How about now?" Burl prodded the man's shoulder
with his boot. "Naw. You're right. I ain't nothing to be scared
of. Is that why you drew down on me when all I wanted to do
was talk? Did you think you could get by with whatever the
fuck you pleased? Was that it?" Burl leaned down so close to
the man that he could smell his piney cologne. The man
twitched and moaned. "You want to know what'll happen to
your family if you say who done this? Won't nobody survive.
Not that wife of yours, wherever she is. Not your kids. Not
your grandbabies." He stood up straight and spat on the
man's chest. "Not nobody."

Burl had one last look around before he headed out,
extracting and lighting another smoke. He made his way
down the steps and to his car, dragging deep on it. He gestured at Greek to back out, motioning with his hand that
held the cigarette. Then he got in his car and followed him.

They wound back the way they came on Avawam, blew
past the guard shack, and turned back up toward 25, topping
out near the I-75 on-ramp. They got back on, going south
now, making their way toward the new bypass in Richmond
so they could head out to Greens Crossing. Eight or so miles
up the interstate, a state police cruiser rocketed by them in
the opposite lanes with its sirens blaring and blue lights
ablaze. Burl took a moment to consider the wisdom of what
he had done.

CHAPTER

8

I T'D BEEN YEARS since Burl had gotten his hands dirty like that. Greek had been handling all that work, or delegating it, since coming back from overseas. He'd worked for Burl while he was still in high school, but he'd come home more valuable after his tours with the Rangers in the Middle East. Burl hadn't planned for what happened at Boone's Trace, but once it got started, he lost himself. What he gave that man would've been far better served cold by Greek or one of the boys. That had been his intention going in.

Burl bid his phone to dial, and soon an outgoing call rang in the cabin of his car. Greek's voice followed a faint click. "Yeah."

"I want you to take lead on this thing," Burl said to his dashboard.

"Roger that."

That was all they spoke on the fifteen-minute drive from perhaps the straightest neighborhood in Madison County to one of its sketchiest. Situated off 52, headed toward Irvine, residents of Greens Crossing took up well more than their share of the Madison County District and Circuit Court criminal dockets. Most who turned up in court were low-level addicts and therefore thieves, but the sod-growing

Begley clan represented the upper crust. Criminals, yes, but not so petty.

Greens Crossing and the offshoot roads held a mix of trailers and single-family homes. Much of the land was cleared, but thick stands of trees also crowded the asphalt at certain points. The Begleys' place wasn't even the only sod farm out there. There were three. Another lay on the left just before the biggest landmark in Greens Crossing: Richmond Raceway. The raceway sat in the crook of a ninety-degree bend. It roared to life on weekend nights and was fixing to as Burl and Greek made their way past. The Begleys' sod compound lay a half mile beyond.

The metal sign denoting the Begley Turfgrass Sod Co. was mounted between two posts, and as old as it was, it was surprising that it only had two bullet holes in it. In the distance, a massive sod irrigation system stretched hundreds of feet across fields, section after metal section arcing over bright grass below.

Down a long gravel drive, at the center of it all, small copses of trees sat at the perimeter of a chain-link-fenced yard around a white two-story siding farmhouse and two steel barns that had better than a half dozen vehicles parked around them, including more than one Mustang, some pickups with pipes running up the back of their cabs and decals on their rear windows, various work trucks, a flatbed trailer with rolls of sod loaded on it, and an empty one farther out.

Distant behind the farmhouse but down a fork of the same drive was another cluster of buildings. Two of the buildings were nearly identical brick houses barely half the size of the main house that sat among tool sheds, a carport, and some other outbuildings.

Greek pulled in ahead of Burl and came to a stop in the dirt-and-gravel drive thirty yards from the big farmhouse. A brindle pit bull emerged from a plywood doghouse on the porch and short leg ran straight for Greek's car. Its tail was docked, and its teeth bared. It had the build of a scaled-down rodeo bull.

Rather than get out, Greek laid on his horn. A thin boy in his early twenties, in a black Tractor Supply hat and dirty white T-shirt with the sleeves cut off, came out the door and called the dog back. The dog went to him reluctantly. Looking the two cars over, the boy took the dog up on the porch and managed to get the pit in the house, yanking on its collar the whole way.

Only when the boy came back out toward Greek's car did Greek get out. He had a black holster strapped around his chest. Burl rolled his windows down but stayed in his car, the engine running.

"Something I can help you with?" the boy asked.

"I need DeeDee Spoon."

The boy looked down and wiped his brow below his hat brim. "She ain't here."

"You sure."

He glanced up at Greek, rubbing his hands on the front of his pants. "Yeah. She ain't here."

"She ain't here now or she never was here?"

"Uhhh. I don't think she ever was here."

"That's weird." Greek took his phone from his pocket and held it for the boy to see. "Her phone's here. I tracked it."

The boy's head snapped up. He squinted at the screen. "Oh." He scratched the side of his face real hard. "I don't know. Let me—let me see what that's about." The boy turned and went back inside. Once the porch door opened and closed, Greek went around to Burl's open window.

"That boy's lying."

"No shit, he's lying. Fidgety as fuck. You see him jump when you said her phone's here? Maybe now they'll send her ass out."

Greek leaned against Burl's car, staring at the house. The driveway was more dirt than gravel, really. Light brown and dry, unlike the richer-looking soil in the fields. The whine of engines at the raceway was on the slightly smoky air as dusk descended. The voices of children playing and a dog barking somewhere in the distance cut through the sound of the cars.

When the door at the house opened again, four men came forward. The first boy who had come out had the pit bull on a leash now, the dog pulling so hard it looked like it could get loose any time it wanted. They were all led by a man with a sun-damaged bald head, speckled brown like a hawk's egg. He had an uneven gray beard, a bent nose, and two cauliflower ears that sprouted from him like chanterelle mushrooms on a log. He wore caramel-colored Carhartt overalls with nothing under them. An abundance of long gray chest hair protruded from the top. Burl knew this man to be Clovis Begley.

As far as Burl was concerned, it was Clovis and his ilk who were responsible for countless lost lives and souls in his mountains. It was people like him who necessitated the black lights Burl installed in the bathrooms at his gas stations so users couldn't find their veins to shoot up. It was people like him who'd led DeeDee to the life he was currently trying to retrieve her from. In Burl's mind, weed was all good and zero harm. The junk Clovis and his family peddled was all bad and pure harm.

Of the other two coming out behind him, one of them was bigger than Greek and dressed in dirty work clothes. The last man was built about like the one with the dog, but a lot cleaner. He had on a polo shirt with a gold chain spilling out of it. His dark blue Atlanta Braves hat still had the gold sticker on its flat brim.

Burl reached for the .38 in his ankle holster before he tapped Greek on the hip. "Let me get out." Greek gave him space to open the door, and Burl stepped out, dropped the gun onto his seat, and stood inside his open door.

The four men from the house stopped ten or so yards from Burl and Greek. Bald-headed Clovis said, "Boys, what is it we can do for you?"

"Clovis," Burl said, "surely to God you know me. I'm also sure that boy told you we tracked my daughter DeeDee's phone here. We're trying to figure out where she's gone to."

"Yeah, Burl. I know you, and we was just talking about it. Cargo says he was out somewhere, and he done found the thing. He was wanting to get it back to somebody, but being as he didn't know whose it was, he wasn't too sure how to do that. We're glad you come by. Go on and give them the phone, Cargo."

The big one walked toward Burl and Greek. Neither of them moved. He held the phone out to Greek, looking down at him. He grumbled, "Here you go." Greek took it, and the man began to recede.

"Hold on now," Burl said. "Where was it you said you found it?"

Clovis started, "He—"

Burl shouted over him. "This boy ain't mute, goddamn it. He's got my daughter's fucking phone. I'd like to hear from him how he come to have it. I'm still trying to figure out how come it takes four of you all and a dog to bring us a cell phone."

The big man's forehead furrowed. He looked to Clovis.

Clovis wiped the sweat off the dome of his head. "Thing is, we was trying to figure out why it took two of y'all to come after it, one of you wearing a hand cannon for all eyes to see."

"Cargo," Burl said, "Greek here's been calling and texting that phone. If you was holding onto it for DeeDee's sake, why not answer the damn thing and tell us you had it? Sure would've made this easier. Where was it you said you found it again?"

Cargo's lip twitched like he might offer an answer. Before he could, Clovis cut back in. "Cargo ain't on trial. He done give you the phone back. You got no more business here unless it's thanking him for keeping it safe. Don't none of us know where your daughter's at. Sorry about that."

Burl knew what it was to stonewall. The more you tell about anything, the more likely you are to get tripped up on something that's not true, and the more likely you are to give away something that is true that you don't want out. Clovis was trying to give away as little as possible. Burl's stomach started to pull knots because Clovis knew exactly who Burl was, knew exactly what Burl did, and he knew that this tactic would lead nowhere good. That meant whatever he was keeping from Burl was even worse.

Burl fixed his eyes on Cargo, more determined than ever to shake something loose. "You're awful big to have your daddy do all the talking for you. He's treating you like a god-damn baby. Why don't he want you to tell me where you got DeeDee's phone?"

"Come on, Cargo." Clovis waved Burl and Greek away with the back of his hand. "It's time for these two to go on."

"Why don't he want you to tell me if you seen her?"

Cargo walked away, and when he reached the other three, Clovis said, "Go on now. We're done out here." The Begleys pulled back toward the house as a group, but their eyes stayed on Burl and Greek as they went. The pit bull still strained at the lead. They all sidestepped up the porch and gave one last long look before going in the house.

Burl still stood in his car door. "Fuck, Greek. This ain't good."

"No. It's not."

"Can you get into her phone?"

"I don't know. Looks like it's about dead. I'll have to charge it. If there's a call, I can answer, but it's got a passcode, so that's about it."

"I got no earthly idea what it'd be. Maybe her mother or her brother would know. I don't. You know she don't let me in on a goddamn thing."

"You want me to call them?"

"You'd probably do better than I would right now. Call our boy at post too. See if he's got any idea how to crack it, but don't say how we got it."

"I'm sure you saw that cruiser going north. You want me to poke around about that too?"

"Naw. See if he mentions it, but don't ask nothing. I may have left our friend with enough reason to keep the law off my scent." Burl reached to his seat, picked up his gun, and slid it back into the ankle holster. "I'm going to head back the Irvine way. Take 89 down. If they are looking, I doubt any will be looking for me that way."

"That's probably right."

"Just prepare yourself for one thing. If nothing pans out on DeeDee's phone real quick, we going to have to snatch up one of them Begley boys and see what the hell they know."

CHAPTER

9

MAKING HIS WAY toward Estill County, Burl placed a call to Sheriff Horne to tell him to send someone back to DeeDee's to see if she had turned up. He wasn't optimistic, but he was praying for it. After passing through Irvine, the cell signal got real sketchy, and the night got dark. From there on, the only thing Burl did was steer behind his headlights, listen to the radio, and smoke cigarettes. For the first time in as long as he could remember, he felt helpless.

Burl was someone who willed what he wanted to happen to happen. If anyone in his orbit didn't do what he wanted, he made them do it. If they weren't willing, they got willing. The only people who ever seemed to frustrate him were his family. Maybe because they were the only ones who didn't really fear him. Not the way everyone else did. He couldn't make DeeDee stay off drugs, no matter how hard he tried. Now he couldn't get her to turn up. He couldn't make Darron straight. He couldn't stop Colleen from condoning him. Hell, as it turned out, he couldn't even make her be faithful.

After the reality of it had a chance to set in, Burl wasn't altogether shocked that Colleen had strayed. Even though he loved her—intensely in his way—he'd had someone on the side since they were first married. At times more than one.

He and Colleen had continued to have relations throughout, which he mostly instigated. It wasn't that she didn't satisfy certain of his desires, only that his desires overran those bounds. He'd never considered for a minute that hers might as well.

She no doubt knew about his indiscretions because he scarcely tried to hide them, and Jackson County was small. That's why he was surprised he'd never found her out. Keeping it out of county and using Darron as her cover must have been the keys to it. Burl and Darron never spoke, and Northern Madison County wasn't on Burl's radar. There just wasn't anything up there for him to care about. It was mostly just a bedroom for people who worked in Lexington.

His wife cheating was the least of Burl's problems, although his reaction to it may have boosted it up some. It was his uncertainty over DeeDee that had turned to torment. He'd grown ever harder on her with the years, but there was a time when she brought a shine to his eyes much the same way Chelsea did now. Burl ran around a lot for business and with women, but when not doing either of those things, he was mostly home on his farm. DeeDee had once been his little sidekick in a way that Darron never was. She was a daddy's girl for the first dozen or so years of her life.

Burl always kept animals on the farm, even though the main purpose was growing marijuana. Livestock gave him one more outlet to launder money, and he wrote the feed, supplies, and equipment off his taxes. A whole lot of the supplies and equipment were real useful to someone growing pot.

DeeDee took such an interest in the animals that she swore someday she'd be a veterinarian. That was an interest Burl could get behind. When she asked him to get her the Barbie veterinarian playset, he sent one of his boys to the Walmart in Berea to get it that same day. When it wasn't at the Berea Walmart, he sent his man on to Richmond, then

Lexington. He finally found it at the old Toys R Us on Nicholasville Road and ran it straight to Burl's place. DeeDee went to sleep that night with the new doll under her arm.

By the time she had hit high school, she sneered at the thought of being a vet, but it was little DeeDee with the doll under her arm that Burl still pictured now that she'd gone missing.

When he pulled up his gravel drive, Burl expected to see Waylon and Johnny run out to greet him. Colleen typically turned them loose and let them stay out when she was home, but there was no sign of them. The garage was around back where the gravel turned to concrete and Darron's old basketball goal still stood. After raising the door and beginning to slide in, he found a void where he expected Colleen's Mercedes.

Looking at the clock, it was possible she and Chelsea were still at dinner if they had stopped to eat inside somewhere. Possible. But knowing Colleen and knowing the scene she had just left and her disposition, that felt unlikely.

He went inside and looked around to see if they had come and gone, but as far as he could tell, things were as he had left them. Waylon and Johnny were locked up and keening in their cages in the mudroom. He turned them loose and went to the front door, where he released them galloping into the yard to hike their legs.

Burl stood on the brightly lit porch, looking out into the silvery-smelling darkness, the trees beginning to dance in the slim light of a slim moon holding water obscured by passing clouds, the wind and sky foretelling the coming of rain.

He looked to his phone and found missed calls from Sheriff Horne as well as Greek. There was no cell signal at his house, so all calls went over the satellite Wi-Fi. He called the sheriff first, hoping he had news that would make the vise in his chest loosen, but was disappointed to find there was no change at DeeDee's place. Car home. Her not.

Greek had a little more to say, though he and Burl tried not to give away too much on the phone. "Nobody has her code, and our guy can't crack it."

"So did you reach Colleen or Darron?"

"Both. They're together. She took Chelsea to Louisville."

"Goddamn it." Burl raised his cigarette over his shoulder and flicked it hard as he could. It tumbled end over end, the orange glow spinning like a flaming baton before it landed in the grass. "And neither has the code?"

"Nope."

"So, the phone's a fucking dead end. And all we know is somehow it ended up with those sod fuckers."

"So far. There's been no calls. A couple messages that didn't amount to anything."

"So, our man can't do a fucking thing for us?"

"He said he'd do an Ashanti Alert if you want."

"What the fuck is that?"

"An Amber Alert for adults. He's not really supposed to, but he said he would."

"Naw. I ain't putting this shit out there like that. There's some fuckers who know where she's at and it's those fucking dopers. No point in asking the whole goddamn world when we already know who to ask. What do you got going there?"

"I got five cars out that way waiting on someone to leave the nest. I had Christy fly the drone over, but she says it's real quiet out there. She says they ain't stirring at all, but they will."

"You tell everyone not to do no more than's absolutely necessary. If this shit turns too bad, it'll hurt our chances of seeing her back safe. Once we get my girl back in the fold, that's when we consider our options."

"Understood."

"You call me the second you hear anything."

"I will."

"Anything."

"Roger that."

Burl hung up and put flame to a fresh cowboy killer. He squinted out at his dogs in the yard. He contemplated calling Colleen but knew damn well it wouldn't lead anywhere good. She would be agitated as hell, and he most definitely was. He pondered why his dogs didn't read any distress from him and come to be near, as they say dogs are perceptive of such things. All he could make of them were small glints of light reflecting off their black coats in the darkness. Nothing more.

10

A GENTLE RAIN FELL and brought the smell of earth into the air. A dirt bike buzzed in the distance and drew nearer and nearer to Burl's front porch. He sat with a short glass and a cigarette, rocking slow, Waylon and Johnny sprawled out alongside.

Whitney had texted him a half dozen times. The first couple she was trying to get him to reconsider Red Lobster. The next few she was asking why he hadn't responded. He texted back, *I'm tied up*, just to get her off his back. That didn't work at all. It only prompted her to send three more texts. He wished he'd never responded. His mind was elsewhere. Mostly on DeeDee but strayed some to Colleen, which didn't make him feel any better.

Once the high-pitched two-stroke cleared the woods, Waylon and Johnny rose and began to bark. "Hush now." Burl waved a hand at the dogs. "It's Clarence or Toby, and y'all know it."

The bike rounded the house, its headlight beam the first thing to come into sight. Once the bike itself did, there was no doubting it was Clarence. He made it look top heavy carrying his squat two hundred and fifty pounds. He had about five black T-shirts and wore one every day. None of them seemed quite long enough to cover the bottom inch of his sagging gut. This one hugged him all over because it had gotten wet in the rain.

As he dismounted, Burl said, "What do you know, Clarence?"

"It's quiet out there." Clarence ascended the porch steps. "We thought we had us a raccoon creeping around the chicken coop, but now we think it might be a bobcat. We found some tracks over there, so we moved one of the trail cams."

Clarence and Toby worked the evening shift in the field office, which was located inside one of Burl's indoor marijuana grow rooms a good mile from his house. Times being what they were, Burl didn't grow outside anymore. He used a combination of grow rooms and greenhouses, and between the two he could grow just about anything he wanted. He relied on Middle Fork, a creek that bisected his property, for all his irrigation needs.

The field office was full of monitors that displayed the dozens of trail cams spread throughout the eleven hundred acres of Burl's farm. In addition to the trail cams, Burl had another thirty-six conventional security cameras at key points on his property. Each night, either Clarence or Toby would ride to the house and give Burl an update.

"Don't be letting that bobcat get any of my birds, now. I already lost me a momma goat today, and her kid. Mother Nature's had her share of my property."

Clarence stood beside Burl's chair, dripping just a little on the porch planks. A sidearm jutted from his hip at on odd angle on account of his overhanging fat. "Me and Toby rode by there. Looked like you got one back from her. We seen the dead vulture up there in the goat field. You want us to get it strung up to warn them other bastards?"

Burl drew in through his nose. "I'm of two minds on that. This afternoon, I'd have told you to go on and get it hung, but now I'm thinking better of it."

"We dragged it out of the field and put it by the fence. The goats was spooked by it. It's the damnedest thing, but them other vultures won't touch it. They'd just as soon let it rot as eat it, but they'll eat damn near any other fucking thing."

"Yeah. It's the only time they're picky about their carrion."

Clarence peered in the house, then around. "You home alone tonight, Boss? Where's Mrs. Spoon and the baby?"

Burl took the edge of his lip in his mouth. "They took a little trip, Clarence. Headed out on the goddamn open road."

"Well, that sounds like fun. Where they gone to?"

"Goddamn. Canada. I don't know."

Clarence scratched his wet head. "When they coming back?"

Burl stood up slowly, looked Clarence in the eyes, and slapped his meaty face good and hard one time, and it sounded like someone had dropped a raw brisket on a kitchen floor. Clarence stepped back and put his hand to his face where he'd been hit.

"Quit asking me fucking questions." Waylon and Johnny swirled around the men, alarmed by the confrontation. "I don't know when they'll be back, dummy. Get your fat ass on that fucking bike and get the fuck out of here so I don't have to answer no more of your stupid fucking questions. You got it?"

Clarence backed down the porch. "I'm sorry, Burl. I didn't mean nothing."

Burl pointed into the distance. "Get the fuck out of here, you fucking half-wit."

"I'm sorry."

Burl shook his head. Clarence hurried his thick self back to the bike, kicked it alive in the rain, turned it, and was gone away as quick as he could go. Burl shook his head.

"Jesus Christ. What the fuck?"

He took his glass from the floor beside his chair and turned up the last remnants of his bourbon, leaving only melting cubes. He flung the glass down the porch, where it shattered. The dogs cowered away. Then Burl turned back to his ashtray and kicked it the other way down the porch. He stared at it and the trail of scattered butts a moment. He looked down, grabbed the rocking chair he had been sitting in by both arms, lifted it, swiveled toward the yard, and flung it out there. It landed with a crack, and one arm splintered. Burl huffed at the top of the porch, looking out on what he'd done. Then he looked at his two cowering dogs.

"Let's go in the fucking house."

He opened the screen door, let the dogs in, and followed them before ripping the screen shut. He slammed the inside door so hard that the pineapple sign flapped away and then back into it with a slap. The door strike rattled every pane of glass across the front the house. The broken rocking chair still lay there in the grass.

11

SLEEPING WAS UNREALISTIC. Burl had tried, but it was a goddamn joke. He was up on the couch around two in the morning, watching an old movie on the TV, having a smoke, when his phone vibrated. It was Greek.

"What do you know?"

"We got us one. Where you want it?"

"Arizona."

"Roger that."

Arizona referred to Phoenix Products, which was in Sandgap and had nothing at all to do with Burl. It just happened to be in the Northern Jackson County Industrial Park off 421, and Burl happened to have a warehouse nearby where he stored his mowing equipment. In that way, the warehouse got its name.

"One more thing," Burl said before hanging up. "Send someone after the farmhand. You know who I mean?"

"I do."

"Make sure he brings his gear."

"I'll make sure."

* * *

Burl was the first to make it to Arizona. He'd pulled his car in through the garage door and closed it behind him. The fluorescent lights were on, and he was seated atop a zero-turn mower. The place smelled like gasoline and decomposing grass, which irritated Burl because it meant his guys weren't hosing down the equipment like he wanted. A couple of the lights flickered continuously, creating a slight strobe effect and buzzing. Having nothing else to do to kill time, he smoked.

A car engine arrived outside, and the garage door went up. Greek pulled in, behind the wheel of his Challenger, with Pot Roast in the seat beside him. Pot Roast had gotten the name because he liked to eat pot roast. He'd talked about it in jail one time when he was nineteen, and another inmate offered to tattoo it on his shoulder, and he said okay, and that was his name after that.

Greek killed the engine, and he and Pot Roast got out. Once the engine noise quieted, there was a thumping noise. "I told that fucker if he dented my trunk, I'd bury him," Greek said.

Pot Roast uncapped a twenty-ounce Mountain Dew bottle with no label, spit deep black into it, and recapped it. "I don't think he believed you, Greek."

Greek went around back of his vehicle, leaned over, and shouted, "Cut that shit out!" The banging stopped.

Burl climbed down from the mower. "So, who'd you send after Seth?"

"Jared."

"How far out you think they are?"

"He was well ahead of us coming back. Just had to fetch him." Greek pointed toward his trunk. "Pot Roast located this one going out for Sonic. We got him corralled shortly after that. I called you. Then I sent Jared."

"I believe this boy was buying for everyone because he placed a hell of an order," Pot Roast said. "We was able to pin him in and hog-tie his ass."

"Any cameras at Sonic?"

"There were," Greek said, "but that ain't going to be a problem. I negotiated that and took care of it myself."

"What about his car?"

"Pot Roast drove it and left his truck there. We dropped it off out back of Hill Top. We didn't want to bring it over here."

"Pot Roast's truck could be a problem. We'll need to go get it."

"I'll take care of it," Greek said.

"We could send the wrecker. Ain't no wraps on it yet."

Greek creased his nose. "What if someone comes looking? It'll take too long getting it hooked up."

"You right," Burl said. "We just got to drop someone over there. It don't need to be you or Pot Roast, though."

"Won't be no video until first shift comes in."

"Y'all don't need to be seen over there again. Tempting fate." Burl spat on the concrete. "Let's drop Christy. They won't be expecting no woman."

"We'll put her out a ways off from it and have her walk over."

Burl nodded at Greek. "Get Toby on that when we're done here. Let Christy know he's coming."

Greek stepped away and got on his phone. Pot Roast hooked his dip from behind his lip, uncapped his bottle, and dropped it in. He went into the back seat of Greek's Challenger and pulled out an oversized Sonic bag. He raised it in Burl's direction. "You want a burger?"

"Naw."

"They was free."

Burl didn't reply. Pot Roast shrugged and went into the bag. He unwrapped a cheeseburger and took down a third of it in one bite. The whole thing was gone in less than thirty seconds. He was still chewing when he went back in the bag for another. He was on his third when Greek rejoined them.

"It's took care of."

Mouth full, Pot Roast asked him, "You want a burger?"

Greek wrinkled his nose. "No."

"We can't do nothing until Seth gets here," Burl said. "Twiddling our goddamn thumbs. Except Pot Roast. He acts like he ain't ate nothing in a week."

Pot Roast wadded an empty wrapper. "I'm a growing boy."

Greek drew close to Burl. "You serious about doing this?"

Burl jutted his chin at Greek's car. "That all depends on him. If he don't think I'm serious, then I'm goddamn serious."

Greek clinched his eyes and sucked air in through his teeth. "I think I'd rather kill him."

12

J ARED LIKED TO go off-roading, and the tires on his truck
reflected that. The drive to Seth's required crossing a dry
creek bed, which after the rain wasn't necessarily dry. That
made Jared the obvious choice to fetch Seth. His tires were so
knobby that the men inside the warehouse could hear him
pull in the driveway coming off 421. Unlike Burl and Greek,
he didn't have an opener for the garage door, so Greek went
out to meet him and to make sure it was who they were
expecting.

Greek came back and raised the door before the mud-
crusted Silverado rolled in. Jared climbed out of the driver
side and said, "What do you know, boys?" His boots were
similarly muddy. His black T-shirt had an arrowhead on it.
His beard hung lower than his ponytail. Burl sort of grumbled but didn't really answer.

A light-headed fellow with bedhead, who wore glasses,
stepped from the other side with a bag under his arm. His
reddened eyes called out for more sleep. Burl had made Pot
Roast set up a folding table in the middle of the room. The
drowsy fellow went to it and unpacked his equipment. "So,
what does this boy weigh?"

Pot Roast scratched the side of his head. "I'd say he's, like, one forty, one fifty. He ain't too big. What would you say, Greek?"

"He ain't over one sixty."

Burl gestured at Seth. "You get yourself situated. The rest of y'all, pull in." Greek, Pot Roast, and Jared drew close and dropped their heads toward Burl. "All I need you three to do is hold him. I don't want you to say shit. I don't want you to do shit." He pointed two fingers in the direction of Greek and Pot Roast. "Y'all got him taped up, and we're going to keep him that way. In fact, I don't even want you to untape his mouth until after I've had my say—you got it?"

Three nods, and Pot Roast said, "Yep."

"If we do this the right way, he'll tell us whatever the fuck we want."

The four men separated, and all stood watching Seth arrange his instruments. Burl lit another smoke. Greek was still as a stone. Jared chewed at a callous on the palm of his hand. Pot Roast nudged Jared in the ribs. "We got some Sonic burgers if you want one. They was free."

Jared side-eyed him, his hand still pressed to his mouth. "Are you serious? Maybe later. Not now."

"I was talking about later."

"Y'all shut up," Burl said, with the cigarette bobbing in his lips.

Seth finally turned and all eyes went to him. "I'm ready."

Greek led the two others to the trunk. He popped it using his remote. They all stayed a couple steps back. There was some thumping and groaning when the lid went up. The boys just stared into the trunk, seeming to wait it out. After twenty seconds or so the thumping abated. "Y'all get his legs," Greek said.

Greek, Jared, and Pot Roast hauled a man out of the trunk with a green T-shirt tied around his head so he couldn't see. Greek untied the shirt and took it off. It was the boy who had handled the pit bull hours before. They carried him around to where Burl and Seth stood. Greek had his torso while the other two handled his lower extremities. Duct tape bound his ankles, his wrists behind him, and his mouth. His hat was gone, but he still wore the dirty jeans and sleeveless white shirt he'd had on when last they saw him. They set his feet down, but Greek kept hold of him, making sure he stayed upright.

The boy's eyes were pink and leaking. His hair matted where the hat had been. His face had clusters of strawberry scrapes on it, as did one of his shoulders. His chest huffed hard, and he could barely get all the air he was trying to push and pull in and out of his nose.

"Calm down, boy." Burl dropped his cigarette. "We just want to talk to you. Maybe if y'all was a little more forthcoming when we was out your way you wouldn't be here now. If your daddy thought we was just going to accept that 'we found it' bullshit about my daughter's phone then he's fucking crazier than I thought."

The boy's body shuddered as he tried to catch his breath without a whole lot of success. The body odor coming off all the men was powerful, but the boy's was fearsome, filled with every bad hormone a body knows how to make.

"We know you all know more than what you said, and if you didn't, you'd have said more. I just want my girl home safe. That's it. If you all ain't done nothing, you got nothing to worry about. We'll turn you loose, and if y'all are smart, that'll be the end of it." Burl drew close and looked square in the boy's eyes. "You understand all that?"

The boy nodded with the whole top half of his body.

"All right then. We gonna peel that tape back from your mouth, and I want you to tell us your full name. Nothing else. Not another word. Just your full name. You got it?"

More exaggerated nodding.

Burl pointed with just his pinkie at Jared. "Peel it back."

Jared brushed his jostled ponytail off the side of his neck, then put his hands to the tape at the side of the boy's face. It didn't come easy, and it made the slightest noise as he picked at the corner then drew it back. The boy's face wanted to stretch with the tape, and as it came, it left behind harsh red where it had been. As soon as the tape cleared the boy's lips, he gushed air in and out and continued to for some time.

"Get your breath now," Burl said, "and tell us your name."

The boy huffed some more before finally getting out, one syllable at a time, "Ken-dall—Gen-try—Beg-ley."

"Good, Kendall Gentry Begley. You followed directions. Now, I want you to think before you give me your answers, because lying ain't going to go nowhere good. I'm interested in the truth, the whole truth, and nothing but the truth, so don't fuck this up. Now I want to know, how'd y'all get DeeDee's phone? Where is she?"

Still sucking wind, he said, "I don't know nothing. My brother found that phone. I just—."

Burl grabbed him by the front of his shirt and yanked him closer. "Shut the fuck up, Kendall. I warned you." He looked to Jared. "Tape his fucking mouth back."

The boy started to shout, but Jared slapped the tape back on. He kept trying to holler, and now the tape wouldn't stick as well, so he was garbling some stuff out that couldn't be understood. Greek cranked his arms up behind him, and the boy really squealed then. "The roll's in the trunk," Greek said.

Jared went around and came back with the silver duct tape. He ripped off eight inches and dropped the roll to the ground. He yanked the old piece off fast and slapped a new piece on and held it tight to the boy's face, letting his hand rise up tight under the boy's nostrils, blocking his breathing altogether. The boy thrashed harder, and when he did, Greek cranked his arms again, and he thrashed even more.

Pot Roast stood back watching. He winced. "Goddamn."

Burl cut his eyes hard at him. "You shut the fuck up too."

Jared finally took his hand away, and Greek let his arms back down. The boy hyperventilated through his nose again as hard as he had at first. He looked like he was having spasms.

Burl looked on, unaffected. "You done fucked up, Kendall. We're talking about my daughter here. It's an insult to me and to her for you to spout that bullshit. You're the same boy who said he didn't know nothing, and not a minute later y'all come out with her phone. We know y'all know more than you're saying and that ain't going to just pass by. We ain't at war yet, but you're fucking up whatever chance you have to avoid it."

The boy shook his head hard. His hair that wasn't pressed down flew side to side.

Burl one-finger summoned Greek to bring the boy closer to Seth. "Since you just fucking lied to me after I told you that would go bad, now it has to go bad." Burl directed his thumb at Seth. "This man here's going to take one of your nuts."

The boy started thrashing again. Greek cranked his arms up again.

"Calm down now. He's going to put you out first with a nice shot of ketamine. You won't feel nothing until you wake back up. And like I said, he's only going to take one for now. He's done about a thousand hogs, so it might take him a minute to get the hang of castrating a man, but I got faith in him. He's what you call a side cutter, so he'll do the cut in the side of your sack, squeeze your nut out, and lop it off. Shouldn't be too complicated. We'll even bag it up for you to take home if you want. His stuff's all clean, so you don't got to worry about nothing. Show him your knife."

Seth approached the boy with what looked kind of like an X-Acto knife in a blue plastic casing. The tip of it was

shaped like a hawk bill. He brought it about a foot in front of
the boy's face. The boy's eyes got wide as groundhog holes.
He whimpered something awful.

"People's always saying how they'd give their left nut, so
I'm thinking that's the one we take first. What do you boys
think?" Burl scanned the men around him. All bobbed their
heads and said, "Yep," except for Pot Roast, who said, "I
guess that makes sense."

"Okay. So, what we're going to do now is put you out.
Since your family's a bunch of dopers, you might have took
ketamine for fun, but what it's really for is putting people to
sleep. It don't last too long, so after you wake back up, you'll
have another chance to say what you know about DeeDee.
You tell the truth, and you'll still have one nut to work with,
and that ain't too bad."

Seth had gone back to the table and come back. He
stood before the boy now and showed him a syringe stuck
into an upside-down vial. Seth pulled the plunger, drawing
the liquid into the syringe, eyeballing the scale on the side.
He withdrew the needle from the vial, and depressed the
plunger just a bit, flushing out the air. The boy's eyes
wouldn't leave it.

"I guess you don't got to roll up his sleeves." Burl bumped
Seth with his forearm.

Seth said, "Nope."

"So, Kendall, when you wake up, you going to be one nut
light, and you by god better have some truth to tell. Remember something when you going out: I done gave you a chance."
The boy started to thrash and squall through the tape again.
Burl looked to Jared and Pot Roast. "Help hold this fucker
still."

The two grabbed a hold of his ribcage. Greek jacked his
arms up behind him again; Seth grasped his bicep with his
left hand while bringing the needle to the ball of his right
shoulder. The boy was still trying to move but couldn't. His

head was wrenched in the direction of the syringe, eyes locked on it. He screamed into the tape.

Seth had just punctured the boy's skin when Burl said, "Hold on. Hold on." The boy looked on Burl, his eyes pleading. "Kendall, did you change your mind?" Burl pulled in close, looking right into his face. The boy's head jackhammered up and down, sending tears into the air. Burl looked at Jared. "Pull the tape."

Jared had barely got a corner loose when the boy blurted, "She fucking OD'd, man!" Slobber spilled out as he spoke. Jared ripped the rest of the tape off quick. "She fucking OD'd," the boy shouted again.

CHAPTER

13

BURL HAD THE boy by the throat. "Where is she?"

He wailed, "I'm sorry."

Burl tightened his grip. "I don't give a fuck what you are. Where is she?"

"He took her."

"Who took her?"

"Cargo. Cargo's the one that took her."

"To the hospital."

"No." The boy shook his head. "Somewhere else."

Burl drew back and threw a right that rocked the boy's head, but the rest of him didn't move because he was held so tight. "Where else?"

The boy's head sagged after and blood ran from the corner of his already tape-ragged mouth. He slurred now. "I don't know. I'm not sure. She OD'd. She was with Micah and she OD'd. He brought her to the house, and she wasn't hardly breathing. Daddy was pissed. He was so pissed. He Narcaned her. It seemed like she was better, but she wasn't right."

"You didn't call no one?"

"Daddy said not to. He said we shouldn't call nobody. He said she'd be okay. He said she just needed to sleep. Daddy told Cargo to dump her somewhere to sleep it off. He said not to be seen with her, just leave her. I swear to god I don't know where he took her. I swear to god. Daddy said it was better if Cargo didn't tell, so he didn't tell. Only Cargo knows."

"Bullshit."

"It's true. I swear to god it's true, but it's not his fault. It's Micah's. Daddy made Cargo take her because Micah wouldn't do it, and he don't trust none of the other boys. Micah wouldn't do nothing. He's no good. Cut his fucking nuts off. He deserves it. I didn't do nothing. I don't mess with no needles. None of that. Neither does Cargo. That's all Micah. Don't take my nuts. Please, god. Cut Micah's nuts, not mine. I won't tell nobody about this. Please god, just don't cut my nuts."

"Where's Cargo?"

"Daddy sent everyone away except family and told all of us to stay at home. We didn't have nothing to eat, though. I was supposed to get everybody Sonic and come right back. We didn't think nobody'd find me."

"You think they went out when you didn't come back?"

"I don't know. Daddy probably sent somebody looking."

"Where do you think Cargo would take DeeDee?"

"I don't know."

Burl jerked the boy forward by the shirt. "I said where do you think? You don't gotta know for sure. I want to know the places you think he might dump her."

"I—I don't think he'd dump her. He liked her. I can't see him doing that. Cargo ain't like that."

"Then where would he go?"

"I don't know. Maybe his mother's. That's the one place."

"His mother's?"

"Yeah. Cargo don't got the same mom as me and Micah. Daddy used to go with her."

"Where's she live?"

"In Irvine."

"Where?"

"In town. I don't know the address. I can find the way, but I don't know the address."

"What's her name?"

"Chandy Saylor."

Burl looked at Greek. "Hand his ass off."

Jared stepped behind the boy and took hold of his arms like Greek had them. Pot Roast stood close by. The boy didn't fight. He didn't do anything except breathe hard and shudder. Seth stood down and put his syringe back on the table.

Burl and Greek stepped away from everyone else and lowered their heads together. Burl was shaking just a little. Almost imperceptibly. His voice was low. "What do you think?"

"I think he's telling the truth, but he's guessing."

"It's all we got. We got that and we got Cargo. I don't think Cargo's going to be as easy to obtain as this boy. We got to try, though. Send Jared and whatever boys you can back out Greens Crossing, and see if anything presents itself. You, me, and this boy gonna ride over to Irvine and find the mother. Hope to god she's got DeeDee. What else we got?"

"Unless you're ready to get the law in it, that's it."

"Naw. All they'd do is get in the way of what we got to do. We know what bastards seen her last. We know that now for sure. Only way we find her's through them motherfuckers and the law don't got the measures we do."

"I'll tell the boys. How you want to get Seth back home?"

"Call someone out here to pick him up. We got to get going. We'll drop Pot Roast off at Hill Top and have him move this boy's car over here. He can ride home with whoever comes to get Seth."

"I'll take care of it."

Greek went to dispense orders. Pot Roast held the boy up while Jared retaped his mouth, and the boy didn't fight it. Then he retrieved the green shirt and tied it back around the boy's head. He and Pot Roast deposited the boy back in the trunk. Seth repacked his hog castrating gear into his bag. Burl went to his phone. He knew she wouldn't see it until morning, but he wrote Colleen a text: *Stay gone and don't tell nobody where you went*

14

WHEN DARRON WAS young, Burl would take him out on the farm, and he'd mostly hang around where his father was, watching him work and helping where he could. Trying to please him. Even so, they didn't talk much. As he got older, Darron started to roam the property on his own, riding a four-wheeler out, then hiking the far reaches of the family land for hours on end. Burl was always pleased with that, as he felt a boy ought to push his own bounds and flex his independence. What that meant to Burl and what that meant to Darron turned out to be two different things.

DeeDee was different from the start. She chattered to Burl all the time. He liked to take her with him when she was little, and she'd talk his head off much the same as Chelsea did now, but he couldn't turn his back on her, or she'd run off into the woods after whatever it was that caught her eye. A bug, a bird, a squirrel—anything. Generally, Burl would notice she'd stopped talking, look around, and find that she was out of sight, and when he called to her, she called back, and he'd track her down, no sweat.

That pattern was one they had repeated countless times, but the year she turned six they got a late March freeze that burst one of Burl's irrigation pipes overnight. By daytime it had gotten just warm enough to thaw so that when he found it, water was gushing from the damaged pipe, unchecked, and flooding the base of one of his grow houses.

It took Burl a good five minutes to close the valves and assess the damage. As had happened so many times before, DeeDee wasn't there when he looked up, so he called to her. No call came back.

Burl walked in an ever-widening loop, shouting, but nothing changed. "DeeDee. Come on out now, girl. This ain't funny."

Burl searched the ground for some sign of her footfalls or something that would give away which way she had gone, but he was no tracker. He scanned the hillsides for her red coat. Green and orange buds were just beginning to spread open on the trees. Shoots only now threatened to rise from the mud. The wind blew, birds called, the nearby creek riffled, but there was no sound of his daughter.

Not quite panic set in. His pulse quickened to the point he could hear it in his head and feel it in his chest. His throat was cinched some when he radioed to his men to come help him look for her. When they arrived, he gave them firm instructions: the search would not stop until DeeDee was found, and Colleen wasn't to be told anything.

Because he didn't know which way she had gone, he sent men in all directions. He couldn't bring himself to look the place he least wanted to find her, but he did have one of his men head down the creek bank, searching for her.

The boys rode away on four-wheelers and dirt bikes, covering more ground than they might have on foot, but the growl of their engines negated the chance they might hear DeeDee if she called out.

With every passing minute, Burl's insides cramped tighter. After a half hour of four men finding no trace of DeeDee, he called them back.

"I can't hear shit with y'all buzzing around. She can't have got far. She's not but six. I want y'all to get off your bikes and four-wheelers and just fucking walk and listen."

As they all went back out on foot, a level of dread had begun to set in, and Burl's imagination spun out grim thoughts. It's not that Burl couldn't call the law to help look; it was just that he could only call so much of it. The local boys were more or less all bought. Even so, that didn't mean he wanted any one of them on his land looking around. What they didn't know was for the better. The Kentucky State Police were a bit trickier. He always had one or two boys down in his pocket from post seven in Richmond, and they tipped him off and diverted attention away from his doings, but it was by no means across the board. A full-out search involving KSP would be absolutely no good. Too many variables he couldn't account for.

Burl was sidestepping up a hillside nearing the crest, considering that they might need the sheriff's dog, when a voice came over the radio, "I got her." Burl put his hand to his chest.

DeeDee was already back with some of the other men when Burl reached the grow house. Her red coat was covered in dirt, but she looked none the worse for wear. She was smiling and chattering at the men.

One of his older men approached Burl, "I found her wandering. Apparently, she'd holed up on us for a bit."

Burl knelt in front of her and hugged her to him. "DeeDee girl, where'd you go?"

"I thought I seen a horse. I was chasing it."

"A horse? Why would there be a horse out in these woods?"

"I don't know, Daddy." She waved her hands beside her face. "I thought I seen it go over that mountain. When I went after it, I found me an old log, and I got in it because I was being a raccoon."

"What happened to the horse?"

"I wasn't after it no more because I was a raccoon. Raccoons don't chase horses."

"Didn't you hear me calling for you?"

She giggled. "No."

"We was scared to death. We've been looking for you for almost an hour. We was hollering for you and everything."

"I got sleepy. I was a sleepy raccoon. I was sleeping in that log."

"You fell asleep?"

She looked around at maybe something, maybe nothing. The wind blew her hair into her mouth and she wiped it back out. "Uh-huh."

Burl snugged DeeDee to his chest. "Never again, honey. Never go off chasing nothing like that again. You scared your old daddy to death. You just stay where your daddy knows to find you, okay?"

DeeDee patted her father's back with him still squeezing her to him. "Okay."

15

Some sections of 89 between Jackson and Estill County twisted the shape of ribbon candy. Greek took the curves up and down the mountain at a rapid clip with Burl in the passenger seat lighting cigarettes end to end. He'd left his Cadillac at Arizona but grabbed three packs of Reds from the carton he kept in the back floorboard.

The sun was still down, and the previous evening's rain had all dried up. Greek's headlight beams were the only light for long stretches, spotlighting the green walls of foliage that bordered the edges of the road. Fewer than five cars came the other way over the course of thirty minutes of driving, and Greek overtook only one going the same way. He scarcely slowed before swinging out and passing it on a double yellow. Even with an automatic transmission, the Hellcat could fly.

The terrain flattened as they approached the Kentucky River. Once he had cell signal, Burl checked his phone, and he had one missed call from Whitney and a bunch from Christy. He dialed Christy.

She answered, "Boss."

"You get it?"

"No. They was crawling all over it."

"Who was?"

"I don't know. I come across the lot headed to it, and two guys come out my way. Out of nowhere. I just ran."

"They say anything?"

"They was hollering at me, but I didn't even try to listen. I was booking it. They was lying in wait."

"Fuck. What'd they look like?"

"I don't know. I didn't get a good look. I seen them out of the corner of my eye but that was all the look I needed. They was nothing special, but they was after me."

"Where you at now?"

"Toby picked me up out back of the drugstore and we come back. They was no use in staying around. Like I said, they was lying in wait."

"Y'all didn't drive back by to get a look?"

"Seemed too risky. They was using that truck like it was bait or something. We didn't want to get caught."

Burl had his head in his hand. He thought about ten different things, but all he said was "Okay," and hung up.

Next, he dialed Jared. "You out there yet?"

"Yeah, Boss."

"What do you see?"

Jared gave a long pause before answering. "It's four in the morning. There's nothing. We're keeping an eye on them, but I doubt anybody moves for a while."

"I just talked to our girl," Burl said. "She says they was crawling all over the truck. Said she had to abandon it and get away."

"They ain't moving out here. You want us to go over there and see what we got?"

"Send one car and have a look. Everyone else stay put. Ain't but one of them that knows what we need to know. I'd just bet that big bastard's holed up where you at."

"I'll get a car out there to slow roll it, and we'll stay here keeping watch. We can fly the drone over when the sun comes up."

"Do that," Burl said, and hung up. Unsatisfied by both calls, he glared at his phone for a mile, trying to figure out what else he could do. What other call he could make? He couldn't come up with anything. Even if Whitney was still up, calling her back would only lead to frustration for both of them.

As they neared 52 in Irvine, Burl leaned forward. He pointed to the right side of the road and directed Greek to turn into a dirt pull-off shrouded by trees and brush. Once obscured, they both got out and went to the trunk. Greek hoisted the boy out, removed the green shirt from his head and carefully pulled the tape from his mouth. His hands and ankles remained taped. Greek had to help him stay upright.

Burl put his hand on the boy's shoulder. "Okay, Kendall, we need you to show us the way to Cargo's mother's house. Do us all a fucking favor and don't do nothing stupid. We shown you mercy, now you got to show us some appreciation. You do that, and maybe all this can come out okay. I find my daughter, you go on home, and we call this thing a truce."

The boy's face was a mix of scratches and cuts, the blood somewhere between scabbing and still wet. "I'll do whatever you want. I swear."

"We're gonna put you in the back seat." Burl unholstered the .38 from his chest and showed it to him. "I'll be back there too. You ain't going to do nothing but tell us where to go and otherwise be good and quiet. You make a scene, you do anything out of the way, I'll pack you full and we'll dump your ass in the gravel pit and not think nothing else about it. I don't want to do that, so don't make me."

"Man, I swear to god, I ain't gonna do shit. I want you to find her so fucking bad."

"We on the same page then."

Greek put the boy in the seat behind him, and Burl climbed in on the passenger side. Burl had his revolver drawn, but the boy was taped, so he didn't train it on him.

The boy directed Greek to turn right onto 52, headed toward downtown. They crossed over the bridge at the Kentucky River, then turned right at the old cut-stone courthouse and headed toward Ravenna on River Drive. The old Twin walk-up restaurant on the left and the BBQ place were both unlit and desolate in the early morning hours.

As they approached Meade's Do-It Center to the right, the boy said, "It's a left up here." The street was South Madison Avenue. At the end of South Madison, the boy had Greek go right on Broadway, then take a left on Cherry Street. The streetlights lit scant patches. The lights at the majority of the houses were dark. They were close together, and most were clad in siding. With a few orange brick exceptions, most were white with black shutters. There were no curbs and no sidewalks; the street sat level with the yards. Leaning forward now, the boy squinted at the houses as they passed. "I been here a hundred times with Cargo—it's just dark is all."

Greek rolled slow, and the boy craned to the right side, unbuckled. "It's coming up here on the right." He peered hard that way. "Shit. We just passed it. That was it." Greek hit the brakes and the boy's head went unchecked into the back of his seat. Greek backed the car up and brought it in up next to the grass yard in front of one of the white houses.

The home had a short, oil-stained driveway, but no garage. There was no car parked in it. The porch was built of block with slender white pillars supporting the roof above it, and the wooden swing that hung from it faced the street. A single bulb fixture burned yellow beside the door. The interior lights also all seemed to be on.

"You sure this is the one?"

"Positive. That wreath on the door there. You can't see it, but it's got her initials on it. It says 'CS.'"

"Go see what we got," Burl said to Greek.

Greek got out slow, his head swiveling methodically, taking in his surroundings. He made his way to the porch, where he rang the doorbell with the knuckle of his middle finger and waited. Burl rolled down his window and peered at the house, looking for signs of movement. Greek rang the bell again after twenty seconds or so. Another twenty seconds passed before he knocked three times, hard enough that Burl could hear it from the back seat over the sound of the running engine.

Greek looked to Burl and pointed at the doorknob. Burl nodded. Greek tried the knob with his hand wrapped in the bottom of his shirt, and it opened right up. He disappeared within.

The boy was still beside Burl, his head tilted back. Burl laid his gun on his own leg, fished out a cigarette, and sparked his Zippo. The smoke fled out the open window. Outside, all was still.

Greek had been in the house several minutes when headlights cut the night behind the Challenger and slowly closed on their position. An aged red Chevy Cavalier, rolling on a mini spare, pulled up alongside Greek's car and slowed to a stop. The silhouette of a small woman with short hair looked into the car. Burl looked back at her and smoked. The boy looked her way, then at Burl. "That's Chandy."

Burl holstered his gun, elbowed his door open, and flicked what was left of his cigarette into the grass. He went around to the woman's window, and she lowered it. "Is that Kendall in there?" she asked.

"Yes, ma'am. You Chandy Saylor?" Burl squatted to see in and found the woman's face stricken. Her eyes red, swollen. Her skin blotchy. "Something wrong with you?"

She looked straight ahead, turning her eyes so that he couldn't scrutinize. "I've been at the hospital."

"That's no good. I hope everything's all right."

"Who are you and why are you in front of my house?"

"I was wondering if you seen Cargo lately."

She still didn't look. "Why are you looking for Ryan?"

"That's his name, huh. Well, it seems that my daughter has come up missing, and I'm told it was Ryan that seen her last. She was having a problem. I's hoping he'd brought her by here. I need to find her. I need to find her fast."

She broke. Her hands went behind the back of her head as it fell toward her lap. "Oh, Jesus."

Burl reached in for her, grabbed her by the sleeve and shook it so hard that her entire body rocked. "What the fuck do you know?" He shook her harder still. "Open your fucking mouth and talk." She drew in even tighter.

Greek appeared at her driver door, opened it while sweeping Burl back, reached past her, and threw the car into park and unbuckled her belt in one motion. He yanked her out as she grabbed and clawed at the doorframe, trying to keep him from it. She shrieked before his hand went over her mouth, and he had her vised to him so tightly that she seemed to lose some will to resist.

He passed by Burl, carrying her easily with one hand clamped on her face. "Can you move her car in, Boss?"

Burl hustled around the back of her car and got in the driver's seat without speaking. Greek had her inside her own house before Burl had the car in drive. He moved it into the driveway, killed the engine, got out, slammed the door, and pocketed her keys. He ran across the little yard, up the porch, and through the open front door, pulling it closed hard behind him.

16

CHANDY SAYLOR LOOKED tiny on the couch, both because she was small and because she was so drawn in. Greek loomed over her with his hands on his hips. Burl went straight to her and shook her by the shoulder. "Where's my daughter?"

Her face buried in her arms, she moaned something inaudible. Burl grabbed her arm, shook her again, squeezing now as hard as he could. She looked at him, her face stricken, tear weary. "She's at the hospital but she's not doing good."

"Where?"

"Here. In Irvine. Marcum and Wallace. They don't know her name. I didn't know who she was. Ryan wouldn't tell me. I just took her."

"He just left her here?"

"He wasn't even supposed to do that. His father'd kill him if he knew."

Burl scowled. "Fuck his father."

"You don't know him."

"You don't know me."

"He's dangerous."

Burl jabbed his finger in his own chest. "I'm worse."

"I did everything I could. I took her as soon as I realized how sick she was. I've been there ever since. I've hardly been home in two days. Ryan tried to save her. He brought her to me to try to save her."

Burl looked at Greek, and Greek pointed his thumb at the door.

"Don't tell nobody we was here." Burl grabbed a handful of her sleeve again and yanked her to almost standing. "You hear me? If you're scared of Clovis, you don't know the half of it. I'll soak Ryan in gas and put a match to him while he's still breathing. He'll scream his way to ash. You understand that?" He flung her back down to the couch without her ever answering.

Greek led Burl out the front door. From the porch they saw that the boy was out of the car. He was in the open door of Greek's Challenger, his hands free, hopping up and down because his ankles were still taped. His eyes bugged when he registered they were coming.

Greek's normal calm was lost. He shouted "Aw, for fuck sake!" running for the boy.

The boy lunged in head first and got himself upright. He managed to get it in gear, and the car took off just before Greek reached it, with the tires squealing on the pavement, the driver door still open. He shot straight ahead before pulling a wide and violent U-turn that took the Challenger into a shallow yard up the street, peeling deep stripes in the grass. It bashed into two trash cans on its way back onto the asphalt. One plastic can shot out of the way. The other flew over the top of the car and crashed to the street behind, slinging trash everywhere before it came to a rest. The car shot down Cherry, leaving all that in its wake.

Greek pulled his Desert Eagle and pointed it at the taillights before reconsidering and lowering it. The boy had some trouble taking the turn onto Broadway, as his taped feet must have struggled to stay on just the accelerator or the gas, but he managed it and was soon no more than the fading sound of changing gears dissipating. The very first rays of the rising sun were beginning to unfurl on Irvine.

Greek and Burl stood beside one another staring down the street. Greek reholstered his massive piece. Burl retraced his steps. He'd gone from Chandy's car to her house without ever considering the boy. "I lost my goddamn mind. I left the fucking thing running."

"I thought he was still taped good."

"Don't fucking matter now. We just got to get to the hospital." Burl remembered the Cavalier keys in his pocket. "We'll have to take her goddamn car." Burl jumped into the driver's seat and Greek hunched in the passenger side, too big for the little Chevy. Burl backed out and nearly dropped the transmission, not waiting to get the shifter into first from reverse. He hadn't driven a manual in years. He dropped the clutch and ground the gears down the street.

"Where the fuck am I going?"

Greek's body was bent over his phone. "I'm looking." He tightened his eyes on his screen and thumbed the image larger. "Says it's right off Main Street. Easiest way is to go back like you was going to Richmond, but make a right instead of a left when you get to the courthouse."

Burl didn't respond. He patted his pocket for his cigarette pack, pulled it out, and drew out a cigarette with his lips. There were only two more left. "That little shit got my fucking cigarettes."

Greek just barely turned his head and looked at Burl driving with his hands at ten and two, smoking. "He got my fucking car."

17

B URL PARKED THE Cavalier directly outside the emergency room entrance and left it there. He and Greek went in and straight to the admissions desk. The place smelled strongly of disinfectant and mildly of body odor. The woman sitting at the desk was speaking to an older man in moth-eaten flannel who was holding a clipboard in one hand and gesturing with the other, which was missing the pinkie and ring finger but was long healed.

Burl didn't stop to listen to what they were saying. He pressed himself against the desk beside the man. Greek stood over his shoulder. "My daughter's here, and y'all don't got her name. I need to see her."

The woman drew back in her chair just a little, pulled her hands off the desk, and balled them against her chest. "I'm sorry, sir, I'm speaking with someone else right now."

Burl waved both his hands in front of him and shook his head. "Y'all can figure that out after I seen my daughter. She come in here two days ago with Chandy Saylor, and nobody knows who she is. That's my daughter. She's real sick."

The lady's hands opened, she laid them on her desk, and she regarded him more earnestly, suddenly disregarding the other man. "Okay. There's paperwork you'll have to fill out first. I can have someone up here real quick." She pointed at a small glass room with a desk. "If you'll wait in there, we'll have someone right with you."

Burl nodded now, and he and Greek went the way she'd directed. The woman snatched her phone off the hook, pressed it to her ear with her shoulder, and quickly dialed.

*   *   *

A man in glasses, khaki pants, and a collared shirt with the hospital's logo stitched on the chest had come into the room and explained that they could let Burl see DeeDee as soon as he established Burl's relationship. Doing so required Burl to fill out a stack of paperwork, some of which he couldn't do on his own. Colleen was awake in Louisville, and she provided DeeDee's Social Security number, the insurance number from Kentucky Kynect—which was what they called Obamacare in Kentucky because he wasn't too popular there—and even her blood type. Burl was not the keeper of such things.

Colleen was initially terse until Burl was able to explain, at which point she became all business. Once Burl had all the information he needed from her, she said, "We'll be there as fast as we can."

Burl didn't reply, just hung up. The man took all the paperwork and left Burl and Greek sitting there. Burl's right foot bounced like a jackhammer, and he gnawed his nails. First one, then another, then another, then back to the first. He'd have killed for one of those last two cigarettes but wouldn't leave the hospital. Greek sat very still in the seat beside him, with his huge hands clasped together.

Eventually the man in the embroidered shirt returned with a woman in dark blue scrubs with lank blonde hair, no makeup, and a lanyard around her neck. "Mr. Spoon," the man said, "Dr. Phelps is going to take you to see your daughter."

Dr. Phelps said nothing at all as she led them along. Burl was uncharacteristically quiet during the trudge down the vinyl-tiled hallway, through double automatic doors, and finally to DeeDee's room. His heart raced even more rapidly as he entered, adrenaline coursing through him and making him nauseated.

DeeDee lay slightly propped up, and her eyes were closed. IVs ran into her arms. Her mouth and nose were obscured by an oxygen mask; various monitors around her beeped and pulsed and flashed digital numbers and fluctuating peaks and valleys. Aside from that, the only movement was the up and down of her chest. Her skin looked as pale as Burl had ever seen it, and her long brown hair appeared oily near her scalp.

Burl turned to Dr. Phelps. "Can I touch her?"

"You can hold her hand if you like."

Greek shoved a chair up alongside the hospital bed, and Burl took DeeDee's left hand in both of his and squeezed. "Do you know what did this?"

"Mr. Spoon, I'm walking a very fine line. Per HIPAA, I can discuss with you what I deem to be in your daughter's best interest. I can only do that if your friend steps out."

Greek went for the door. "I'll be outside."

Burl watched him go out, then turned back to the doctor. "We were told she was using heroin. Was this heroin?"

The doctor steepled her fingers. "That would not be inconsistent with our findings. It appears it was more than that?"

"Fentanyl?"

The doctor drew a portion of her lower lip between her teeth. She nodded.

Burl dropped his head atop his hands, clutching his daughter's. "Goddamn them. Goddamn them." Without raising his head, he said, "What're you gonna do?"

"Mr. Spoon, she was administered naloxone both before she arrived and after she was admitted. You've probably heard it called Narcan. So far, she hasn't shown significant improvement."

"How long will she be like this?"

Dr. Phelps's expression was as stoic as she seemed able to will it. "I don't know. She's not—she's not trending favorably."

He looked up at her, his mouth agape. "Are you saying she's dying?"

Her steepled fingers had woven together and were twisting. "I can't say, but if you believe in prayer, she needs it. If her body doesn't respond very soon, she won't last. If there are any loved ones who would want to see her, they need to ger here as soon as possible."

Burl gazed at the doctor as his face fell. Something like poison passed through him, making him sick in a way he wished he had never had to know. The doctor looked back with an expression of concern but with a weariness that suggested the frequency of such tragedies had reduced them to nothing more than the low points in her working days.

CHAPTER

18

CLOVIS DIDN'T SLEEP at all after Kendall went missing. At first he hoped Kendall had just gotten delayed coming back. As mad as it would have made him, he was hoping Kendall had defied him and had gone to see his girlfriend. Disobedient but safe would have suited Clovis just then. After more than an hour passed, he sent Micah to look for him.

When Micah called back to say he had tracked down Kendall's girlfriend and she hadn't heard from him and that there was no sign of him or his car at Sonic, Clovis's heart iced. Micah said the Sonic employees had gotten sketchy when he asked if they'd seen anything. The manager had volunteered that their cameras weren't working without being asked. It was then that Clovis became near certain Burl Spoon had gotten his hands on Kendall. He blamed himself for letting him go. Clovis knew he could send as many men out looking as he wanted, but there would be no finding Kendall if Burl didn't want him to.

Still, he sent men out. All he could do was pass the time, pacing the floorboards of his farmhouse and praying to a god he scarcely thought about for some sort of intervention. The intervention came in a form he least expected. The car

Spoon's muscle had driven the previous day thundered up the drive with Kendall behind the wheel and the sun rising behind him.

Clovis called in his other two sons, his cousin Ephraim, and Ephraim's son Ronnie, who he called "nephew," being that Ephraim may as well have been his brother, having both been raised by Clovis's father, Clayton Begley. They circled up in Clovis's house to hear what had happened to Kendall, and to decide what to do next. Kendall's account of what they'd done to him caused Clovis to seethe, but he was grateful nothing worse had befallen him. When Kendall told where he had taken them, Cargo's face fell. Clovis went and stood over Cargo while Cargo's head sagged between his knees and he trembled.

"Is that what you done, you big dumb motherfucker?" Clovis bent at the waist so his mouth was right beside Cargo's ear. "You done took that junkie to your momma's house?"

"I couldn't just dump her," Cargo said, not raising his head.

Clovis swatted straight down on the back of Cargo's head. It sounded like a wooden bat hitting a baseball. "You what?"

Cargo's huge frame bolted upright, and he was on his feet. He stood several inches taller than his father and stared him in the face, with tears welling in his dark eyes. He rubbed the back of his head. His voice cracked. "I said I couldn't dump her. She's a human being."

Clovis looked off to his right, away from his son. Cargo stood pat. Clovis's hips twisted and his open right hand shot straight into Cargo's left cheek before he could react. Cargo tumbled straight back onto the chair where he had sat a moment earlier, and it splintered as Cargo crashed to the floor. He started to twitch up as fast as he landed. Kendall shot between his father and Cargo and lay on top of his brother. Kendall threw one arm up, shouting for them to stop. Ephraim grabbed Clovis by the shoulders from behind, but Clovis shrugged him off easily. Micah stood back and watched wordlessly as his father stood over his two brothers.

"Is that junkie worth any one of us going to prison? Is she? She's going to die anyway. If not this time then next time. Or the time after that. Now you've connected us back to her. Fuck sake. Do you not know how the goddamn law works?" Clovis glanced fingers off the side of his head. "If she dies, that could end up on us. It's not just a fucking trafficking charge. You understand that? You stack trafficking and manslaughter, and it's twenty years. You willing to give twenty years for her? Because now one of us might have to."

Cargo had stopped trying to rise. He lay there with Kendall across him, both looking up at their father with fear in their eyes.

"And that's not even taking into account the fact that Burl Spoon knows for an absolute certainty who it was that done it. He ain't going to try to law nobody. He's going to try to kill us." Clovis slapped his own chest. "I say what I say for a reason." He directed a finger around the room at everyone. "You're willing to fuck this family over one little junkie bitch? What is wrong with you? Goddamn it. You got no fucking sense at all."

Nobody spoke. Nobody moved except Ephraim, who patted his cousin's back gently now. Clovis glared a bit longer before heading upstairs to his bedroom without another word. He slammed the door. He sat on the edge of his bed with his chest heaving.

He hadn't sat there long before he got to feeling bad about hitting Cargo. He hadn't been that angry since Micah showed up with the Spoon girl, clearly overdosed. He'd told him more than once before not to fool with her. He could tell the instant he laid eyes on her the first time that she was a user. He knew damn well what that could mean if it went bad. It was almost like that risk was what drew Micah to her.

He always had some girl, so why did he need this one? It was like she was forbidden fruit he couldn't resist.

Clovis had the same impulse to hit Micah when he had come in screaming for Narcan for the Spoon girl. They kept the Narcan on hand in case there was a mishap with the fentanyl. It was for them, not a user. They were so busy trying to revive her that Clovis didn't lash out. Once he had sent Cargo off with the girl, he still had an urge to lay hands on Micah, but he had time to consider what would happen if it got away from him. Clovis knew well his own capacity to hurt a man. Cargo was big enough that Clovis had never registered the same concern for him. He knew Cargo could take it.

It was Micah who should've known better than anyone the peril he had put them all in. He and Clovis had decided together to cut the heroin as much as they could and offset it with fentanyl. Fentanyl was cheaper and more potent than heroin, and the users didn't seem to care about the difference. When their buyers started to become bodies at a rate they'd never seen before, Clovis got worried. Not about the deaths so much, but about sales.

Micah had eased his concerns about sales slumping. "Right now, if anybody ODs, all anyone else wants to know is where they got their shit. These fucking junkies are that stupid. Somebody ODs, and they think it means it's the good stuff. They come looking for it."

Overdoses were good for business. That was all Clovis had to hear. There were junkies, there were people, and there were Begleys. The last were worth the most, and the first weren't worth anything at all. All they were was fuel in the Begleys' fire. They existed only to burn. They chose their own lot, and as far as Clovis could tell, they enjoyed the burning.

Micah had brought menace into their house. Clovis had tried to cast it out only for Cargo to bring it right back. Now Clovis had to figure out how to clear the place of it. He eventually lay down in his bed with everything but his boots on. He was exhausted, but he did not sleep. His mind churned, seeking an answer to their most pressing problem: Burl Spoon.

By the time Micah pushed the door open to tell Clovis one of their boys at post had called with an update about DeeDee Spoon, Clovis had moved past the urge to strike out at his own. Now he would have to try to save them.

CHAPTER

19

Holt Peters was asleep on a mat when someone shook him. He came to ready to swing on whoever the hell it was that woke him, until his cellmates got him to understand that he was being called to booking over the radio. He made his way down the long hallway in his dirty green Madison County Detention Center jumpsuit and bright orange rubber slides. Only one of the snaps on the front of the jumpsuit worked, so it hung wide open.

The Madison County deputy jailers all knew Holt because of his frequent flyer status, and they knew what he was about. He received a deference from them that he kind of liked. He knew none of them wanted to be looking over their shoulders when he was out, much less worrying about what he might do while he was in.

Captain Simmons was at the desk in booking, typing at a computer keyboard with a landline phone receiver wedged between his shoulder and ear. He wasn't doing any talking, just listening.

Holt leaned against the doorframe, his earlobes drooping sadly where he'd had to take out his gauges after he got booked in. "What's going on, Simmons?"

Simmons raised one hand and signaled for Holt to wait a minute. He finished up his call, pecking hard at the keyboard. He eventually thanked the person he was talking to and hung up. He picked up a bag of clothes and personal items he had on the desk beside him and stuck them out to Holt. "You just made bond."

Holt took the bag and stared at Simmons with his mouth sagging open. "Do what?" He screwed his eyes up. "How the fuck'd I make bond?"

"All I know is, I just put twenty grand cash in the safe and you're about to get out. She said she'd wait for you in the parking lot. Go get dressed while I finish up your paperwork."

* * *

Holt exited out through the sally port, wearing the same clothes he'd had on when he'd been booked in one hundred and thirty-eight days earlier, complete with his own dark brown blood stains. It was after one in the morning, and there was only one person in the half-lit parking lot. He approached the woman who was gesturing him to her from within a shadow. As he neared her and before he could make out her features, she said, "Clovis is across the street. Go see him."

A pickup sat on the other side of North Second in a lawyer's parking lot, with its lit headlights facing the street. The woman walked away without another word. Holt strode toward the truck without urgency.

Clovis motioned out the window for Holt to get in the passenger side. As a natural reaction to the circumstances, Holt opened the door and checked the back seat to make sure Clovis was alone, and he was. Clovis looked straight ahead, but Holt looked at him, blinking rapidly. "You paid my bond?"

"I did."

"Why? I mean, I'm damn glad to be out. I'm just—why'd you post my bond?"

"Because I need you to do something for me. Something you'll be good at. Before we can talk about that, I need you to tell me one thing."

"What is it?"

"You know what they're saying you did to that little girl?"

"Yeah."

"Did you?"

Holt raised both his hands. "What do you think, Clovis? You know me."

"I do know you, and I'm asking." Clovis turned to Holt with hard eyes. "Well? Did you?"

Holt put both his hands on his forehead. "Hell no. She's lying. Goddamn. The cops is lying. They all lying, man. I don't know why. I didn't touch her. I don't know what happened to her, but it wasn't me. Fuck."

"Okay. You say you didn't do it; you didn't do it." Clovis nodded. "We had to start there. Now that we got that lined out, I got something I need done. If you don't want to do it, we can do a bond surrender, and they'll put you right back inside. If you do want to do it, we can use that bond money to get you a paid lawyer."

"Paid? Who?"

"Lane Spicer."

Holt balled his fist and pumped it, then put it to his mouth and kissed it. "Fuck yeah."

"He said if I'd assign him that bond, he'd represent you on what you're facing. First I got to know if you'll do what I'm asking."

Holt was off-kilter smiling now. "I don't give a shit. I'll do whatever. Fucking public defender was selling me out anyway. He ain't worth a shit."

"Good. That's what I was hoping you'd say. I need you to do some work for me that my people can't do right now. If you were to help me out, at the end of this we'll be square. You won't owe me anything."

"Yeah. Cool. Whatever."

"You ready to get to work?"

Holt nodded. "I'm ready. What you want me to do?"

Part 2

Part 2

20

B URL ROCKED SOMBERLY, staring straight ahead, looking at the same yard, the same driveway, the same tree line he had stared out at for years on end, and yet he knew none of it could ever be the same as it had been before.

DeeDee stayed gone a lot, and somewhere deep inside him constricted the longer she stayed away, but eventually she always came up that drive and that knot loosened. Now it felt like that knot would never go away.

DeeDee hadn't lasted long enough for Colleen and Chelsea to get there. Burl raised hell in her room. Told the doctor to fly her to Lexington. She said they couldn't do it. That DeeDee was already gone. He had only relented when security showed up and threatened him with the police. Greek managed to retrieve him from DeeDee's room. Once Colleen, Chelsea, and Darron arrived, he took Burl on home, and he hadn't left there since.

Burl's eyes had once been capable of producing tears, but hardly anyone alive had ever seen them. He'd learned young the weakness it betrayed. Even now, after the loss of his daughter, his body reflexively staunched the tears.

The dogs mostly laid down the porch from him. They would get up now and then and wander the yard or nose his hands until he patted their big heads, but he told them to go on, and they would go back and lie down. Both seemed to recognize the state of things and were somewhat somber themselves.

Colleen told Burl she was coming home only because their granddaughter needed them both there. She moved her things to the guest bedroom so that Chelsea could sleep with her. Chelsea woke to fresh grief every time she stirred, and even though Burl wouldn't say it out loud, he had to concede that it was Colleen she'd want when that happened.

Chelsea had spoken only sparingly since arriving at the hospital in Irvine. She'd had a moment to say goodbye to her mother before they'd moved her body at the hospital, but Chelsea's devastation was so overwhelming that they had to take her away.

What little Chelsea said after that were questions of how her mother died, why she died, and about the permanence of it all. Colleen spoke of sickness and struggle and promised a reunion in heaven, as one might expect. Burl became grimmer each time she talked about it.

Darron initially said he wouldn't stay at his parents' house. He'd sworn to Burl years ago he'd not spend another night under his roof. He'd booked a room at Boone Tavern in Berea, where he stayed the first night after DeeDee passed, but Chelsea begged him until he finally agreed to come sleep in his old room. He said he would stay on until after the funeral, and that was it. Colleen and Darron kept to the house while Burl stayed mostly out on the porch with his dogs, and on and off the men who worked for him. Chelsea would go out to sit with him by times, then come back in to be with her grandmother and uncle.

Greek had called for one of the boys to pick him up at Chandy Taylor's house after he returned her car. The whereabouts of his Challenger were still unknown, so he'd been driving one of Burl's spares, a white Malibu. Burl had given

Greek instructions to account for all the men and call them in. Greek advocated for what was between the Spoons and Begleys to wait until after DeeDee was buried, and so far Burl had grudgingly assented.

Pot Roast had stashed Kendall's car at Arizona as he was told, but still didn't have his own truck back. Kendall, of course, had not been seen since peeling off in Greek's Challenger, so both sides still sat on a vehicle of the other's, and a third was up in the air.

The grounds of Burl's land were laden with men armed even more heavily than normal. Not knowing the Begleys' intentions, Greek had told Sheriff Horne to keep deputies near each of Burl's stores. Although Burl had agreed to stand pat for now, Greek promised he would not let him stand vulnerable.

Whatever happened, Burl would stand down only for so long. Clovis Begley had to know that. If Clovis took a notion to press an advantage by catching Burl on his heels in mourning, Greek swore he'd have an answer prepared.

In the few words spoken between Burl and Colleen, not one of them had touched on the events at Boone's Trace, which seemed small in the shadow of what had happened with DeeDee.

The sun had sunk and the porchlights were on and surrounded by frenetic nighttime insects. It was Monday, and Colleen, Darron, and Chelsea had gone into town earlier to see about things. After getting back, Darron had headed out onto the property in the RZR, with Chelsea along for the ride.

In all times of crisis or triumph, Burl took to a front porch rocker with a glass of brown liquor and a pack of Marlboro Reds. Rather than going in and out of the house, he kept an ever-renewing bottle of Four Roses Small Batch with him.

The ice in Burl's glass was long melted so that he was now pouring bourbon into an empty glass, draining it, pouring again, draining it. Colleen came out, ice cubes in one hand and a box of tissues in the other. She dropped the cubes into his half-full glass. Burl looked at it, swirled the ice, turned it up, took down the bourbon, reached for the bottle, and filled the glass again.

Colleen sat in the rocker beside him. It was several minutes before she spoke. She stared out at the same periphery as Burl. "It'll be Friday at one. Visitation, Thursday evening," she said.

Burl's elbows rested on the arms of the rocking chair. He picked between two of his teeth with a fingernail. He sighed.

"We'll stay until Saturday," she added.

He cocked his head. "Who's 'we'?"

"Darron, Chelsea, and me."

Burl jutted his lower lip and nodded. "You decided that, huh?"

"I did. It's not safe here."

"And when do you propose to bring her home?"

"I don't." Colleen smoothed her blouse. "This is no place for her. Or me."

Burl drew out the word, "Right." He took a long swallow from his glass. "You gonna move her in with that man? Is that what you was planning?"

"My intention is to take her into our son's home, where we're welcome. She can't stay here."

Burl leaned forward and set his glass on the porch planks. When he rose back up, he twisted in his chair, looking at Colleen. He pointed his index finger into the wooden arm of the rocker three times. "You think you going to dictate terms to me?" He had gotten to a place of not being able to control his slur. He wasn't trying.

"I'm going to do what's best for her."

"Oh, I see. You think moving her in with a couple queers is what's good for her? What exactly you think she's going to see over there?"

"I don't know, Burl. Maybe people who are civil. People whose entire existence isn't about breaking the law. People who don't strap on a gun the instant they roll out of bed of a morning."

"Naw. There's no better place for baby girl than right here."

"Because that worked out so well for our children." Colleen blotted either side of the bridge of her nose with a white tissue.

"You think you just gonna run off with her? Is that how you think this is gonna go? It won't for very damn long. It's a goddamn judge who decides. You know that. And you know how that'll come out, right?" Burl scratched the side of his neck and gazed into nothing. "Right?"

"Our daughter's dead, Burl. You understand that? And you can't pay any amount of money or threaten her back to life. You don't get another bite at it. DeeDee's gone. Are you prepared to admit that the life we lived is the reason?"

"She ain't gone because of me. I know what killed her, and I know who give it to her."

"My god, Burl, you're blind if you don't see how she wound up where she did. It was years coming, and the whole damn thing started right here." Colleen gestured outwardly, but at nothing in particular. "It started with one of your boys, not them. It may have ended somewhere else, but it started here. I'm not going to see Chelsea go the same way. I won't have it. Not for anything."

"Your own daughter dies, and all you can think about is running off with our only grandbaby. Naw, that ain't happening. Ain't going to work. She needs her papaw. If you ain't going to stand by your goddamn husband, that's your choice."

"You're no husband, Burl. You're not even a father. You don't have any children left. Not that'll have anything to do with you. Are you still convinced you can be a wonderful papaw in spite of it?"

"I take care of my family."

Colleen put her forehead in her hand. "What family, Burl? I mean, really. You and I haven't been married since I don't know when. Not in any real sense. You've always done whatever you wanted with whoever you wanted, and all I ever did was look the other way. It used to hurt me, but there came a point I just didn't care. Then I finally found a little happiness for myself, and you go and shoot the man."

"He drew on me."

"And what did you expect? You got just what you wanted. And then you threaten his wife? His family? My god." Colleen flung her used tissue on the porch. "He's separated, Burl. He has been for almost two years. He only wears that ring for appearances. You won, though. He deleted the video. I doubt I'll ever see him again. He was afraid of what you might do, and he was afraid of what it'd do to his practice if people found out what happened. He's telling people it was a hunting accident."

"Smart man."

"Yeah. Smart man." Colleen's eyes went skyward. "He gave you your way. That's what makes him smart to you. You think you should get everything you want all the time. You got rid of Daniel, and now DeeDee's gone too. Chelsea's got no parents left. Once you get rid of me, you can be that special papaw you always thought you were. You can do the same bang-up job you did as a father."

"Watch your mouth."

"Okay, Burl." She pulled another tissue out of the top of the box and pressed it to each cheek. "You're the father of the year. You'll be the grandfather of the year too if you can squeeze it in between shooting people and buying off the ones you don't shoot."

Burl reeled on one boot heel to his feet. He stumbled to the rail of the porch. Waylon and Johnny jumped up and went to him. It almost felt like they stabilized him. "I ain't

gonna fucking sit here and listen to this shit." He pointed
hard at Colleen. "You ain't talking to me like this."

"Or what, Burl?"

"You just ain't."

"Burl, if you love that baby, let her go. She can't stay here.
It'll only make it worse. I told you now because I want you to
have some time with it. You're the most stubborn person I've
ever known. You're the most stubborn person I'd know if I
lived a thousand years, but if you really love her, you won't
keep her here. You can still be in her life, but not here."

Burl spat on the porch. "Fuck no."

"You know I'm right, Burl. We can't lose another one. I
can't do it. You can't either."

"I said fuck no. She stays right the fuck here."

Colleen shook her head. She never broke eye contact.

Burl pushed off the porch rail and moved toward her. He
leaned just a few inches from her face. "Fuck. No." He didn't
care where his spittle went. She didn't move. She continued
staring straight into his eyes.

Gravel crunched behind him, and Burl swiveled. The
white Malibu appeared, circling up the drive. Greek brought
it to the loop in front of the house near where Colleen and
Burl were on the porch. It slowed to a stop, but the engine
still ran. It sat there for a full minute like that while Burl and
Colleen just watched it.

Greek got out, looking grim. "Can I get a word?"

Burl glanced at Colleen before he went unsteadily down
the porch with the dogs alongside him. Greek didn't move
from the open door, and he'd left the engine running. Burl
braced himself on the top of the door. "What is it?"

"Pot Roast's truck got towed from Sonic. We've located it
at a wrecker lot. I've sent him and Jared after it."

"You think them sod fuckers got it staked out?"

"I got my suspicions. I sent a second car as backup just in
case. I've gave them a route back that should flush out a tail.

Once they're back, I was going to pull everyone out of Madison for the time being. Bide our time."

"Pull back?" Burl's head lolled. He kept hold of the door and stared at the sky. "Why you pulling back?"

"I want things to get more settled here. I don't want any vulnerability."

"Fuck no. They need to feel us. They need to feel what's coming." Burl stumbled back and caught his balance.

"They'll feel us soon, Burl. I can assure you of that, but we don't need this thing popping off right now. You all need to get DeeDee laid to rest. Your family doesn't need to be worrying about those bastards coming back on us right now, do they?"

"I don't go on the defensive, Greek. You know that. Let's pull them back, and you and me ride over there."

"Tonight?"

Burl waved at the air with the back of his hand. "No, fucking next month."

"I don't know about it."

"Nah. We going." Burl started to make his way around to the passenger side of the Malibu with the dogs at his heels. "What do you got in the trunk?"

Greek didn't move to get in the car. "I'm right on top of this. I can go over if you want. See what opportunity arises. You ought to stay here. It don't do us no good to have you out right now. I only came here because I wanted to tell you in person what was going on and see how you all were doing."

Burl stopped short and tilted his head to look at Greek. "I ain't ask you your opinion. I was telling you what we was doing."

Greek didn't move. His expression remained the same. "I'm on it, Burl. I promise. I can get more done if it's just me, and I ain't gotta worry about anybody else. Stay here with your family."

With that, Burl spun precariously and stalked back around the car, stopped square in front of Greek, and grabbed a fistful of his shirt. The dogs pulled back and gave them berth. Their tails were down. Greek was still except for looking up at the porch, where Colleen stood with her arms crossed.

Burl's face was just inches from Greek's, though a good bit lower. "I said let's fucking go."

"I just don't think it's a good idea."

Burl drew back and fired a punch just off-center of Greek's nose that barely moved Greek's head. Greek blinked one eye but otherwise didn't react. Burl squinted at him, still holding his shirt, his right fist still balled. "Let's go." Greek eyeballed him and nothing more. Burl threw two more rights in quick succession with as much steam as he could put on them. Greek's arms remained at his sides. A thin trickle of blood leaked from Greek's left nostril down his upper lip. Greek swiped it with his tongue but still gave no other reaction. Burl drew back again, bringing his fist down below his waist, and launched a wild right hook at the side of Greek's head. This time Greek feinted back just enough for Burl to whiff, and the force of the swing and his own body weight sent Burl careening away, unable to keep his hold on Greek's shirt. He pirouetted, ungainly, and landed half on the gravel drive, half in the grass.

Greek didn't react to any of it, and neither did Colleen, but Waylon and Johnny had seen enough. They leaped to where Burl lay sprawled face down, cockeyed. They nosed at him and licked his face, keening the whole time. "You motherfucker," Burl said.

"I'm sorry, Burl. I just don't want to see anything bad happen to you and your family."

Burl rolled halfway over. "You fucking work for me. You done forgot?"

"Doing the best job I can."

"Fuck you, you goddamn fucking half-wit. You do what I fucking say."

"You ain't yourself, Burl."

"Who the fuck am I, then? You want to tell me that?"

"I don't know, Burl. You ain't yourself."

Burl sat up, the dogs still right in his face. "Burl fucking Spoon's who the fuck I am. I go where the fuck I want, and I do what the fuck I want. Y'all done forgot that?"

"You pay me to take care of things. Let me. You'd be best off right here. I'll be back at oh-eight-hundred and fill you in." He walked by Burl toward the house.

"Goddamn you will," Burl said at his back. "You ain't got a job no more, son. You fucking fired. You goddamn—you can leave that fucking car, walk your happy ass out."

Greek strode to the porch, and for the first time put the back of his hand to his nose, wiping away the blood. He went up a couple steps so he was close enough to Colleen to talk low. She listened to him intently, shrugged, said something Burl couldn't hear from where he sat in the yard, then turned her back on Greek and walked away.

Greek's focus went from Colleen going in the house to Burl, propped up in the yard with both his arms behind him. Burl rocked and swayed in spite of the support. Greek descended the porch.

When he got back to Burl, he stood over him and extended a hand. "Sorry. I guess we can head out."

Burl looked at it, bleary-like. "You goddamn fucking right." He took it and let Greek heave him back to his teetering feet. The two made their way to the Malibu.

Greek and Burl headed back down the mountain into the dark murk below, knifing through it with blazing blue LED headlights. Burl mumbled and grumbled with his head against the passenger side glass. Greek turned toward the route through Estill County. It was a much longer route, and Burl registered it, but he didn't bother questioning it.

21

T HE SUN SHONE through the trees on the east ridge when Greek topped the hill back at Burl's farmhouse. Burl snored rhythmically with only the interruption of the occasional snort and had been doing so for hours. Greek had posted up near the Begleys' place on 52 in Richmond and let Burl sleep. He didn't make any move at all. He only wanted to be nearby so if Burl woke up, he could make like he was tracking something. He'd headed back about an hour before sunup.

Greek was trying hard as he could to keep a stopper in things until they had time to focus on what needed doing. He hadn't entirely figured that out yet, but he had some notions, and he wanted Burl more clearheaded before they made any decision. The Begleys were more than a little dangerous. Mixing Burl and any one of them would uncork all hell. Not that Greek would shy from it; he just wanted things settled and Burl's family sequestered safely before fully deploying their ordnance.

Greek debated the best way to get Burl in the house. He half wanted to carry him like a child, but if Burl woke, the shine he'd cut wouldn't be worth it. He nudged Burl three times, then four, then five before Burl's lids finally cracked. Greek looked at Burl and said nothing. Burl worked his lips a few times before posting his elbow on the door and slowly rising out. He made his way unsteadily inside with Greek at his heels, spotting him. They were met at the door by Waylon and Johnny, who had barked their approach up the porch from inside. Burl told them, "Shut the fuck up, boys," as he crossed the threshold.

Greek followed Burl to his empty bedroom, where Burl fought his boots off like they were leeches, peeled down his dark jeans, and ripped the snaps open on his shirt and let it drop in a heap. He went face first down in only his bright white underwear and tube socks of the same color. His rhythmic snoring recommenced near instantaneously.

Greek knew better than to expect any sort of apology from Burl for hitting him the night before. He could count on one hand the number of times he'd seen the man express remorse for doing someone wrong. More often he'd do them some good turn without ever mentioning why he was doing it. Give them some money. Buy them something. From there he'd just let it blow over without ever saying anything.

The sound of coffee dripping and the smell of it drew Greek to the kitchen. He found Darron staring into the stainless-steel refrigerator with a carton of eggs in one hand and a butter dish in the other, still hunting something else. He glanced at Greek and then went back to the fridge.

Greek considered him a moment. "You care if I get some of that coffee?"

"Help yourself." Darron didn't look his way.

Greek knew the cabinet where Burl and Colleen kept both coffee cups and travel mugs. He took down a lidded travel mug with the National Wild Turkey Federation logo prominent on the side. He looked at the coffee brewing and could see that there wasn't enough to fill more than half the mug yet.

Darron laid the carton of eggs, butter, and a small can of evaporated milk on the counter. He went into cabinets under the huge granite kitchen island and came up with a frying pan.

Despite Darron's absence from Jackson County, the two weren't unfamiliar with each other. They'd come up only a year apart playing on many of the same Jackson County ball teams. When Greek was an undersized senior center who got by on hustle and muscle but missed lots of practices for guard duty, Darron was a junior and the true star of the team—a pure scorer at shooting guard with a sweet stroke and enough wiggle to create his own shot. The only hard surface poured around Burl's house was the basketball court out back. Burl once told Greek that Darron spent the majority of his time at home during his high school years "alone in the woods, in his room, or on that court."

Greek was still Kyle Staley back then, and off the court he didn't give much thought to Darron Spoon, really, but he also knew you didn't fuck with him. Not because Darron was in any way imposing, but because everyone knew his daddy ran Jackson County, and they also knew how he did it. Back in those days, Burl Spoon was known to get his hands dirty. Sometimes very dirty. It wasn't until Greek's return from overseas that Burl had gone on his run of personal cleanliness he'd just recently broken.

A wad of butter sizzled in the pan, releasing the scent into the room. Darron cracked three eggs deftly into a metal bowl before adding a splash of evaporated milk and twisting in some salt from a small grinder. "Based on the dogs, I take it you all just got in?"

Greek didn't avert his eyes from the stream of coffee slowly raising the level in the glass carafe. "Yeah."

"He raise hell all night?"

"Naw. Your daddy mostly slept."

Darron beat the eggs with a fork in the side-turned bowl. "My *daddy*? I think you misspoke. I don't have a daddy."

"You prefer 'father'?"

"I prefer nothing. Whatever word you want to use for it, I don't have one."

Greek barely shrugged. "Okay."

"I mean it. That man's no kin to me. I didn't want to come here, and I don't want to see him. You're welcome to him if you want. How about he can be *your* daddy? If you want him, you can have him."

"Naw. He treats me good, but I don't need no daddy."

Darron poured the egg mix into the heated pan, where it crackled at first contact. "I guess that makes two of us. At least he'd claim you."

"Eh, he's old school's all."

"Yeah. Right. Old school." Darron made an air quote with the hand not holding the spatula. "It's okay to disown your kid so long as it's because you're old school. That excuses everything."

"I didn't say it was right. I'm just saying, this is Kentucky. I don't give a fuck who you fuck." Greek shook his head. "Don't care one bit. But I ain't your daddy, and I ain't lived in Kentucky my whole life. I seen the world. Did you expect something else from him?"

"Honestly, no. But it's not a Kentucky thing. It's a 'people like him' thing. Did you know the homecoming king in Madison County was gay? Like, three years ago. That's right up the road. And the *mayor* of Lexington's gay. Or at least he was. I don't know—he might not still be in office, but their crosswalks are rainbows. People and places can change. There's no excuse for my father except that he's an asshole, and that's no excuse at all."

"Maybe." Greek lifted the now full carafe. "But he's going through a lot."

"Oh, fuck him. He's put people through a lot. With your help."

Greek's reaction was a long unaffected yawn. He filled the mug while Darron worked the eggs on the stove aggressively. He seemed to still be carrying on some kind of dialogue, but it had gone internal. Greek took a sip of the coffee, furrowed his brow, dragged the blue Bybee Pottery sugar jar across the counter, and used the little spoon inside to add a pinch before he affixed the lid on the travel mug.

"Okay. Good talk, bro," Greek said. He took a yellow apple from a bowl on the counter and lit for the front door. Darron stayed focused on his cooking and whatever conversation he was having with himself.

CHAPTER

22

B URL SETTLED INTO a sort of routine the week of the funeral. He took Chelsea out on the farm midday like he usually did. He'd do his normal rounds, and they'd check on the goats. She'd seem to forget things for a bit and even giggle as she ran among them, but then things would roll over her again, and she'd go back to somber. Burl's mood went up and down with hers. He usually started drinking on the porch not long after they got back, and stayed there into the evening. He took calls, and some of his guys came and went, but his only movement was in to the bathroom or to get something to eat, and he didn't do that much.

Like everyone else in town, Whitney had heard what happened. She'd sent a series of texts asking after Burl. Asking if there was anything she could do. The idea that she could do anything for him under the circumstances—or that he would entertain it—struck him as absurd, so he just ignored her messages until she gave up.

It hadn't been at all unusual for DeeDee to go a week without seeing Chelsea, but of course this wasn't the same. DeeDee would always turn back up eventually. There was no predicting it, but she would, and sometimes she'd run off with Chelsea for a bit, and sometimes she'd stay overnight with her at Burl and Colleen's place. Sometimes she'd stay for days at a time. Then she'd be gone again. Chelsea would ask her how long she'd be gone, and the answer was always the same: "A few days." How long that would actually be had always been ill-defined. Sometimes it meant a couple days, sometimes a week, sometimes longer. Now the answer to how long was forever.

Chelsea didn't go to school the last week. Even in the best of times, Burl Spoon's granddaughter could've come and gone from Jackson County Schools without questioning, but any child that young who's lost a parent is given a lot of leeway on school attendance.

Burl was on the porch with his dogs, smoking, when Darron came out and stood beside his chair. The dogs both got up to beg a petting from Darron, which he obliged. Burl kept rocking, and Darron didn't say anything. The dogs lay back down, and Burl and Darron both stared out at the yard's perimeter.

It was Darron who finally broke the silence. He stepped in front of his father and faced him. "So, how're you planning to get to the funeral home tonight?"

Burl didn't look at him. "Greek's picking me up."

"Okay, well, Mom was wondering if you didn't want to all go as a family. She thought Chelsea might like that. Chelsea's at her friend's house with Mom. We could pick them up on the way."

Burl snorted. "A family. All I been hearing from her is how we ain't one."

"Believe me, I can see her point." Darron pushed both his hands deep into his pockets. "But I'm not making this about me. It's about Chelsea. I don't know if that little girl's really grasped what it all means. That it's permanent. I think the least we can all do—the least you can do—is make her feel like she still has a family around her for the next few days."

"I ain't the one trying to break up her family, now am I?"

"I'm not getting into that. That's between you and Mom. I'm talking about today. I'm talking about tomorrow. I'm talking about getting through all this. You and Mom can work out what happens after. I already told her I'm not getting involved."

"Oh, does she think she's going to negotiate?" Burl pressed the tips of his fingers to his chest. "She's going to negotiate taking a child away from her home? *This* is Chelsea's home. You know that? If your mother thinks she's going to take her away from here, she's crazier than hell."

Darron pivoted on his heels and drew his hands from his pockets. He balled one fist and pressed the tip of the index finger into his thumb. "This isn't about a fucking negotiation. This is about a little girl who just lost her mom. A little girl who's sitting in the middle of what's about to be a divorce. Sitting in the middle of what's about to be a war between a couple of fucking outlaws, her own grandfather being one of them. Christ. Take yourself out of it for one second, you selfish prick. Do what's right for your granddaughter, not what suits your ego."

"So now you want to talk about pricks, huh? Your favorite subject."

"Oh, fuck you. You're going to die on this mountain and you're going to do it all by yourself. And I got news for you: nobody's going to mourn you. Nobody. Chelsea'll figure you out, just like I did, just like DeeDee did, just like Mom did. All your money can't buy you family. Maybe money can be your family. It's all you've got."

"Ain't you smart. Ain't you got it all figured out." Burl flicked his cigarette butt all the way out into the gravel. "Guess that college done filled you up. Naw, Chelsea loves her papaw. She needs her papaw. She don't need to go nowhere but here. She definitely don't need to go live with you and your cheating ass mama and whatever goddamn boyfriend you're prissing around with."

Darron shook his head and gathered himself. "Sometimes I have to remind myself that this is what you do. That this is what you've always done. You belittle everyone and everything that doesn't bend to your will. Everyone's beneath you because they don't have the money and power you have. But that's literally all you are: money and power. You don't bring anything to this world." Waylon raised his head as the words got heated, which meant Johnny did too. "All you ever do, all you've ever done, is play life like it's a game you have to win. And it doesn't matter how much you have to cheat so long as at the end of the day you feel like you're winning. But here you are, all this money and power, and you've got nothing. Do you feel like the winner?"

Burl stared into the air. Into the space between something and nothing. He started to say something more than once but didn't.

Darron lowered his voice. "Have you started figuring it out yet? You don't have one thing left to cling to except a granddaughter whose life is only going to be worse if she stays with you."

Burl cocked his chin Darron's way. He was calm. "It ain't my fault you turned out a faggot and your momma turned into a goddamn whore. I done the best I could for both of you. What's come of you couldn't be helped by me."

"You're making my point."

"So, you agree with me?"

"I'm exactly the person I'm supposed to be," Darron said, his hand on his heart. "And whether you can comprehend it or not, I like who I am. I'm proud of who I am. Being raised by someone like you, it was hard to get here. And I'm well past caring what you think, and Mom's the same. You don't matter. Not to either one of us. All that money, all that power, and the people who should care about you the most don't want anything to do with you. So, what do you have to show for it all?"

"You real proud, huh?"

"Yes, I am." Darron went for the door. He paused and looked at his father again. "Not everyone makes it, you know. I wasn't always sure I would."

Burl regarded his son. An iridescent beetle clattered onto the porch and landed on its back, then buzzed its wings until it flipped upright.

"Fuck it. Ride with your damn lackeys. They're all you have left. You might as well get used to it."

Darron pulled open the screen hard and let it slam back behind him. Burl turned his head, thinking he might say something at Darron's back. The dogs looked from the door to Burl, unsettled and agitated. Burl kept looking at the door for a bit. Eventually he turned back, drew out a fresh Marlboro, and put it to light.

CHAPTER

23

JACKSON COUNTY'S POPULATION was spread out among a number of small communities. Of the county's roughly thirteen thousand residents, only around eight hundred of them lived in the county seat, McKee. The rest were disseminated through Sandgap, and Annville, and Gray Hawk, and Fox Town, and lots of other places, some of which had names you couldn't find on a map anymore.

At DeeDee's visitation it felt like people had come from all of those places. Lakes Funeral Home's parking lot couldn't hold all the cars. They spilled out onto 421, making driving past a hazard. The folks who came to pay respects wouldn't fit inside. The line of people leaked out onto the columned porch and snaked around the side of the low-slung white building.

The evening was warm, and folks fanned themselves with their hands or whatever scraps of paper they might have. The funeral home had a few handheld paper fans to give away, but there weren't nearly enough. Days were getting long, and the sun was still out shining hazily. The folks who showed up made sure to get their names in the book and see Burl and shake his hand.

When he first went inside, Burl was overtaken by the
smells of fresh paint and old carpet. He was just getting accli-
mated when he realized DeeDee's casket was closed. His first
act was to snarl at the undertaker for not fixing her up, and
the undertaker said he could have made her look great, but
Colleen wouldn't have it. She didn't want a repeat of Chelsea's reaction in the hospital. Instead, there was a big, framed
picture of DeeDee sitting on a picnic table with Chelsea in
her lap. They were outside the Frosty-Ette and Chelsea was
staring at her ice cream cone.

Burl's discontent about the closed casket was moot now
because he hadn't done anything to help with the arrangements, and it was too late to open it up. Around the casket
were dozens of sprays of flowers and a handful of houseplants.
All would be dead inside a couple of weeks.

As people passed through, Burl stood at the far end of
the casket with Greek. Some of Burl's other people, including
Jared and Pot Roast, were in the vicinity. Darron and Colleen
were steps away, at the near end, greeting folks first. Their
greetings were warm with sorrow. People recalled their rela-
tionships with DeeDee if they had one, and said what a trag-
edy it was. Colleen and Darron nodded agreement, patted
their backs, and hugged some of them. Burl shook hands but
was somber and had little to say to anyone. He couldn't bring
himself to be any other way. Chelsea lingered near her family
at first, wandering back and forth between Colleen and
Darron, and Burl.

Eventually, Chelsea's friend's mother offered to take her
to the next room and let her play with her friend, and Colleen
said she could go and Burl didn't protest. Getting out of the
house and seeing a friend, in spite of the fact she was in a
funeral home, had seemed to brighten Chelsea's mood to a
place it had rarely been since DeeDee died.

After two hours, people were still filtering through, but
Burl was done. He popped his chin, and that was all the sign

he had to give. Greek and the rest of his people ducked out the side door into the parking lot. Burl scarcely gave Colleen and Darron a glance. They stayed on to greet the rest of the people coming through.

Sheriff Horne was leaned against the hood of his prowler, talking to a local insurance agent. His vehicle was one of three from his department parked in the lot, with uniformed men beside them. As Burl approached, the insurance agent recognized him coming and took his leave.

Burl laid one hand on the sheriff's hood. "I need y'all back here tomorrow."

"We was planning on it," the sheriff said. "How much longer you want us to stick around tonight?"

"Until my goddamn family leaves."

"Will do." The lawman gestured his arm at the surroundings. "Do you really think they'd come hurt somebody here? That they'd do it at a funeral?"

"I don't know what they'd do." Burl motioned for Greek to head for the car. "I only know what I would."

24

Burl sent Pot Roast by Opal's Restaurant to get him some supper while Greek drove him back to the farm. Opal's was his favorite spot, and it sat right around the corner from Burl's arcade, over which was Burl's business office that doubled as a poker room on Saturday nights. He hadn't been by there or Opal's in better than a week.

By the time Pot Roast got to Burl's house with the food, Greek had left on a run over to Hill Top Grocery. Most of the dealers Burl supplied picked up their product at the little grocery and gas station. Because of the money and merchandise that came and went, it was Burl's second most tightly secured location after the farm.

Burl had told Pot Roast to get himself some dinner too, so they sat together, eating at the island in Burl's kitchen. Burl hadn't been eating much but was picking with a silver fork at a piece of fried catfish in a white Styrofoam container that had "vegetables," one of which was macaroni and cheese, in the other compartments.

Pot Roast had just about polished off a slab of meatloaf and a roll, but his soup beans were going begging. He had a half-empty bottle of blue Gatorade beside his food. He ate with plastic utensils he'd gotten at Opal's. He was talking between oversized bites, and Burl wasn't saying a whole lot.

"I got me a suit," Pot Roast said. "I never had one before. I've only ever wore a tie a couple times. I thought it was only right that I should have a suit on if I was carrying DeeDee's casket."

Burl looked up from his fork and nodded.

"I had Greek tie the tie for me, and left it that way on the shirt. If it comes untied, I'm out of luck. I'll just have to leave it dangling, I guess."

Burl took a moment to respond. Things were taking a little longer to sink in. "One of the boys'll tie it back for you."

"Yeah, I guess." Pot Roast stabbed the last big hunk of meat loaf, big enough for three bites for most people, and put the whole thing in his mouth. He chewed real big for a little bit, and before he was done, said, "I just want to be respectful is all."

Burl had a single green bean on the end of his fork, with a small shred of bacon dangling from it. "I appreciate that."

A car approached up the gravel drive, unseen from where Burl and Pot Roast sat, but heard. Outside, Waylon and Johnny barked it in. It could be heard circling around the back of the house, and one of the garage doors went up. That meant it was Burl's family. Doors opened and closed, and voices drifted up from below. Colleen and Darron came up the stairs, followed a moment later by Chelsea who had a well-worn blue stuffed rabbit that her mother had given her under an arm.

Darron set down a Dairy Queen bag on the island. He opened it, looked in, took out a small wrapped burger, and laid it out near a chair. "Here you go, Chelsea." He got out a larger sandwich, looked at it uncertainly, and started to unwrap it.

Colleen put down a couple of drink cups, one of which had a red spoon sticking out of it, meaning it was a Blizzard.

Pot Roast wore a sunnier expression than anyone else in the room. He said, "Hey, Mrs. Spoon."

Colleen pursed her lips. "Hello, Pot Roast."

"I was just telling Burl that I got me a suit for tomorrow. To be respectful."

Colleen laid her palm flat on the granite and patted it a couple times before responding. "Thank you for that, Pot Roast."

Chelsea made her way around the island and leaned into one of Pot Roast's legs. "Pot Roast," she said in a singsong voice. She'd always liked him. He tended to be cheerful and was always ready to talk to anyone, even little kids.

He patted her on the back. "Hey, big girl. You got your rabbit."

"Yeah." She looked up at him. "We got us some Dairy Queen. What're you eating?"

"I was eating meat loaf. I done ate it all, though."

She cocked her head. "Meat loaf? You're not supposed to eat meat loaf. You're supposed to eat pot roast."

"I know. They was all out. This was the next best thing." He wiped his mouth with a napkin, balled it up, put it in his container along with his plastic knife and fork, and laid the spoon from the soup beans flat in the space where the meat loaf had been. "I ought to get on to the house. Dolly's gonna be wanting her dinner."

"Dolly? Who's Dolly? Is she your girlfriend?"

"No, darling, she ain't my girlfriend." Pot Roast opened three doors on the kitchen island before he found the one that housed the garbage can and tucked his takeout container into it. "Dolly's my dog. She's a pretty little pointer, and she's probably missing me about now."

Colleen had Chelsea by the hand and was leading her to the sink to wash up. "Can you bring her over here sometime?" Chelsea asked him as she climbed onto a little step stool so she could reach the water.

"If your nana and papaw say it's okay, I will. She'd probably run off into the woods first chance she got."

"I want her to meet Waylon and Johnny." She looked at Colleen. "Can Dolly come over, Nana?"

"We'll just have to see."

"Course she can," Burl said.

Chelsea peered at Colleen. "Papaw says she can."

"We'll just have to see."

Darron stood at the end of the island, eating a chicken sandwich and looking from one of his parents to the other. Pot Roast looked uncertain. He picked up his Gatorade and capped it. "Well, I'll see you all." He seemed to think about something else and couldn't quite decide on what. He finally added, "Soon."

Darron raised a hand. "All right, Pot Roast. You be safe getting home."

Pot Roast nodded but didn't say anything else before heading for the door.

Chelsea called, "Bye, Pot Roast," as he headed away.

25

COLLEEN GOT CHELSEA situated with her cheeseburger and a cup of apple juice she poured from a bottle in the fridge. The little cup had characters from *Frozen* on the sides. Chelsea's mood had been up and down all day. At times she was tearful and nearly inconsolable. At other times she tittered on as if she'd forgotten that anything had happened. Time, as short as it was, had already begun working on her.

Burl lingered in the kitchen with his supper container in front of him, but not touching it. It was the first time everyone who was staying in the house had been in the same room together more than fleetingly. Burl wasn't acting himself, Colleen noticed. Not that his disposition was too much different; he was just noticeably quieter. If he got wound up, he still ranted and cussed a blue streak, but he wasn't dominating conversations like usual. He wasn't lashing out as often. He seemed more within himself. Colleen had resolved not to rouse him from his introspection if at all possible.

She hadn't begun to eat yet as she'd been getting Chelsea set up, and offered Darron something to drink. When she finally sat, she watched Chelsea before she spoke. "Chelsea, I was wondering, would you want to go to your little friend's house on Saturday? Kaitlyn's mom said she'd love to have you over again."

Chelsea took a bite of her burger and appeared to be thinking it over. "Um, I want to, but when can she come here? I want her to be here at our house. I want to take her with Papaw to see the goats."

Colleen glanced at Burl. She knew if she could get Chelsea to Kaitlyn's house, they could leave from there for Louisville without Burl raising hell. If she could establish that Chelsea was going to her friend's, she hoped it would throw him off the scent of their departure. "Maybe some-time, but Saturday she's invited you to her house."

Darron stayed quiet, but his eyes studied his dad. Burl's demeanor didn't crack.

"But when can Dolly come over?" Chelsea asked.

"Oh, honey, I don't know," Colleen said. "Pot Roast is awful busy. We'll just have to see."

Burl's eyes snapped up. "Now no. He ain't too busy. He'll bring that dog over."

Colleen took a moment to choose her words. "I just don't know when it'd be. I'm sure Pot Roast would be happy to bring her to see you sometime. We'll just have to see how things go."

"Tomorrow night." Burl nodded. "She'll be here tomor-row night."

Chelsea set down her burger on the wrapper, and her face rose. "Really?"

"You can bank on that, sugar. Ol' Dolly'll be here tomor-row evening for a visit."

"Did you hear that, Uncle Darron? Dolly's coming over. Do you think she'll like Waylon and Johnny?"

Darron tapped his middle finger absently on the granite. "I'd say they'll make fast friends." Quieter he said, "I just hope she's spayed."

Chelsea didn't make anything of that. "Can Dolly go see the goats, Papaw?"

He smiled wide like he rarely had lately. "We can take her wherever you want." His smile evaporated just as quickly as it came. "This is your home. You can go anywhere you want to at your own home, and that old dog can go with you."

Chelsea smiled at her grandmother and her uncle. "I bet she'll like the goats. Can Pot Roast come with us?"

"Course he can," Burl said. "You and me and Dolly and Pot Roast'll take us a good long ride all over the farm. We'll have us a big time."

Burl and Chelsea continued on talking about Pot Roast and Dolly and their big plans. Darron and Colleen kept on staying out of the way of it. Colleen's plans to get Chelsea out of Jackson County would come into conflict with Burl's intentions eventually. All Colleen wanted for the time being was to get her daughter buried with some kind of dignity before enduring what was sure to come.

26

H OLT WASN'T FAMILIAR with Annville, but finding the driveway to the boy's trailer had been easy. Micah Begley knew just where it was and had given Holt a phone to use that showed him the way. Holt had lost his own phone before he got locked up, and it had run out of minutes anyway.

It was just after one in the morning, and the moon wasn't throwing much light. He had parked his truck off the side of the road and walked the couple hundred yards up to the boy's trailer, toting his tire iron in one gloved hand. Clovis had given him gloves and had been adamant that he wear them. There was a power company pole lamp that lit up the area outside the trailer. A bat careened in and out of the yellow light, catching a late dinner in the glow. When Holt got up close, he found a battered wheelbarrow leaned against the trailer, which would make things easier. It was the middle of the night and the boy had a dog penned that Holt intentionally got to barking. It was some kind of hunting dog.

The boy came out on his porch, barefooted and barechested in plaid pajama pants. He shouted, "What is it, Dolly?" and peered into the dark before telling the dog to hush and going back in. But Holt needed him to come off the porch for his plan to work.

Holt thought about it a minute. The trailer sat by itself in a little level spot about halfway up a mountain. What he did was set off the alarm in the boy's truck, and that did the trick. The boy ran out into the drive, packing a pump shotgun, but Holt blindsided him with the tire iron before he had even racked it, and the boy went straight down. Holt dropped the tire iron and trained his Ruger on him, but the boy was out.

Holt got him zip-tied at the hands and ankles and got his flashlight out and loaded the boy up in the wheelbarrow and found a pretty well-worn path into the woods. The dog went absolutely wild the whole time, its constant barking and crying echoing off the mountainsides. Multiplying. Nobody was listening, but Holt still wished it'd shut the fuck up. He was able to roll the boy a hundred yards before the path got too steep. He dumped him out at the base of a rise.

The woods smelled green and mossy, and it was a comfort to Holt as he got to work. He set his flashlight on a fallen branch and trained it on the boy. He was breathing shallow but was still out. Holt could still hear the dog, distant, and the echoes of its pleading barks. Holt hoisted down the boy's pajamas and underwear to below the knees, where they were stopped by the zip tie. Holt took his case knife from its holster on his belt and opened it. He'd never threatened to cut a man's nut out before, but there was a first time for everything. To be honest, Holt wasn't real sure why Clovis wanted that, but he was real adamant. That was the message he wanted sent. That he could get to this boy, and if he wanted his nuts cut out, he could get it done.

Holt dug between the boy's legs with his left hand and grasped his junk like it was a weed he aimed to pull. The whole thing was real slack and loose, but still, he thought that'd be enough to wake the boy up. It didn't. The boy was out, and Holt was a little stumped about what to do next. If he didn't tell him he was going to cut his nuts, how would Clovis's message get sent?

What Holt decided to do was give the boy a stick. Just a tiny one. Jab him in the junk just hard enough to draw a little bit of blood, and that way the boy would come to and would know just how serious Clovis was about the whole thing.

Holt put the tip of his blade right up against it, pressed it a bit, then at once gave it a good hard poke. It wound up going a good bit deeper than he'd intended. The reaction was instantaneous, and more than Holt had wanted. The boy came to, screaming and flailing like all hell, clobbering Holt across the face with his zip-tied hands. At that point, instinct just took over, and before he knew it, Holt had stuck the boy a good dozen times in the bare chest and neck. The boy's screaming and moving pretty well stopped after the blade had gone in three or four times, but Holt kept at it, even once the boy'd gone flat and still.

Holt drooped back onto his haunches and stared at the glistening knife in his bloodied hand. Night bugs chattered away all around him, and in the distance that dog still hadn't quieted down. Holt's heart was thumping, and he sat there a minute, waiting for the adrenaline to slack off before getting up. He wiped his knife in the brush and closed it, picked up the flashlight, and trained it on the boy. His pants were still down, and he was real pale wherever he wasn't stabbed and bleeding. Holt had fucked it up, that much was undeniable, but was it really his fault? Clovis had given him a fucked-up plan, and as fucked-up plans are known to do, it got fucked.

The mess he was looking on now was a problem in need of a solution. He'd told Clovis he didn't think threatening a man with cutting his nut out was going to be as easy a job as he made it out to be, and Holt felt vindicated about that. He'd done the best he could under the circumstances. How could Clovis fault him for that? But Holt knew damn well he would.

After a bit of deliberation, Holt loaded the boy back in the wheelbarrow and rolled him off the path and into the brush.

Initially, he'd considered wheeling him all the way to his truck and hauling him off and dumping him somewhere else, but what good would that do? It was far as fuck to his truck, and he'd get blood in the bed and have to wash it out, and what if he got pulled over? He didn't have any shovel, and he wasn't going to hang around and look for one. No, he'd just get him as deep into the woods as he could, and hope animals found him and took care of him before anyone else did.

After he'd gotten the boy dumped in the woods, Holt started the long walk back to his truck, thinking about the best way to explain to Clovis what happened. When he reached the level spot by the trailer, the little dog was still going crazy in its pen, snarling at him as he went past. The sound of the dog carrying on combined with the thought of Clovis giving him hell when he got back for fucking up the job became more than he could take. Holt stopped and listened a moment before he turned back.

The pen was one of those chain-link numbers, with a doghouse inside and big steel food and water bowls. The closer Holt got to the dog, the farther it backed into the corner of its pen, before eventually cowering into its house, still barking and baring its teeth, with only its head sticking out. He decided to shut it up.

Holt drew the Ruger and tried to draw a bead on the dog's head, but it was too dark in the pen, and he couldn't aim the gun and his flashlight at the same time. He'd have to get closer for a better shot. He lifted the latch on the gate and opened it. Before he could even raise the gun again, the dog darted out of its house and ran at him, then leaped past as he kicked at it. He fired three rounds as it dashed away. Before he could squeeze off a fourth, it was across the lit lot and up the trail into darkness. He gazed after it, the gun still aimed where it had just been. But it was gone.

The night was quiet now except for the ringing in his ears and the vague sound of his boots on the gravel as he walked away. It drowned out the bugs altogether. The only movement now was the hungry bat that carried on pirouetting around the light.

Holt would head west in his truck toward Livingston, where he had family. He knew he could hook up with I-75 North from there. He'd be on the interstate about forty minutes, and his radio didn't work, so it'd be a pretty boring ride. Once he got back to Richmond, he thought a stop at Hardees was in order. He'd hit the drive-through for a two pack of sausage biscuits before going home. When he got back to Greens Crossing, he'd go to his mother's to sleep before telling Clovis what happened. Clovis had told him not to call him or any of his people, but to come see him when it was done. That could wait until he'd gotten some sleep. He'd been up all damn night.

27

ABOUT AN HOUR before DeeDee's service was scheduled to start, Burl was outside Lakes, having a smoke by himself. Whenever anyone threatened to approach him, Burl gave them a look that advised them not to.

Family and pallbearers were supposed to arrive no later than eleven. The service was at noon. Just like everything else, Colleen and Darron had chosen the pallbearers. They'd picked DeeDee's three male cousins from Colleen's side and filled the other three spots with Pot Roast, Clarence, and Toby. Of the six, Pot Roast was the only one still not there. He lived pretty far out in the county, and Burl figured he was probably fighting with his shirt and tie.

The first stir of the day rippled through the few other folks gathered outside when an Acura with dark tinted windows pulled in the parking lot, and a Black man in a dark suit got out, talking on a cell phone. Lots of eyes met, including those of the deputies standing guard. Burl's stayed fixed on the man. All seemed to be silently asking what this was all about and what should they do about it.

Although rural Kentucky and Southern Appalachia as a whole were a lot more diverse than many people believed, Jackson County was one pocket that still fit the old stereotype. It was more than ninety-nine percent white, and of the few people who lived there who weren't white, almost none were Black. So an unknown Black man in an expensive car at DeeDee's funeral was subject to extra scrutiny. Especially from Burl.

The man lowered his phone and pocketed it as he approached the entrance. Smoke still rising from the cigarette in his lips, Burl had begun to pivot the man's way. Just then Darron and Colleen emerged from the building, approached the man, and hugged him, one after the other, Darron patting the man's back as he did and saying something into his ear. Darron took the man by the arm, and the three of them went inside, looking straight ahead, not acknowledging that the eyes of every last person outside the funeral home were trained on them. A silence had fallen over everything when the man had first turned up, and the instant he was inside, it broke, and conversations that had been paused restarted or began anew with the fresh topic of what they had just seen.

It wasn't until twenty after and Burl was back inside, seated on the steps by the pulpit, that Toby pointed out Pot Roast still wasn't there. "Why'd you wait so fucking long to bring it up?" Burl said.

"I'm sorry, Burl. I don't know." Toby cowered. "It ain't like him. He usually runs on time."

"Maybe he's fighting his tie," Clarence said.

"Hell, it's been too long for it to be that," Burl said.

"Yeah. I guess he'd have come here for help by now," Clarence said. "I'd offer to run out there and get him, but there ain't time to get to his place and back is there?"

Toby's eyes were down. "I should've said something sooner. I kept thinking he'd show up."

Burl scowled as he stood up. "Let me go tell Horny."

Toby nodded. "Who you want to have be a pallbearer if Pot Roast don't turn up?"

"I don't fucking know." Burl rose from his seat and pointed vaguely at the doorway coming in. "Have Jared do it."

"Okay, Burl."

Sheriff Horne was out front of the funeral home, shaking hands with people as they went in, looking like he was hosting the event. He had an election to win, after all. Not for more than another year, but for any Kentucky sheriff worth his salt, every community gathering is a campaign event for the next election, Burl Spoon in your corner or not.

Burl stood away from the sheriff, by himself, and gestured him over. Horne came to him like a dog that'd been called. "Y'all about to start in there?"

Burl waved a hand in his face, quieting him. "I need you to hush and listen. Pot Roast ain't here. Something ain't right. That boy would be here if they wasn't something wrong. I need you to send a car out Annville by his place. I can't spare none of my people."

"I'll send someone right now."

"I want to know what they find out."

"Okay, but I don't want to bother you with this, Burl. Let me and my boys handle it. You be with your family."

"I ain't ask you your opinion what to do. I told you. I want to know what y'all find."

"Okay, Burl."

Burl tightened his eyes on the sheriff before turning and going back in the funeral home. Inside the lobby, Colleen, Darron, the man from the Acura, and Chelsea all stood close together, talking quietly. Chelsea had her blue stuffed rabbit by the arm. It hung forlornly. Now and again, someone would come up to them, shake hands and pat on Colleen and Darron. Burl was still carrying himself in a way intended to keep everyone away. He'd shook enough hands and heard enough "I'm sorrys" the day before to last him until his own passing.

When Burl saw Whitney come in wearing a short dark dress, he gave her a look intended to tell her to stay away too. But she wouldn't keep her eyes off him, even while she signed the guest book. She came straight to him after and laid her hand on his forearm before he took one short step back. "Oh, Burl. I'm so sorry." She had a little silver swallow pin near the collar of her dress.

He nodded and said, "I thank you for that."

She put her hand on his arm again, and he moved away again. He looked just long enough to see that Colleen, Darron, the man, and Chelsea were all watching Whitney and him. She said, "I just feel horrible. If there's anything I can do, please tell me."

He looked her square in the face. "Yeah. I guess you ought to go in and pay your respects now."

She reached for him one more time and said, "Burl, I—" But before she could touch him, he scooted away again.

"I said go in and pay your respects, and leave me be." His voice rose for the first time. He glanced at his family again, and they didn't pretend not to watch. Neither did anyone else.

Whitney lowered her hand, and her eyes took a shine. She walked away from him slowly and went into the sanctuary.

Colleen separated from the others and came Burl's way, her forehead knotted. He stared at his tight-closed fist in front of him, his thumb digging its nail into the side of his index finger. He never looked up when she drew close.

"Don't you treat that little girl poorly on my account, Burl. I don't care a thing about it. She's just trying to get by in this world." Colleen seemed to be waiting for Burl to say something back. He always found something to say back. But lately he was coming up short some. Colleen seemed to decide that if he didn't have anything more to say, she didn't either, and she walked away.

Burl sat on the center aisle with Chelsea beside him. Colleen was on her other side. Chelsea leaned her head into her grandmother's bosom, but her little hand clutched her grandfather's on her other side. Darron was beside his mother, and the man they had greeted in the parking lot was beside him to his right. The two conspicuously held hands. Burl peered down the row at them intermittently, his brow creased, but he never moved from his seat nor said a word.

The service consisted largely of hymns and scripture but was punctuated by a short sermon from a preacher who had known DeeDee a bit when she was young but who had hardly seen her the last fifteen years. He told one story about something she'd said to him at his church when she was a kid that Burl thought he easily could have just made up. He told a couple other anecdotes about her that he'd apparently gathered from Colleen and Darron. He ended up moralizing about the evil of drugs and the scourge they caused the community without ever coming out and saying that he was talking about drugs. Then he leaned into the old "she's going to be waiting for you all in heaven" routine and wrapped it up. Chelsea cried silently. Colleen sobbed real low and pulled Chelsea closer. Darron cried stoically, with the man next to him stroking his arm. Burl grimaced. He did not cry.

The preacher ended by explaining the procession to the cemetery for those so inclined, and then invited folks to the family life center at his church for a reception. Ushers directed the attendees out, beginning with Burl and his family. Burl passed by DeeDee's coffin and went out the side door, looking for Sheriff Horne. Horne was leaned into his cruiser, talking loudly on his radio. He spotted Burl coming and ended the conversation. He wore a pained expression and no hat on his sweat-slicked head.

Burl spoke first. "What'd we find out?"

"It ain't good, Burl. It ain't good at all."

"What the fuck's happened?"

"Boy ain't around, but his truck's there and his front door's hanging wide open. Vultures is circling up the mountain. My man ain't went up there yet, but he's fixing to."

Burl's mouth sagged open. His face was drained out and stricken of a sudden. He looked over the folks exiting the funeral home, seeking out his wife. She came out the door with Chelsea in tow and Darron and the man from the Acura close behind. Burl's boot heels clacked hard against the asphalt toward her.

Colleen dabbed at her eyes with a tissue, and her face was drawn. Her expression turned stark the instant she saw Burl's face. "What's happened?" she said.

"I don't know yet, but I can't go to the cemetery. I need you and the baby to ride with Clarence and Toby."

"We're not riding with them."

Burl pointed at her chest from inches away, and his voice rose. "You need to do what I say right now. This is goddamn serious."

"I won't."

Burl's voice fell in volume and pitch. "You and the baby need protected."

Darron put a hand between his parents and edged his body in close. "They'll be fine with us."

Burl snorted. "Oh, so you and this fella here are gonna protect them?"

Darron locked his eyes on his father's but pulled his thumb at his companion. "Michael is a sergeant with Louisville Metro. I think he can handle it a lot better than any of your marijuana mafia idiots."

As Burl looked the man over, the man's expression never changed. He shifted the right panel of his suit jacket to the side, revealing a silver and gold police shield on his belt. Burl's gaze went from the man to his son, to his wife, and then to Chelsea. He knelt beside her. "Papaw's got to go check on something, Peanut. You take care of your nana, and I'll get home later, and we can go see the goats, okay?"

Chelsea looked at him, red-eyed, and nodded faintly.

Burl rose back up and looked at his son. "Keep your mother and the baby safe."

Darron put his arm across the back of Colleen's shoulders. "We will."

28

CLOVIS HAD WAITED all morning on Holt, but he never did turn up. It was going on one in the afternoon when his patience ran dry, and he decided to go by Holt's mother's house to see if he was over there.

Some sort of Hyundai was parked outside the little brick ranch, as well as Holt's truck. Clovis had considered having one of his boys ride over with him, but in the end decided it'd be better if it was just him. He topped the steps to the porch, pulled back a loose screen door and rapped on the red-painted wooden door. He stood waiting in his usual tan overalls, and he also wore a red ball cap with "Lake Okeechobee, Florida" stitched into it above an image of a largemouth bass with its mouth agape.

A yappy dog started in, and a woman kept telling it to hush because it was going crazy barking. Holt's mother pulled the door open with the small brown guard dog still carrying on in her arms. She knew Clovis. Everybody out Greens Crossing knew everybody else, but they especially all knew Clovis. She said, "Hello, Clovis."

"Hidy, Pauline. I seen Holt's truck. He here?"

"Last I checked he was still asleep. He might be up now, with Mitzi cutting such a shine." She raised her dog up a few inches. It was still growling quietly and sputtering out the occasional small yip. "He was out most of the night. Sun was about up when he come in. I thought he'd fell in with a girl or something, and I'd not see him for a day or two."

"Well, I need to talk to him if you don't care to get him."

"No, I don't care to. Why don't you come in, and I'll put her up so she don't jump on you."

"Naw. Send him out here if you would. I'll be in my truck."

Holt's mother nodded and walked off, leaving the door open. Clovis let the screen swing shut and went back to his truck.

He'd been waiting five minutes, which was five minutes longer than he wanted to wait, when Holt came out the door, looking like reheated death. He seemed in no particular hurry to get into Clovis's cab, and by the time he opened the door, Clovis's blood had gone from being up to spilling over.

"Get in this fucking truck already."

"That's what I'm doing," Holt said.

Clovis looked at him and shook his head, then stared straight out the front window at nothing for a moment so he could stifle himself from strangling Holt right then.

Holt pulled the door closed and sat there. Clovis moved his mouth like he was chewing, waiting for his ire to recede. "What's going on?" Holt said.

"What's going on? You were supposed to come straight back and let me know how it went. I don't even know if you made it out there."

Holt was just as sedate as could be. "No, I went out there."

"Did you find that boy? Pot Roast?"

Holt nodded. "Yep."

Clovis waited on him to go on, but when he didn't, he finally said, "Well? What happened? Did you get the point across?"

Holt shrugged. "I guess you could say that."

Clovis cuffed Holt in the back of the head so fast that Holt didn't seem to even see it. It rocked his whole body forward. Holt was wiry and not short, but he weighed maybe a hundred and sixty pounds. Clovis went six foot three and two hundred and forty pounds of dense muscle. At fifty-eight years old, he was still packed tight.

Holt's hands both balled, then the left opened and he shoved Clovis square in the face. Clovis scarcely flinched. His big right hand fired out, clamped Holt's neck, and constricted so hard that Holt's eyeballs jutted about a half inch apiece. Holt clawed at Clovis's arm and kicked his legs, but all he succeeded in doing was persuading Clovis to jam his head back against the passenger window and tighten the vise on his trachea even more.

"Quit playing fucking games with me. I'll take whatever's left of your carcass to the jail, drop your ass in the parking lot, and get my bond money back." He'd still not relaxed his grip any at all, and Holt was still flailing, his face hovering on some shade between red and maroon. Clovis just stared at him, watching his coloring change. "When you're ready to tell me what you should've told me at my own damn house six hours ago, I'll let you have a breath.

Holt finally quit thrashing and went slack, whether involuntary or a choice, Clovis wasn't sure. Whatever the reason, he released his grip, and Holt heaved in a deep breath and damn near hyperventilated trying to get his air back. The red of his face fell away gradually, but the finger marks on his neck stayed angry.

Once Holt was finally somewhat composed—although still gasping a bit—Clovis said, "Did you give that boy my message or not?"

Holt's forehead was in his hand. "I tried to."

"What's that mean? Did you or didn't you?"

"I tried. I got the drop on him and everything, like we planned out. I got him bound up. But then, you know, he attacked me. I wasn't expecting it."

"Shit. So, he got loose from you?"

"No, he never did get loose." Holt made eye contact with Clovis. "I had to stab him."

"You what?"

"I had to stab him."

"I heard what you said. I'm just trying to understand why you had to do that if you'd got him bound up."

"He was bound up, but he hit me anyway." Holt pointed at his face where he'd been hit. "I ain't just gonna let someone hit me."

"So, you stabbed this guy and left him there? You don't think he's told his boss by now?"

"He ain't gonna tell him nothing. I stabbed him, I don't know, six or eight times. He's deader than hell. I left him out in the woods."

"You *what*?"

"I left him. What was I supposed to do? I wasn't going to take him with me, and I didn't have no way to bury him. His dog was carrying on, so I tried to shoot it, but it ran off. Everything was quiet when I left."

Clovis didn't say anything. He blinked a half dozen times.

Holt threw his hands up. "What?"

Clovis's straight right snapped into Holt's eye like his arm was spring loaded. It made Holt's head ricochet off the window. He was instantly a noodle. He twitched a few times but was out. Blood gathered in a curved line at the base of his orbital and began to weep down his cheek. Clovis looked over him, seemingly lifeless, and hit him again with the same fury.

29

BURL HAD TOLD Sheriff Horne not to activate his lights and sirens until they were well away from the funeral home. He finally initiated them before the turn onto 290 in downtown McKee as he blew through the red light. Greek was on his bumper, doing the same, smoking his tires, making the turn with Burl in the seat beside him. The sirens screamed down the tree-shrouded two-lane the full ten miles to Annville and then out the side roads that wound their way up to Pot Roast's trailer.

What meager gravel was left on Pot Roast's driveway coming in was sprayed into the brush by the two cars as they tore up the hill, headed for the police vehicle that was already sitting outside the little house trailer. The deputy had his campaign hat hanging from his hand and his weight leaned against the car. His jaw hung slack, and his skin was pale as lime. The sheriff, Burl, and Greek all sprung from their vehicles and went straight to him. Horne shouted, "What'd you find up there?"

The deputy, not twenty-five years old and new to the department, could only get out, "Lord have mercy."

Circling vultures were like a flare, marking the spot from above. Sheriff Horne warned Burl he was going to compromise his crime scene, but Burl stalked up the rising trail without paying him any heed. At the top, blood that had turned brown was spilled all over the trail and streaked into the woods. The path into the brush was becoming worn now. Burl tromped into the blood-painted undergrowth ahead of the others, still wearing his suit jacket from the funeral. The first thing he saw were two vultures crouched on the ground up ahead just past the overturned yellow wheelbarrow. The birds hopped a few feet before they alighted as the men crashed their way closer. When Burl finally saw the body, he didn't look away. Greek fell in beside him, and he didn't look away either. The sheriff and the deputy couldn't keep their eyes on the dead man.

Pot Roast's hands and ankles were zip-tied. His pants were down. His head was tilted back, making it look like he was gazing off into the woods behind him, but the birds had gotten to him, and even if he had been alive, he had no way to see anymore. The wounds on his chest and neck were so numerous it was hard to tell how many times he'd been stabbed and whether the vultures had made it worse. A cut on his groin was significant and looked black, making it unmistakable.

Dolly lay balled up in the brush fifteen feet away, looking exhausted, keening. She watched the men surround him, unmoving, inconsolable.

Burl wiped his forehead with the back of his hand and spoke through clenched teeth. "There was no fucking call for this. No fucking call." He spat straight down and stared at where it landed a beat.

Greek muttered low, but there may not have been one full word formed. The two lawmen were mute.

"They's gonna be some widows and orphans over this."

"He's got to come off this hill," Greek said. "We can't leave him here."

Sheriff Horne finally spoke up. "I got to call the coroner, first. I have to. Lowell's got to clear it."

"Some fucking mystery," Burl said. "Only a fucking blind man would have to wonder at what they done to him. Whoever done this—whoever the fuck that was—is going to suffer. I promise they'll suffer. Fucking left him for the god-damn birds to eat."

"I tried to keep them off of him," the young deputy said. "I run them off when I come up, but I had to go down the hill to meet y'all and they was back on him before I was even halfway to you. The poor dog had done give out."

"They ain't touching him again," Burl said. "I'll kill every fucking vulture in this county. They ain't touching him again."

"He was moved here," Sheriff Horne said. "Dragged."

Greek drew his head back. "Well, no shit. What gave it away?"

"I'm just working through my crime scene, Greek. Mentally. Putting it together."

Burl looked at the sheriff, his expression sour. "Don't strain yourself. They ain't going to be no charges. Not unless you plan on trying some fucking corpses."

"If I don't work this scene, how do you intend to figure out who it was that done this?"

"I ain't that particular. I'm willing to live with some mistakes."

"You can't kill a whole family of men, Burl."

"Naw. You probably right about that." Burl slapped the back of his hand against Greek's forearm. "It's going to take some help."

Greek shook his head. "I don't give a fuck what you say, I'm pulling his goddamn pants up and getting him out of here. What you need to look after is that wheelbarrow. Who-ever moved him had his hands on it, and the handles are bloody." Sheriff Horne gave weak resistance while Greek hoisted Pot Roast's plaid pajama pants. The sheriff gave up his protest and directed the young deputy to help Greek carry Pot Roast's body out of the woods, by the feet and hands, into the clearing. There they waited for the coroner to come do his part. Burl stared into the clear sky above them, where the black vultures continued their slow aerial carousel, hop-ing for another chance to extract life from something that no longer had one.

30

Clovis snaked his arms under Holt's armpits and dragged him to his mother's porch, with his heels skidding across the ground, then knocking on each step going up. The thumping set the little dog to barking again. Clovis dropped Holt with no regard for how he landed on the porch.

The instant Holt's mother opened the inside door, her face fell, and her hand flew over her mouth. She started to say something before she registered Clovis's lethal expression.

"He'll live. He don't deserve to, but he'll live."

She pulled in the air to say something and again stifled it. She cinched her finger over her lip and willed herself to stay silent.

"Get him the fuck out of Greens Crossing. Not tomorrow. Not tonight. Today. Get him the fuck out of here."

"What's he done?"

"He's got people killed." Clovis pointed down at him with his huge open hand. "I was trying to avoid it, but it ain't no question about it now. Only question is who's it gonna be. If I got anything to say about it, it ain't gonna be mine. But I don't want him nowhere near this place."

"I don't know where to send him." The dog squirmed in her arms and let loose a bark. She said, "Hush your fucking mouth," and smacked it on the snout. It yelped and went still. "I know he ain't done what they say he done to that little girl, but people don't care to know the truth. No one will have him."

"Think harder. You got kin somewhere, I'm sure."

"His daddy's brothers are down in Rockcastle. He might could stay with one of them." She looked on her son, bleeding, still, but breathing. Her face was weepy.

"I don't care—just not here. Long as I'm on Greens Crossing, he can't be. You understand that?"

She dabbed at her eye with the hand that wasn't holding the dog and nodded. "It ain't his fault he's this way."

"Then it's yours. Clean up your fucking mess. I've got worse shit to do." Spittle flew from Clovis's mouth. He turned his back on both of them and headed down the steps. Holt's mom pushed the screen open, set her dog down, and knelt beside her son. The dog skittered around, agitated. She patted Holt's cheek, trying to wake him. Clovis slammed his cab door and cranked the V8.

31

Greek didn't leave Pot Roast's body until the coroner arrived up the mountain with Sheriff Horne. Wouldn't. Burl paced back and forth on the trail, muttering things Greek mostly couldn't make out. The sheriff and his deputy had gone down to the trailer to meet the coroner, and the deputy had been left there to do a sweep, look for evidence. By the time Greek arrived back down there with Burl, a second older deputy named Ashcraft, who unfailingly wore a black knee brace on the outside of this uniform pants and walked with a slight limp, had turned up with a camera. He was marking places on the ground with little numbers and taking pictures, with the first deputy watching what he was doing.

Ashcraft was crouched just outside the dog pen, shooting something. Greek said, "What've you found so far?"

Ashcraft lowered the camera. "Shell casings. Three of them. All nines right here inside the dog's enclosure. They's some footprints here in the mud. I'm getting me some pictures of them too."

Burl's lip curled. "Tried to kill fucking Dolly. That dog ain't hurt nobody." He stared at the hillside. "What're we gonna do with her?"

The young deputy spoke up. "I can take her home with me, if that's all right. I'll treat her good."

Ashcraft stood and looked to Burl and Greek. "Is that okay with you all?"

Burl spat on the ground. "I reckon. She can't go home with me without Pot Roast."

"There's a leash in the trailer," the deputy said. "I'll take it up there and see if I can get her to come back down with me."

"Y'all need to be looking at that wheelbarrow," Greek said. "There's some handprints on the handles."

Ashcraft said, "I'll go up with my kit in just a minute."

Greek jutted his chin at the trailer. "So you been inside?"

The younger one bobbed his head. "I was earlier. Before I found him."

"You see anything out of place?"

"I didn't notice anything. I mean, it was messy, but it looked to me just like a regular old mess."

"I'll go in and look around after I see about the wheelbarrow," Ashcraft said. "I might find me some prints in there. I'll shoot it anyway. Might be something we're not seeing right now."

"Y'all been into his truck?" Greek asked.

"No," said the young one.

"If I can go inside and get his keys, I'd like to have a look."

Ashcraft stood and seemed to think about it a moment. "I guess it won't hurt nothing, but let me get you some gloves."

Once he had gloves on, Greek was able go in and locate Pot Roast's keys without looking all that hard. They were right by the door in a little ceramic tray that looked like somebody'd done a shitty job making in art class. Greek lingered a moment longer after spotting something else. Pot Roast's new suit hung from a hook on a door, with the dress shirt in it. The tie Greek had tied for him hung loose around the neck. Greek took a deep breath before going back out.

He walked the perimeter around Pot Roast's truck, looking it over. He knelt down a few places and peered at the underside. Then he clicked the fob, the truck chirped, and the lights flashed. He opened the driver door. Burl and the deputies stood by, watching Greek search the truck.

At once, Greek said, "Fuck." He came out holding a small black box no bigger than a Zippo lighter.

"What've you found, Greek?" Burl said.

"That's a tracker," Ashcraft said.

"They didn't even hide it good, just wedged it under the seat. I told the boys to search it before they brought it back. That's a fucking failure."

"Goddamn it," Burl said. "Who was supposed to search it?"

"Pot Roast and Jared."

Burl's exasperation was drawn into the lines of his forehead. "Ain't nothing to say to Pot Roast, but Jared knows better. Where all's Pot Roast been in it since it come back?"

"Everywhere."

"Everywhere where?"

"Fucking Hilltop, fucking Arizona, the back way into the farm." Greek shook his head slowly. "Goddamn everywhere."

"My fucking house?"

"Your house."

The young deputy said, "Oh God."

Burl's eyes pulled back wide. He pivoted for the car, almost running, and Greek blew by him, making for the driver door.

CHAPTER

32

LONG SPANS OF elevated sprinklers hovered above fields of green grass that lay on all sides of the Begleys' main house, spraying the water that kept the crop fit for harvest. The air smelled of wet turf, even inside the old farmhouse with the windows closed and central air running full blast.

Although the place was over a century old, the guts were modern. Clovis had modernized the electric, the plumbing, the HVAC—everything—better than a decade earlier. They'd taken out the old window air units, dropped the high ceilings just a bit, and run ducts through the entire place. Then Micah had added surveillance cameras and smart controls to everything just a couple years back. That way his father could keep up with the place from Florida and know who was coming and going. Micah had also programmed lights to go on and off each day when his father was gone, to make the place look lived in. It'd take a brave soul to try to rob the Begleys, but out Greens Crossing people were on drugs, and though drugs didn't do anyone much good, one thing they did tend to do was make people brave.

When Clovis took off his hat, his forehead still wore beads from the time he'd spent outside rounding up all the boys and bringing them in his house. Each and every one

who worked in the fields had taken to slinging AR-15s across
their backs before going out, and some wore sidearms as well.
The ARs were leaned every which way just inside the door,
like umbrellas on a rainy day.

Clovis paced while he spoke; the men sitting around him
on couches included Cargo and Kendall. Micah was on a
backward chair, and a couple other boys were standing back.
The boys who weren't sons, Clovis called "nephew," even if
they were some other relation, and one of the older ones was
his cousin Ephraim, who, along with Clovis, knew the most
about growing grass, having both been raised by the original
sod man in the family, Clayton. When it came to seeding,
fertilizing, and applying pesticides, he and Clovis determined
the regimen, and Ephraim saw to the execution. There were
half a dozen spitters between them, all either green twenty-
ounce Dew bottles or wide-mouthed Gatorades. Nobody was
smoking, but a couple had vapes.

Clovis gathered himself before beginning to say what he
had to say. He was like a preacher launching into his sermon.
"Listen up, boys. I need your ears." The movement and the
other mouths in the room stilled. He waited a moment longer
for absolute quiet. "I's trying to avoid a war I knowed was
probably coming. Now goddamn Holt Peters has guaranteed
it, and he's guaranteed it'll be bloody. Burl Spoon won't have
it no other way."

Cargo was shaking his head and glaring at Micah. "So's
it's going to be we kill them, or they kill us? Last man
standing?"

"Naw. It don't gotta be," Clovis said.

"How do you figure we avoid it?"

"That's the thing. We got a few things going for us they
don't got. First is, we all kin." Clovis patted his heart. "Burl
ain't hardly got no real family. What he's got's employees. His
boy's done run off to Louisville and is a-carrying on. If we
take Burl out, that boy ain't going to do nothing about it.

They say his wife don't want nothing to do with him neither. He ain't got no one else around him who ain't on his payroll. The only one of them's likely to take revenge if we take down Burl's that pale one works for him they call Greek. That's the boy that was out here with him. That's all according to Micah's boys at Post, which is something else we got going for us they don't know about."

The two state troopers at Post 7 who gave Micah intel had sourced it from one of the troopers Burl had under his thumb out of the same post. Nobody aside from those two knew their connection to the Begleys, but Micah was their steroid and HGH source via a contact he had out of Johnson City, Tennessee. One of the juicing troopers was weight-room crazed, and the other was cheating in the local MMA circuit. Whereas Burl's troopers were simply on the take, the two muscleheads were reliant on Micah for their gym candy.

"So, if we take down Burl and Greek, that'd end it," Kendall said.

"That's what we're hearing from Post. They say it's them two and not much behind it. I don't reckon any of his real kin would raise a hand to defend Burl, even if they had the chance." Clovis took a red paisley handkerchief from the front pocket of his overalls and wiped across his forehead. "Burl and Greek, they're a two-headed snake. Cut them two off, and the snake likely dies."

Micah leaned in on the two front legs of his chair. "So, which one do we want to take first?"

"Either one, but if you only had one shot and you could take your pick, I don't know." Clovis gazed at the ceiling. "I can see it two ways. You take out Greek, and Burl's not near as fearsome without him. Maybe some of the other boys start second-guessing and dropping off." He replaced the handkerchief in his pocket. "You drop Burl, and what are they fighting for? Greek'll likely keep coming out of principle, but none of them other boys got much to fight for once the man signs the checks ain't there to do it no more. None of them stands to catch nothing from Burl once he's gone. His wife and his boy'll inherit all he's got, but from what we hear, ain't neither one of them got an appetite to keep up his operation. That's the end of the Spoons in Jackson County. All them boys is out of work."

"So, who do we make, you know, the priority?" Micah said.

Clovis snuffed in and rubbed the toe of his boot on the floor. "I'm going to say Greek. If Greek's protecting Burl, he's more vulnerable. If he ain't got to worry about Burl, it's untelling what moves he'll make against us. But I got thoughts on that too. There may be a way to take them both."

"What about his family?" Micah said.

Clovis stroked his beard. "No. Not yet anyway. The way I see this, I don't think they come into play. I ain't saying they're off the table, because they ain't, but if we do this right, I don't believe they'll be any part of this."

Micah peered up at his father. "What about the boys working for him?"

"We won't do nothing that'll cost us a shot at the two we most after, but depending on how things play out, we might be in a spot to pick them off as we go. The less of them we got to worry about, the better."

"What about calling in Detroit?" Micah said, referring to their heroin connection, with several of their operatives local. "I could probably get a couple of them boys out here to back us up."

"Naw," Clovis said. "This is a family matter. What I've got planned needs to stay to our kin. You bring anyone in from the outside—even one—and it'll get beyond us. I already made that mistake once. We keep this to just us in this room, just to our blood, and we can keep better control of it. The only thing we might need from them's some equipment. Didn't you tell me they got them some kind of sentry gun at their stash house? Fires on its own?"

Micah raised his brows. "Not only do they got one, I helped set it up."

"How's that thing work?"

"It's hooked to a laptop. You can program the range. When it's armed, it fires at any movement in that range. Goddamn raccoon got in their yard, and it shot the fucking thing to pieces. We had to adjust the range after that."

"You reckon they'd be willing to part with it?"

"They might rent it out for a couple days."

"That ain't gonna work. If what I got planned comes off, they ain't getting it back. Tell them to name their price. I'll go whatever, but we need it today."

"I can ask 'em." Micah shrugged.

"This ain't really an asking kind of deal, son. We need that thing. I'm sure they'd part with it for the right price. We'll pay enough they can replace it five times over."

"Okay," Micah said. "I'll get it."

Kendall had a pained look. Of the three of Clovis's boys, he was the most on edge. Clovis could hardly blame him given what had happened to him. "What happens if the sheriff from over there gets involved. What do we do about him? What about his people?"

"We ain't going back over there. Not now, anyway. That's another one of our advantages. Burl Spoon's coming to us, and it's gonna be real soon. I got no doubt. The man's vengeful. He ain't going to wait no more. Might take a day or two, but not longer. Maybe shorter. And that's why we go to be ready. We take Spoon, we ain't got to worry about no sheriff, because who does he serve? He's just like the rest of 'em. Once that money dries up, he ain't going to put his neck out. Why? What for?"

"How do we protect the house? How do we protect the farm?" Micah asked. "That sentry gun'll help, but the range ain't that big. It'll only do so much. What else're we gonna do?"

"That's simple. We ain't going to protect neither one," his father said. "We're protecting our family. The farm he can't hurt. The house? I can always build me another house. We may have to give up some vehicles too, but it'll be worth it if we can get through it."

Cargo sat up straighter. "Are you serious?"

Clovis nodded. "That's our other advantage. We're gonna move us some things out, but this house ain't family. And vehicles we can replace. They're coming. I have no doubt. And as long as they don't catch us out, this house'll be their target."

"What're we gonna do once they get here?" Cargo asked.

Clovis wetted his lips. "How many Tannerite targets you got left?"

"Five or six," Cargo said.

"We'll need those." Clovis turned his eyes to Ephraim. "How much AN we got in the barn?"

Ephraim eyed his cousin blinking. "You serious about this, Clovis? Fertilizer?"

"I'm damn serious. The man blames us for his daughter, and now Holt's gone and killed another one of his, and in a terrible way. Burl'll kill every last one of us if he gets the chance. I don't think he stops until he does. We know he's coming. This ain't no time for half measures."

"We ain't got much fertilizer on hand, Clovis. Hardly a cupful. We're out of season. I ain't ordered any but I might could get some."

Clovis bit his bottom lip. "I can't have you doing that. If we do what I'm thinking about, the Feds'll be on us, and we can't have anyone say we were out looking for fertilizer today. Not even from another farm, because who knows what anyone would say. We'll use what little we got, but I got me an idea that don't require hardly any." He turned to Micah. "After you get back from seeing Detroit, we got to spend some time lining up what all you can make this house do."

"I can make it roll over and sit if you want."

"We're going to need it to do both." Clovis looked at everybody else. "What I need from the rest of y'all is every bag of flour and every bit of powdered sugar you got. Bring whatever you got on hand, but don't go buying anything. Just bring what's in y'all's houses. What else we need are the barn fans. Between those, and the HVAC fans, and ceiling fans, we ought to be able to kick us up a hell of a dust storm."

Cargo's chin wagged open. "What the fuck are we making, Daddy?"

"A goddamn tinder box. A dust bomb." Clovis strode away with purpose, headed for the front door. Without looking back he said, "And some of us are going to be spending nights in the root cellar, so prepare yourselves for that. Now let's fucking go. We ain't got a lot of time and we got a lot to do before they get here."

33

GREEK HAD BLISTERED across Jackson County from Pot Roast's trailer to Burl's house. Burl had a .38 gripped tight the whole ride there. Greek threw rocks around the hairpins of Burl's long wooded drive leading up the mountain to the level spot where his house laid.

Waylon and Johnny, tearing across the lawn, raising hell all the way to the car, was a reassuring sign, but Burl's already thundering heart seized when he first spotted a man standing on the porch with a pistol aimed at the sky. "What the fuck?"

"That's the cop, Burl. From the funeral. The one with Darron." Greek slowed his pace, pulling up out front and parking the car.

Burl jostled his head side to side. He'd lost his bearings—he was rattled. Burl was accustomed to doing the rattling. He'd forgotten he still had the gun in his hand when he got out. He tucked it back in his waist as casually as he could manage. Waylon and Johnny had split up, and one was nosing Burl, and the other Greek.

"Where is everybody?" Burl hollered, gathering his composure as he headed for the porch, slapping Johnny on the back, trying to do something that felt normal. "Everything okay here?"

The man holstered his weapon back beneath his suit jacket. "Everything's ten-four. We were a little alarmed hearing the car come up like that. I should probably go in first and let them know it's you, because Darron was going after a rifle."

"There's no call for him to do that." Burl said.

The man cocked his head. "The rate of speed you came up and your weapon being unholstered tells me there was at least some cause for alarm." He turned and went in the front door.

Greek glanced at Burl and shrugged. "A fucking Black cop," Burl said. "Christ almighty. Darron sure can pick 'em."

Inside, the officer had met Darron, who was headed for the porch with a hunting rifle. Darron was now at ease, but the weapon still hung from one hand pointed at the floorboards.

Burl and Greek stopped a few steps back from them while the two spoke in low tones to one another. Burl rubbed his palms up and down the thighs of his suit pants. "What was you planning to do with that?"

Darron eyed him. "Right. Because I forgot how to shoot when I left."

"That's not what I meant."

"What did you mean?"

The man cut in. "I'd like to assess our situation here, if we could. Are we concerned about some sort of incursion here?"

Burl looked at Greek, whose face was steely. "Naw," Greek said.

"Then why the urgency coming in? Why the unholstered weapon?"

"We just didn't recognize you is all," Burl said. "Once we done that, we was fine."

The man had fallen into cop-speak. "That might explain the weapon, but not the high rate of speed."

Burl tapped a toe while he drew out his cigarettes. "What's your name, son? I don't believe we was properly introduced."

"I believe we were, but it's Michael. Sergeant Branham if you want to be formal."

"Okay, Michael. So, you know, Greek here's prone to a lead foot is all. And I ain't been myself. For obvious reasons."

Darron laid the back of his hand across Michael's chest. "No. Whatever's going on was serious enough that you didn't go to the cemetery. Now you're trying to act like you aren't torn up, but you obviously are. Something's up. What's going on?"

"It's like I said. Everything's all right. Was a false alarm."

Darron held his father's eyes a moment. "We're not stupid."

"It don't matter if you believe me or not—" Burl started to say, and then the sound of approaching sirens reached the house. The four men went to the porch, Darron still carrying the rifle.

Two Jackson County Sheriff's vehicles burst over the hill, flying toward the house with their blue lights ignited, sirens wailing. Waylon and Johnny went batshit. Burl threw up both of his hands like a third base coach trying to get them to slow. He forgot he'd called Horny and asked him to send cars to his house. Cars that he and Greek wound up beating there.

Darron shouted over the din of the cruisers, "Everything's fine, right?"

CHAPTER

34

B URL WAS NEVER one to admit defeat easily, but even he had to be realistic about the current situation. He couldn't keep Chelsea by himself, and he couldn't make Colleen stay at the farm with her. And what would he tell Chelsea when she asked after Pot Roast and Dolly? In light of what he intended for the Begleys, and especially in light of what Colleen and Darron now knew, packing them all off to Louisville under the eye of Michael was about the only move that even made sense.

Burl had what could best be described as an arsenal in his home. He gave Darron a Sig Sauer to take with him and asked Michael if he needed any additional guns or ammo. He declined. "I have a shotgun and a rifle in my trunk. Back home I've got a lot more than that. There's no need to worry about us being properly armed."

Colleen owned a Sig that Burl had bought her years ago, and knew well how to fire it. While she wasn't an enthusiast, Colleen was no stranger to guns. She'd been around them from the time she was a girl. Burl had always wanted her to carry the Sig, but she never did. He insisted she take it with her. "I'll put it in the glove box" was the most she would concede.

"You need to be armed."

"I'm caring for a six-year-old girl, Burl. I'm not walking around packing a gun. I'd hope we'd be safe enough in Louisville that I won't end up in a goddamn gunfight."

"You don't know what people are liable to do."

Colleen put her hand over her heart. "But you know what you'd be liable to do. You'd go after someone's family, wouldn't you? Their wife and kids and grandkids. They're all fair game. This is some life we've fashioned for ourselves, Burl Spoon."

"Look who's got all high and mighty. I ain't seen you complain about nothing we've had these many years, or heard you ask no questions."

"I don't absolve myself, Burl. Not one bit."

"Don't go too hard on yourself, now, Leenie." He put his hand on her arm. "Only took you thirty-five years to decide you was above all we done."

"I wish I was above it. I just tried not to think about it too much, and that's no better than being right down in it. Now all I can hope for is some grace and forgiveness, and a chance to do better by Chelsea than I did by DeeDee and Darron. What else have I got? And the best thing I can do for her right now is get her the hell out of here."

"She'll be home soon."

"She'll be back when it's safe," Colleen said. "If it ever is."

Colleen, Chelsea, Darron, and Michael left out in three cars. Burl instructed one of the deputies to lead the caravan to I-75 through Berea and all the way to the Fayette County line before peeling back. Before they set out, Burl sat with Chelsea in her room.

"You'll be back home before you know it, Peanut."

She sat on her pink bedspread in her pink room, surrounded by a bounty of stuffed animals and toys that looked like a store display. "Why ain't you coming with us, Papaw?"

"I wish I could. Papaw's got some business here at home. I'll be here waiting on you to come back."

"How come you never go to Uncle Darron's with us? You don't ever come."

"Your papaw's not meant for cities." He knelt down and looked right into her eyes. "He's meant to be in the mountains. You get me in the city, and Papaw breaks out in hives and swells up." He smushed his shoulders and chest up, trying to make his face look fat, swollen. "It ain't no good. It ain't no good at all. That's why we got to get you back here to your papaw soon as we can."

"When can I come back?"

He put his hands on both of her knees. "Your Papaw's got some planting to do. Soon as me and Greek get everything planted, you can come on back home for good."

35

G REEK HAD GIVEN up on trying to talk Burl down. He would have liked more time to plan, and more importantly, he wished they could wait for even a small element of surprise. Given everything that had gone on, there was little chance the Begleys wouldn't have their guard way up the next couple days. But it's hard to stay on high alert like that for very long. After even a few days of uncertainty, the Begleys' discipline would break down. People like their routines, and even in the face of danger, they fall back into them. If just a few of the Begleys slacked off, Greek would favor the conditions.

But Burl was not to be dissuaded. His cheek did not turn, and his vengeance was seldom allowed to cool. He'd wanted to act before DeeDee's funeral, and Greek had held him at bay. What happened to Pot Roast only confirmed to Burl that it had been a mistake. "We hit them, and they don't get a chance to do what they done to Pot Roast. We was weak waiting," he told Greek. "I ain't going to be weak again. I ain't repeating my mistake."

Having given up on stalling for more time, Greek had agreed to move on the Begley farm early Sunday morning, two days after DeeDee's funeral. But he'd devised as low risk a plan as he felt he could get by with. Something that would deliver the fury Burl demanded without getting everyone on the team killed. Greek knew damn well there wasn't any plan Burl would accept that didn't risk casualties, and he'd been involved in more than one supposedly "low-risk" operation that had turned sour.

Over a dozen boys and Christy stood in Burl's kitchen, jockeying for position around a laptop screen. Two of the men were deputies from the sheriff's department, including Ashcraft, who had collected the evidence at Pot Roast's place, and a younger fellow named McWhorter, kind of a cowboy who was a friend of Pot Roast's, looking for some get-back. All were dressed in black, brown, navy, or dark camo, either what Greek had told them to wear or provided. The kitchen smelled heavy of man sweat and cigarette smoke.

Burl had ceded the lead to Greek, who was taking them through the layout of the Begley sod farm on Google Maps.

"There are basically two focal points. First you have the main house and the two metal barns nearby. Further down the drive you've got the smaller houses and outbuildings." Greek pointed to the screen as he spoke, and paused here and again to make sure everyone had a chance to see and absorb.

They were going in at four in the morning, under a waxing moon, with the understanding that they wouldn't use lights unless absolutely necessary, so they needed to know the terrain.

Between Burl, Greek, the sheriff's department, and the McKee Police, they had marshalled three tactical helmets with affixed night vision goggles, one pair of night vision binoculars, five regular tactical helmets, nine Kevlar vests, some smoke canisters, flash bangs, tear gas, and gas masks. Greek would lead team one; McWhorter, team two; and Ashcraft, team three. The plan was for Burl, who they were calling "Rooster," to hang back a bit with the binoculars and supervise from afar.

Clarence, who was deemed too fat for any of the teams, was driving a cargo van full of men. Burl and Greek were coming in a separate car driven by Christy that had a little more speed. Burl, Greek, Ashcraft, and McWhorter would all communicate via hands-free two-way radios. Christy's car and the van were each coming in on Greens Crossing Road off 52, and both would park a quarter mile from the sod farm on the other side of a wooded area near the raceway. Four men plus Greek, Burl, and McWhorter would proceed on foot through the trees and emerge south of the main house. McWhorter and one of the men would split off to sweep the barns, then set up in front of the house.

Jared was to drive Ashcraft's team of four in a Suburban that he would bring in from the north on Charlie Norris Road and then onto Concord Road, where they would park near another wooded area and walk in a shorter distance. The two vehicles from the raceway would move to the Concord Road position.

After the assault on the house, all the men would sprint to that position, and the vehicles would flee north into Clark County before circling back through Estill on 89 and back into Jackson County.

"Team three will canvas the two smaller houses and out-buildings before we take the main house," Greek said. "They'll disable any vehicles parked there before continuing on. We'll leave one man back to pin down anyone who tries to come out of those houses after the shooting starts. Don't let them reinforce the main house."

Burl broke in. "Now, boys, them two houses is the most likely to have women and kids in them, so we trying to avoid anything going off there. Sweep them outbuildings, slash them tires, and keep moving except for the one. Some of them bastards we're interested in may be in them houses, but it'll have to wait for another day unless you can get a shot at them in the clear. I don't want them houses shot up, or you're likely to do some collateral damage."

Greek eyed Ashcraft. "Who do you got in mind to leave back?"

"I was thinking Toby."

Greek pointed at Toby. "You can pop some rounds in the bases of the porches, and they'll get the point. If they got any of their vehicles parked out front, light those up too. Spray rounds where you won't hit anybody, but where they'll hear the impact. They likely won't want any part of it. If they keep coming, mow 'em down."

"You got that, Toby?" Burl said.

"I'll ping everywhere but where the people's at unless they show out."

"Okay," Greek said. "McWhorter'll sweep the barns with team two before establishing a position in the barn directly in front of the house. That one's maybe thirty yards out, just inside the fence." Greek gestured at the barns on the screen. "If there's occupants in either of them, we'll reassess and might have to change it up. Keep in contact."

McWhorter said, "Okay."

"We know they got at least one pit bull in the main house," Greek said. "May have other dogs. Not sure about in them other two houses. If there's dogs out either place, we'll take them out. I don't want anyone getting taken down by a fucking dog. Ashcraft and McWhorter both have suppressed .22s. Let them deal with any dogs. That's also how we'll take out the lights."

Ashcraft tapped Greek on the shoulder. "What time you thinking we're all in position at the main house?"

"I'm hoping we can sweep the outbuildings and be in position by zero four fifteen." Greek indicated the east side of the house on the screen, the front. "We'll start by taking down any dogs and the lights on the house. We'll take any cameras we can see, but if they've got any, they're well hid. After that we'll deploy smoke from our position in the barn. There's twice as many windows on the front as on the back, and all but one of the exterior lights." He pointed at a pole visible on the map. "There's one pole light in the yard out front. Don't nobody bother it. If that's the only light they got, and that's where we lay down smoke, that's where their eyes should go. It's just natural."

He pointed at some objects near the barn on the screen. "Right here you can see some equipment, metal boxes, and their sod hauling truck. We saw the same thing when we ran the drone over. That stuff stays there just about all the time. McWhorter, after you throw the smoke from the barn, move up and take cover. Make sure you're behind something good and solid. When I give the signal, you're going to be firing blind, so keep under cover and make sure you're firing high. Spray the second floor. Once we've got their attention drawn to the front, we'll come from the northwest and southwest simultaneously with the gas. There's only one window on each of the sides. That's where the gas'll go in. That's why we need your trajectory high." Greek looked at McWhorter. "We can't have you hitting any of our personnel. If the only light's out front, and there's smoke out there, and you're firing on them from there, that's not where they'll come out. They'll come pouring out the back, where it's dark. Me and Ashcraft's teams'll have us a shooting gallery."

Greek continued assigning positions and duties and checking and double-checking that everyone knew their roles. He put police response time to the sod farm at eight minutes after shots fired, at the absolute quickest. He allowed three minutes from first shots fired until pulling back to the vehicles. The chance of the police response coming from the north was near zero because there was very little development or population that way, and all attention would focus on the farm, making the northern route a cold trail out.

If for some reason they couldn't get close enough to the house to gas it, or if the Begleys had gas masks and didn't come out, they'd fire as many rounds into the structure from three positions as they could, and hope for the best. Burl wanted blood quickly, and Greek intended to give it to him, if possible without losses. He hoped whatever the outcome, it would satiate Burl at least long enough to come up with less blunt tactics.

Before the boys loaded up, Ashcraft spoke out to the group. "Nobody should be taking a cell phone out there. Police'll check cell tower activity, and none of you boys' phones need to turn up on it."

Burl gestured at the drivers. "We got us a burner phone for each vehicle, and I got one with all the numbers in it, and they all got my burner's number in them. You got to remember, don't power those on until we get there, and you got to power them back off once we get on our way. We'll bust 'em all up once we get back. I don't need y'all fucking that up, now."

"One other thing," Greek said. "If anything happens out there, if anyone isn't able to rendezvous at the vehicles for any reason, the Shell station at Speedwell Road is open twenty-four hours. Ditch your gear and make your way over there. We've got fifty dollars and a phone number for all you all with your gear. Go in there like nothing's up, get you a pop, a bag of doughnuts, and a TracFone, and call the number we gave you. Don't just buy the fucking phone—buy some other shit. We'll have another car waiting up the way to come pick you up. Whatever happens, if you get picked up by the law, you don't say shit. Not one fucking word. Just silence. If y'all do this just the way I got it plotted out, we ought to all come out of there clean."

"And boys, don't forget"—Burl pointed his finger at the ground—"I got three thousand cash waiting on every last one of you all when we get back."

A couple of the guys whistled their approval.

"What if you ain't a boy?" Christy spoke up.

"Naw. You right. I shoulda said 'boys and Christy,' but you knowed what I meant. Anyway, I should also say, pay attention to what Greek said. If any of y'all get picked up, you know I'll take care of your lawyer just like always, and I'll take care of your family until you get out, just like always. That is unless you talk to the law. Any of you all do that, your families'll still get took care of, but not in the way you want. You understand?"

There was a universal grunting assent.

"Remember"—Burl stood straight and pointed hard at them—"these sod fuckers, the Begleys, is responsible for what happened to DeeDee, and they done killed Pot Roast like a goddamn dog and left him to get ate. What we're fixing to give them, they deserve every fucking bit of. Think about that when you sight them in, and don't fucking miss."

36

THE AIR WAS warm and nearly moonless. Crickets continued their chirping, which had begun when the sun went
down. It was due back up in just a couple hours. A drizzle of
sweat trickled down Kendall's forehead. He couldn't move
much, and he'd drunk most of a sport bottle of water through
a big bendable straw. His bag of Mingua Beef Jerky was long
gone. He'd pissed twice into a Gatorade bottle. He was itchy,
the straw smell was tiresome, and a few bugs had found him.

Kendall would have rather been with his family, but
Clovis had decided he was the one who ought to be out in the
far barn northeast of the house on account of him being the
smallest, a crack shot, and due some revenge for being kid-
napped and tormented. It took them nearly two hours the
first night to rearrange the straw bales up in the hayloft, hiding him deep inside with his scoped .308 peeking out through
a hole they cut in the metal roof. The second night it was
easier. As much as his brothers had complained about spending nights in the root cellar hidden under a flatbed trailer in
the yard, those accommodations seemed pretty plush compared to what Kendall had gotten.

At the front northeast corner of the farmhouse, tucked in
alongside the concrete porch in what looked like a random

pile of bricks, was an eight-inch channel Kendall hoped he could thread under pressure. It was angled so only a shot from his position could make it to the center. His brother Micah had called it a "death star shot."

Before they put the Tannerite payload into the bricks, they'd had Kendall practice on gallon jugs of water. In daylight, at a little over a hundred yards, with no stakes, he'd burst them every time. But now it was dark as hell. He was using a night vision scope he'd only ever used to hunt coyotes. He hadn't had a chance to practice with it on the death star, and no shot he'd ever taken in his life had this kind of stakes.

Micah had a radio and Kendall had an earpiece. They'd tested it from down in the root cellar. It had rung clear even from underground. Micah would monitor and run the house via a laptop and a collection of phones. When he gave the word, Kendall was supposed to fire his round. Supposed to thread the needle.

Kendall's barn was the older and smaller of the two, both prefab galvanized steel numbers. They'd unbolted the ladder and pulled it out after they'd got Kendall set up. Unless someone turned up with a ladder or who could jump fourteen feet high, there was no getting into the loft with him. There was a sub panel in each barn that they'd hidden with equipment. They'd killed the electric to both.

The root cellar in the yard had been dug out over a hundred years ago at the same time the house was built. It had fallen into disuse once the house got electricity. It didn't regain its usefulness until Clovis discovered a lucrative supplement to sod farming in cocaine trafficking. He'd stored product down there until relatively recently. It was cocaine that had seen the farm through some lean years it might not have otherwise survived.

As Clovis told it, he had stumbled his way into trafficking. He'd bought some powder while down in Florida on a trip with his now deceased wife. That had led him to make some connections that brought him deeper into it. After a good number of prosperous years in coke, the demand started dropping off. That was when he switched lanes to moving pills, and sourced those out of Florida as well.

It was only after Micah was old enough to steer the operation that the Begleys shifted their focus to heroin, which Micah got through a Detroit connection. He also dabbled in performance enhancers, but those weren't the source of any real profit. They were more of a personal interest and the way into the hearts of certain law enforcement personnel. The family didn't bother with anything Clovis termed "hippie shit," so they stayed out of marijuana, molly, and other psychedelics, which attracted what Clovis considered undesirable clientele.

He was unrepentant about what they did sell. "People die from fucking French fries and cheeseburgers every day. That's just business. We're no different."

The family's trafficking enterprise was for the most part under Micah's wing now, with Clovis still calling some of the consequential shots. In the interest of spending five months of the year in Okeechobee chasing fish, he'd ceded much of the day-to-day. It was Micah who had overseen the transfer of everything they used to keep in the root cellar to a storage unit just up the road on KY 52.

Kendall and Cargo had little to do with the drug enterprise. Clovis said they "lacked the constitution." He kept them busy mainly with the sod farm. Micah's closest collaborators were cousins and an uncle. Nobody operated within their inner circle who wasn't family.

Clovis swore Burl Spoon and his men would come within four nights. That was the number. Clovis was adamant. The prospect made Kendall absolutely sick. As much as his father wanted him to have vengeance, Kendall didn't crave it. All he'd ever wanted was to get away with both his testes, and he

had. He feared Burl more than he hated him, and he was terrified of what would happen if the plan didn't work. The sun
would be up soon, though, and he'd started to think nothing
would happen before morning. That meant he'd have to go
back up in the loft the next night, but he was happy for even
a short reprieve.

But then one of the dogs started barking, and he heard
hushed voices inside the barn. It was about then that the
other dog started in. His father had made him tie his pit bull,
Ramsey, to a porch post, as well as Cargo's Staffordshire,
Kong. "Where there's dogs, there's people," Clovis had said.

Cargo had spit fire. "So, we're just going to sacrifice
them?"

"What do you value more? Your fucking dogs or your
family?"

"Why's it got to be our dogs? Let's go get some other
dogs."

"That ain't gonna work, son," Clovis said. "This ain't some
other dog's house, so they ain't going to want to protect it.
Beside that, we ain't got time. I'll get you another fucking dog."

Cargo's eyes glinted as tears gathered. He had walked off
and hid his face. He didn't say anything else about it, and
when it was time, he had tied Kong up like he was told, but
he sat with him for ten minutes, talking to him and hugging
his neck. Kendall had watched him do it and knew he had to
do the same.

When Kong and Ramsey began to sound off, there was
little doubt in Kendall's mind just what that meant. He'd
been braced for it since the sun had gone down more than six
hours before. Upstairs lights in his father's house came on as
planned. Micah had every switch and outlet at his fingertips
down in the root cellar. Moments later, another lamp lit on
the first floor.

The whispered words of men Kendall didn't know entering the barn below quickened his pulse. He gripped the stock

of the gun but kept his finger on the trigger guard and off the trigger for the time being.

He could hear only footfalls and muffled words he couldn't make out until the voices were at the end of the barn closest to the house, right below him. He held his breath because even his breathing seemed loud. Everything that itched was suddenly fifty times worse, and a rivulet of sweat rolled into his eye. With his breath held, he could hear nothing but bug chatter, the dogs barking, and the low sound of the voices. For the first time, he could make out the words in spite of Ramsey and Kong.

One of them said, "First barn's clear, team one, you copy? We're moving up."

Another voice said, "I can't see shit."

"Shut up. I'm trying to hear." The voices went quiet for a moment before the first one spoke again. "Yeah. Dogs first, then the lights."

Kendall had an urge to cry out that he stifled. He had to keep telling himself losing his dog would save his family, but that was cold comfort. He liked the dog better than most of them.

The second man said, "Where are you?"

"Right here," the first one said. "I'm looking right at you. Reach out and grab my arm. This night vision's a fucking trip, man. Hang on and follow me close. I can see everything."

"You get night vision, a fucking helmet, a vest, a radio, and I ain't got shit."

"You got you a gun, didn't you?"

"And I'm keeping the fucking thing."

"Fine. Now shut up," the first one said. "We got to move. You got my six?"

"Your what?"

"Fuck. My back. You got my back?"

"Oh," the second one said. "Yeah."

"All right. Let's move."

"Hold on."

"Why? Wait. What's that smell?" The first one said. "Did you bring your vape? Are you fucking vaping right now?"

The other man's voice came out strained, like he was holding his breath. "I just needed one pull." He exhaled. "I'm fucking nervous, man. It calms me down."

"Put that fucking thing away."

"Fine. Jesus. You ain't gotta get all bent out of shape like that."

"Just put it away and let's go."

"Okay. So fucking sensitive."

"Just shut up, and come on." The first man's voice began to move away.

The second man muttered something else, but now Kendall couldn't make it out. It wasn't until the footfalls faded that Kendall let out his air and rubbed at the sweat in his eye. His gulping for breath seemed louder than ever. What he anticipated next was gunfire. After that it would be his brother's crackling voice. The sound to follow he could only imagine, but even with the ear protection he would put on before firing, he was scared to death of it.

37

GREEK AND TEAM one knelt roughly thirty yards from the southwest corner of the main house, in relative darkness. Air still hissed from the slashed tires of the Chevy dually and Mustang that sat between Greek's men and the structure. The shine of the rear floodlight didn't reach their position, and the lights that had come on inside the house would only make it more difficult for whoever was in there to see out. He couldn't see any movement at the house, but he could hear a pair of dogs barking, howling, pleading. They had left Burl crouched down about fifty yards behind them with an AR slung over his shoulder, watching through night vision binoculars.

Greek confirmed via radio that McWhorter and his man were at the larger barn, directly east of the main house, and in position to take out the dogs and porch lights on his command. He was still waiting on Ashcraft and team three to take position northwest of the old house. It'd been a few minutes since he'd confirmed that the outbuildings at the other houses had been cleared, the vehicles had been disabled, and that nobody was stirring over there.

In addition to the porch lights, there was one small floodlight high up on the back of the old farmhouse. The plan was for Ashcraft to take it out with a suppressed .22 simultaneous to McWhorter taking down the dogs and the porch lights the same way, leaving only the front pole light shining. Greek scanned the location where he expected team three to settle, and could make out the men leaping the fence and dropping into place. There was very little cover around the house, but there was an old maple and a few bushes at the yard's perimeter, just inside the chain link on that side. Just as the men stilled at the base of it, Ashcraft's voice came across the radio. "Team three in position, waiting on your command."

The dogs continued their desperate barking at two different pitches.

"Rooster," Greek said, "we've got all teams in position and ready to fire."

"Let's get it started then," Burl came back.

"All right, boys," Greek said. "Counting down to zero."

Hearing Greek give the command, the men around him all tensed and stilled.

"Five, four, three, two, one. Zero."

The shot from Ashcraft's gun made no intelligible sound, but a muzzle flash shone in the dark. The sound of the glass breaking on the floodlight came through the dogs ranting. Sparks kicked from it as the backyard went dark. The racket the dogs had been making on the porch silenced all at once. The visible light extending from the sides of the front of the house soon dimmed.

A sudden volley sounded out from the front of the house. The *pop, pop, pop* of a rifle split the air. McWhorter's frantic voice came over the radio. "We're under fire! We're under fire!"

Greek's demeanor didn't change. "Throw the smoke, team two."

McWhorter was shouting, "Smoke, smoke, smoke," when it cut out.

Moments later plumes of smoke became visible, rising up over the house from the front. Gunshots continued to rattle for another few seconds before dying out.

Greek got back on the radio. "Team two, I need you to move up, and when you're in position, start firing. Put it all on the second story. You hear me? Second floor, nothing low."

McWhorter's voice came back, "Got it, got it, got it."

A few seconds passed before rapid gunshots ripped through the night one more time. First one gun, then another, then another, and it was hard to tell when one shot started and another ended.

McWhorter came over the radio, screeching, "We're under heavy fire."

"Hold your position but keep firing," Greek said into the radio. "Team three, gas it. Go." Greek tapped the man beside him on the back. He took off, crouch-running for the house in a tactical helmet and vest. The space between the cars and structure was all open but relatively dark. It didn't take but a few seconds for him to close the gap. In the time he did, the gunshots began to slack a little. He reached the house and hurled a tear gas cannister in the window before turning and sprinting back, no longer maintaining his crouch. The man rounded the corner of the dually and slid back behind it, near where Greek was positioned, like he was coming into home plate. Across the yard, Greek could see Ashcraft's man return to his position as well.

Greek said over the radio, "Hold your fire. Look for movement."

The firing at the front of the house stopped at once. Greek's command seemed to have ceased it entirely. He squinted into the goggles, but it was nothing but green glow around the contours of the house. No figures.

Burl came over the radio. "What do we got?"

"No movement, Rooster," Greek said.

Ashcraft said, "Same here. I'm not seeing nothing."

From McWhorter came, "Still real smoky up here, but we ain't seeing nothing. They ain't shooting at us no more, neither."

"Give it a second," Greek said. He scanned all over the house, and all was still. Nobody was coming out, and he couldn't make out any movement inside. "Team two, when they fired on you, where'd it come from?"

"First floor," came the answer.

"Can you see anything in there now?"

"I mean, there's still a lot of smoke, but from what I can see, there's nothing."

"Move in," Burl said over the radio.

"Hold on. Hold on." Greek lifted his goggles off his eyes and raised his AR. "Let's light it up first, boys. All positions." He waved his finger at the house and started firing himself.

Guns blazed on the house from three sides without ceasing for a full twenty seconds. Greek had positioned the groups so there was no crossfire, but bullets strafed the house all over. The men dropped magazines and replaced them and kept slinging lead. Even in the dim light, debris could be seen flying off the house, and a cloud of dust filled the air around it. Even in the slim light, the excess of dust was evident.

Finally Greek said, "Hold your fire. Hold your fire, all positions." The firing tapered off a few men at a time. He got back on the radio. "Is anyone taking fire?"

Both Ashcraft and McWhorter responded no.

"We need to move out."

"Naw, naw, naw," Burl shouted over the radio. "Go finish them motherfuckers off. I'm coming."

"We got tear gas in there, Rooster," Greek said. "I don't know what we're going into."

"Y'all got masks. Get in that fucking house. There's no fight in them."

Greek had followed a lot of orders he didn't like. Orders that he didn't agree with. It was a familiar feeling. Just for a second, he questioned following this one. Something was off, and he hesitated, but something else that had been ingrained in him took over. "Team two, maintain your position and hold your fire. Team three, masks on."

He elbowed the man beside him who'd thrown the gas cannister. "When we hit the door, you're going to hit it with the flash bang through the window. It needs to be simultaneous." The man withdrew the explosive cylinder from his pack on the ground, made his way to the corner of the truck, and scanned left to right.

Greek pulled the gas mask from the clip at his waist and raised it. Before putting it on, he said into the radio, "Let's go, boys—we're taking the house." He shucked his helmet with the night vision, dropped the mask onto his head, pulled it down over his face, and pulled it tight. He raised his rifle back up and crouch-ran for the house, with his men at his heels, just as Ashcraft's team did the same. Burl was still behind them somewhere.

Everything Greek could see was made slightly fuzzy by the mask, and his peripheral vision was gone. He could just make out Ashcraft with his uneven gait and his two men approaching off to his left. Their only entry point from their angle of approach was the back door, which he thought could be breached with one good kick. As he drew near the house, his view became darker and darker, with only the structure in his tunnel vision line of sight. He raised his leg and smashed his boot beside the doorknob, and the door flew inward with a crack. Passing through the threshold, the interior of the meagerly lit house looked like it was thick with dawn-break fog. Then, just for a nanosecond, everything was sound, and everything was light.

38

B URL WAS MEASURING the distance between himself and the chain-link fence around the yard, getting ready to side hop it when it felt like a man twice his size and on fire smashed into his face and chest at a dead run. He somersaulted backward with his arms splayed out, hurtling his gun away as the strap broke, all the air leaving him. He landed on the top of his head, and rather than coming to rest on his back, the next thing that hit the ground were his knees and the toes of his boots as he came down in the lush sod. His ears were jammed closed by the drone of one ceaseless ring. He raised his head and opened his eyes. There was no other man. All he could see in the sky was fire rising up like a dust devil.

Chunks of debris landed all over the yard and further out than even where Burl had gone to ground. The vehicles around the farmhouse were alight. The house itself now appeared only as flame, not substance. The land around where the house had stood and where the vehicles smoldered was on fire as well. He could just make out the now sagging chain-link fence around the yard. The few trees in the yard were mostly gone.

Heat radiated against his face. Burl vomited. His body rocked like a dog's that'd gotten into chicken bones, and what little he'd consumed of late—mainly brown liquor—spilled from him, then dripped from his lips and chin. He put the back of his hand and wrist to his mouth and wiped, still on all fours on the ground. He pressed his knuckles into his ears, trying to plug them, trying to do anything to stop their howling. Liquid dripped from them much like it did from his mouth.

He rose up, teetering, and nearly went back down. He reeled on his feet. His Kevlar vest was still wrapped around his chest, but the long-sleeved black T-shirt he had on under it was in tatters. The only things still holding it to his arms were the shreds of the cuffs.

His urge was to go to his men. To find Greek. To somehow regroup. But everything and everyone was gone or in flames. He gaped at it, his retinas burned out, seeing but poorly. It felt like the ground under him was tilting, and he was on one foot, trying to regain his balance, the other leg not working well.

Then he ran. Awkwardly, lamely, with one legging dragging, he ran north toward the pickup point where a van, a car, and a Suburban waited. Every so often he lost his balance and fell. Each time he got back up. His lungs were shredded, and the air that came in felt like acid, but he wouldn't stop until he reached the vehicles that would take him away from the horror into which he had just cast his men. He wanted to sprawl out and just lie. There would be plenty of room for that. Burl and Toby would be the only passengers going back home.

39

WHEN KENDALL TOOK off the industrial earmuffs he'd put on before the explosion, he heard what sounded like hurricane winds. A warm glow illuminated his face through the hole in the barn roof. His awe at the scene outside was shot through with bafflement. Micah had screamed in his ear that the gas was on and he'd powered on the fans and HVAC system in the house, that the dust bomb was ready to ignite, but Kendall couldn't see his target when he put the gun to his cheek. The smoke was too thick. He had never fired a shot.

He rolled and kicked and dug his way out from under the straw bales. They may not have seemed heavy, but as they tumbled on him in the dark, Kendall got a little panicky, like he could suffocate. Eventually he managed to get himself dislodged. Itching and sticky and stiff, he was out.

He took the small flashlight he had carabinered to his hip and used it to make his way to the edge of the hayloft. He found the AR-15 that had been left there for him, and lowered it to the ground with the rope that was tied to the stock. Then he sat with his feet dangling, turned and hung down by his hands before letting go, dropping to the dirt floor in a way that jarred his heels and rattled his molars. The only light in the barn was from the glow of distant flames outside. He picked up the AR, untied the rope, and found his way to the sub panel, pushed over the gear in front of it, and flipped the breaker back on. With that, the inside of the barn lit up.

Kendall scanned down the sight of the AR, but he was alone in the barn. He went to the wide-open doorway and gazed out at the devastation where the house he had been raised in had stood. His adrenaline was so high that the sight of figures running his way hardly raised it, but he jerked his gun in their direction before realizing it was his family running clear of the flames that had reached to the root cellar opening, where they had been hidden.

Micah and his cousin Ronnie led a quartet of men toward the barn. Cargo and Clovis tracked slightly behind them, guns raised. The only person who had gone down the root cellar unaccounted for was Kendall's Uncle Ephraim. Micah and Ronnie entered the barn with their ARs slung across their backs.

"Holy fucking shit." Micah said, coughing and wheezing as he spoke. "How many of them fuckers did we get?"

"I have no idea," Kendall said, looking out at the burning landscape.

"A lot of them."

"I couldn't see a fucking thing."

"I'm telling you, it was a lot of them. The last thing I saw on the rear camera before it cut out was a bunch of guys going in." Micah put his hands together, then splayed them out. "Then *boom*." He laughed and slapped Kendall on the arm before he and Ronnie headed toward the far end of the barn.

The fact was, Kendall's stomach was a wreck. The only thing in the world that consoled him even the least little bit about what had happened was that the bastards had killed his dog.

Without Kendall realizing, Clovis was at his side and his hand was on his shoulder. "You done good, boy. I knew you wouldn't miss."

"But—" Kendall said.

His father cut him off. "You aced it, Kendall. You absolutely aced it."

Kendall's head sagged. "I didn't shoot, Daddy."

Clovis squeezed. "What?"

"I didn't shoot. I couldn't see nothing because of the smoke. I never shot."

"No?"

"Something else set it off. I'm telling you. I didn't. It wasn't me."

Clovis's eyes bored in on him, and he drew his head closer. "Listen here. Just don't tell nobody. They don't gotta know. Far as anyone's concerned, you done it. You were ready to."

"Okay." Kendall nodded. "Where's Uncle Eph?"

"He's pulling out whatever's left of the sentry gun. We gotta get it out of there and get it gone." They'd run a chain from around one of the legs of the gun out into the yard so they could get whatever was left of it out after the explosion. "Remember, you, me, and Micah were asleep in the house when the shooting started. And I was the one who fired back. It's a miracle we all got out alive. You remember that, right?"

"Of course. Yeah."

"Cargo's going to the big barn. If it ain't going to burn all the way down, he'll make sure of it. Ronnie ought to be lighting this one up any second. We got to get."

Micah turned back up beside Kendall and marveled again at the destruction. "Goddamn. It took the cars. It took everything. I knew it'd be big, but I thought maybe." He looked at Clovis. "What the fuck are we supposed to drive?"

THEY ALL FALL THE SAME

"Insurance should take care of it. Might take a while. We got to be patient. Important thing is, we ain't hurt. Not one of us. If we moved them vehicles, they'd have knowed something was up. Insurance would too."

"You think it got Burl?"

Clovis shook his bald head. "No way of knowing. We know we got some of them, but it's untelling who or just how many. Thing we got to do now is finish it up." He turned to the other end of the barn and shouted. "Ronnie, you about ready?"

Ronnie came out from behind a stack of burlap, pouring a trail of gas from a can, headed out the rear door. "Yeah. Y'all need to go on."

"All right, boys," Clovis said. "Time to cover our tracks and get on back in the root cellar. Eph's going to meet us and take our guns. Get there but stay aware. It's possible some of them's still around or hiding." Clovis hacked up from his throat and spit a great wad onto the barn floor. "Burning this barn'll be the last thing Burl done to us tonight. Maybe if we done this right, even if he survived, his ass'll be locked up or on the run. Maybe."

Micah turned from the door and looked at his father. "So, you think it's over?"

"Naw. It ain't over. It ain't going to be that easy."

"We blew up our house. We blew up everything. That don't seem easy to me."

"Easier than dying." The first sound of sirens reached them, though nothing was in sight yet. Clovis backhanded Kendall's arm lightly. "Y'all go on." Then he shouted, "Ronnie, count down from thirty, light it up, and get clear."

Ronnie gave him a gloved thumbs-up. Kendall and Clovis watched him head out the opposite door before heading out themselves. Kendall slowed and turned to watch his father as he stood a moment looking at the scene of devastation where his house had stood just minutes earlier and for over a hundred years before that. Then he saw him grasp the grip of his AR-15 and scan for any movement before lumbering after him.

Part 3

Richmond, Kentucky (June 1, 2020)

A JOINT INVESTIGATION BY the Federal Bureau of Investigation and the Bureau of Alcohol, Tobacco, Firearms and Explosives of the June 1, 2019, Greens Crossing bombing in Madison County, Kentucky, remains open one (1) year after it occurred. The investigation presently indicates that an unknown number of assailants, armed with semiautomatic rifles and military-grade equipment, entered the Begley Turfgrass Sod Co. property during the early morning hours with an incendiary device or devices. The assailants ignited the incendiary devices or devices at a residence on the property, apparently inadvertently or prematurely, killing eight (8) of their number as well as two (2) canines that lived on the property. One (1) of the homes on the property was destroyed in the blast, seven (7) vehicles were severely damaged, and two (2) barns located adjacent to the home also burned. One (1) of the barn fires appeared to have been deliberately set independent of the explosion.

The property owner, Clovis Begley, was one (1) of three (3) residents present in the home at the time of the attack. He alleges that he returned fire on the assailants before escaping out a window along with his sons, Micah and Kendall Begley. He further alleges that the three (3) were able to flee the residence to the safety of an underground root cellar on the property before the incendiary device or devices were ignited. Hundreds of spent rounds were found clustered at numerous locations on the property, including inside the residence.

The deceased found at the scene were all male residents of Jackson County. Many were also known associates of a suspected Jackson County marijuana cultivator and trafficker named Burl Spoon. A 2018 Dodge Challenger registered to one of the deceased, Kyle "Greek" Staley, a purported lieutenant in Spoon's operation, was located intact during a search of the property.

The property owner implicated Spoon in the bombing. The owner alleged that one (1) of his sons, Ryan "Cargo" Begley, who lived in one (1) of the homes on the property that was not destroyed, had recently ended a relationship with Spoon's daughter due to her continued drug use. Shortly thereafter, Spoon's daughter had arrived at the home of Ryan Begley's mother in Estill County while in the throes of an overdose and was taken to the local hospital, where she later died. This account was confirmed both by Ryan Begley's mother and hospital records. Spoon allegedly blamed Ryan Begley for his daughter's death and had threatened members of the Begley family.

Spoon was identified as a person of interest in the bombing within hours of the event. FBI agents traveled to Spoon's home in Jackson County, but he was not located. Evidence at the scene indicated he had recently fled the location. Dogs and livestock were abandoned on the property. Agents suspected but could not establish that Spoon was alerted to their approach by local law enforcement.

Jackson County law enforcement agencies were eventually excluded from the investigation after DNA analysis of human remains found at the scene of the bombing revealed that two (2) of the deceased individuals were deputies employed by the Jackson County Sheriff's Department. Further, equipment recovered from the scene was identified as having originated with that department, as well as the McKee Police Department. Additionally, multiple vehicles and several cellular phones located on the Spoon property were registered to individuals who died in the Greens Crossing bombing, including each of the two (2) deputies.

A search of Spoon's property revealed the existence of a large-scale marijuana cultivation operation that had been intentionally set on fire shortly before the arrival of federal agents. The fire was extinguished, and evidence of the operation preserved. A cache of firearms, a stockpile of ammunition, and equipment was also located on the property. The land and personal property were seized pending forfeiture. Attempts to question suspected coconspirators of Spoon resulted in the invocation of Sixth Amendment right to counsel. Insufficient evidence exists to support charging any of the above-referenced individuals. One (1) year after the event, Spoon remains at large.

CHAPTER

40

IN LATE AUGUST of 2020, Chelsea Spoon had just started her second year of school in Jefferson County. It had taken her a little while to adjust to her new classmates when she first got there. Initially she came home talking a lot about how Louisville kids were different from McKee kids, but by the end of her first semester, in the winter of 2019, she seemed to have settled in. Then the schools shut down due to Covid in March 2020. She completed the school year virtually, on a laptop. This new school year was also starting out virtually, and there was no end in sight.

Chelsea Spoon couldn't say exactly how long it had been since she'd last seen her papaw, only that it felt like a long time. "I'm sure you'll see him again soon," Colleen told her, even though she had no reason to believe it was true. Chelsea didn't ask about him nearly as much as she used to, but she still asked. What she didn't do much at all anymore was talk about going back to Jackson County.

When they had first settled in Louisville, she would ask, "When are we going home? I want to see Papaw," time and again.

"I know, baby," her nana would say, "but we can't go home right now."

"Why?"

"Because, honey, your papaw's had to go away for a while. He's not at home."

"But where'd he go?"

Colleen had picked a place out of the hat, and she chose somewhere she didn't think Chelsea would want to go. "Ohio, sweetie. Papaw's had to go to Ohio."

"Ohio? Why'd he go there?"

"He had some work to do." They'd go back and forth like this a few times a day at first. Then once a day. Then once every few days. Then once a week. Over time it got longer and longer between the conversations, until Chelsea hardly asked at all. She came to accept that they weren't going home, but she still couldn't understand why her papaw didn't come to visit her.

Unlike Chelsea, Colleen Spoon knew exactly how long Burl had been gone. In the first few weeks after the explosion, she was in shock, and also the subject of heavy attention from federal law enforcement. They seemed certain she was withholding information when she told them the truth: she hadn't seen or heard from her husband since leaving the family home the day of their daughter's funeral. The only thing remotely close to contact were the occasional packages that arrived for Chelsea, and she had agreed to inform the Feds before opening any of them. They never had a return address, they were always mailed from Knox County, Tennessee, and each one had a handwritten note in it, from Burl to his granddaughter, along with some toy. The notes never said much more than that he loved her, and he missed her.

Two things seemed to change the Feds' minds about whether Colleen was telling the truth. First, she gave them the name of the doctor she had been seeing romantically, and as it turned out, he hadn't actually erased the video of Burl shooting him, only taken it off the device and stored it elsewhere. He was persuaded to give it to the Feds, and it showed

Colleen leaving before the incident and Burl forcing his way into the home.

They also got a little more convinced when, in December, after six months in Louisville, Colleen filed for divorce in Jefferson County. The case was tied up in court because of the Covid shutdown, Burl's disappearance, and the complexity of it due to their property all being seized. But Colleen had won the race to the courthouse. There was no undoing it. Her divorce and custody of Chelsea were both rooted in Louisville's courts.

Burl had been indicted by the Madison County Grand Jury on assault and burglary charges for shooting the doctor. And since it was on video, the case against Burl was fairly clear cut. In Kentucky, burglary merely means entering a building unlawfully to commit a crime.

After everything Burl had built in Jackson County, and the apparatus he had established there to protect himself from the legal system, his fate now lay in the Circuit Courthouse in Madison County, the Family Courthouse in Jefferson County, and potentially the Federal Courthouse in Lexington.

Despite numerous threats to charge her for the grow operation in Jackson County, and other nefarious aspects of Burl's business operations, nothing had been filed against Colleen. Agents seemed more inclined to lean on her continued cooperation in an effort to locate Burl.

Colleen was surprised Burl didn't resurface immediately, because she knew he'd want revenge on the Begleys. Then a year went by and there was nothing. She'd braced for some grand and violent gesture on the anniversary of DeeDee's death, and then again on the anniversary of her funeral and the bombing, but he never showed himself. Now, nearly fifteen months after he'd disappeared, she had started to experience the tiniest episodes of hope that he'd gone into hiding for good. Whenever she did, she felt foolish. The Burl Spoon she knew would never allow Clovis Begley and his family to triumph, especially after killing his men.

Darron and Michael had done their best to make Colleen and Chelsea feel at home. Colleen was used to having money to burn, but those days were done. She wished for her own place with Chelsea, but it just wasn't possible. She hadn't worked since she was in her twenties, and Chelsea needed someone to care for her, and Colleen was it. Darron worked remotely because of the pandemic, but he was too busy to do more than look after Chelsea part-time. Michael was considered an essential worker during the pandemic, and the police in Louisville were stretched incredibly thin.

The Louisville Metro Police killing of an unarmed Black woman named Breonna Taylor during the execution of an illegally obtained warrant had set off massive protests. Every officer at Louisville Metro was being called upon to work heavy overtime. Even at his rank, Michael was included. As far as the protests went, there was no end in sight.

Michael was hardly home anymore, but Darron, Colleen, and Chelsea were there almost all the time. Darron kept his home office while Michael gave his up so Colleen and Chelsea could each have her own bedroom. Colleen had painted Chelsea's pink, just like the one in Jackson County, and decorated it as close to the old room as possible. They set up a little desk for Chelsea to get on the laptop and go to her virtual classes.

Colleen arranged some outdoor playdates, but there were only so many opportunities. If nothing else, Colleen took Chelsea to the playground at Seneca Park a few times a week just to get her outside. Other than that, the two of them mostly didn't go out.

Chelsea was in her room, playing by herself between classes, when Colleen brought her a snack and a glass of chocolate milk. "How about some Nabs?"

Chelsea had been engrossed in a discussion she was carrying out between Barbie and Skipper, but she looked up. "Um, okay. I'm kind of busy right now, though, Nana."

"I'll set them here for when you're done. I don't want you hungry." Colleen sat on the bed and watched her.

Chelsea held Barbie and Skipper but was kind of stalled out because her nana watching seemed to make her self-conscious. "I guess I could eat now."

Colleen pointed at the crackers. "You want Nana to open them?"

Chelsea wrinkled her nose. "Um, could you make me a grilled cheese?"

"Grilled cheese? You had that yesterday."

"I know, but they're good. That's why I want another one."

After everything Chelsea had been through, losing her mother and then to a great extent her grandfather, Colleen gave her nearly anything she wanted. Although she worried about spoiling her, she worried about Chelsea's happiness more. She got up and headed to the kitchen to make her a grilled cheese. As she left, Barbie and Skipper's conversation started up again.

In the kitchen, Colleen got out a small pan, lit a gas burner, and went into the refrigerator for butter and cheese before taking a loaf of Bunny Bread from the bread box. It wasn't long ago that she thought of it as Darron and Michael's kitchen and felt like a guest. Anymore, it was her home and kitchen too. She thought of it that way and moved around in it that way, which is to say she didn't think much about it at all.

As the melting butter began to sputter and spit, she swirled the first piece of bread in it. Her mind was not on the bread. Her mind was on Burl. After all this time, she still had no idea where he was or what he was doing. The only signs of him were the packages, and they hadn't seen one in months.

Her and Chelsea's world had already been set on its ear, and then came the pandemic. In a way, it almost wasn't as jarring as it might have been if things had been normal. But it made Colleen wonder if it was something about the pandemic that was keeping Burl underground.

The Burl she had known so many years was not patient, especially if he was aggrieved. She kept thinking he'd turn up on their doorstep and try to take Chelsea. She kept thinking she'd feel a tap on her shoulder on one of the rare occasions they left the house. She almost hoped he'd show himself and have it out with the Begleys. At least that would keep him away from her and away from Chelsea. His return was beginning to feel more welcome than the anxiety of his prolonged absence.

41

AUGUST WAS WINDING down, and Clovis Begley's new home still wasn't done. He had managed to stay patient while he waited for the insurance company to pay the money. Once he had the funds, his patience was tested by contractors who worked slowly or didn't show up at all and who really didn't seem to care whether he liked it or not, because good luck finding someone else.

The insurance company had delayed paying the claim on the grounds that the ATF and FBI were slow to release the preliminary results of their investigations. While they said there was no question that a criminal act had taken place, it was unclear who had committed it. The evidence pointed to a plotted attack. The fact that the Begleys had known ties to drug trafficking raised suspicion, as Clovis knew they would. The counter to that was the obvious question: What sane person would blow up his own house, destroy his own vehicles and equipment, and burn his own barns?

The insurance company eventually relented, and construction got underway. Nearly fifteen months after the old one had been vaporized, the new house was under roof on the same site, but there was still a long way to go. The barns and the vehicles were taken care of soon after the insurance paid out, but a twenty-five-hundred-square-foot house was another story.

The explosion had displaced Clovis, Micah, and Kendall. Kendall moved in with Cargo in his little house on the property. Cargo only had his daughter every other weekend, and Kendall had taken to staying at a girlfriend's most of the time, so Cargo was still mainly on his own. Clovis had moved into the other house on the property with his cousin Ephraim and his wife, but he'd stayed gone to Florida for the better part of the last year.

Micah had moved into a modest house he bought in one of the cookie-cutter neighborhoods behind the car dealerships on the new bypass. He laughed at the fact that his neighbors all hated him. On a street full of young families and empty nesters, Micah kept different hours, drove different speeds, and played his music at a different volume than the rest of his neighbors.

Clovis was in Richmond for a few days, but not for much longer. He'd come in to oversee the construction of the new house, but Okeechobee and uncaught fish were calling him back. He was to meet Micah and the general contractor at ten in the morning out at the house to go over a punch list. Micah was supposed to be keeping an eye on the jobsite for him in his absence. Clovis deemed Cargo and Kendall too soft to deal with the contractors.

CHAPTER

42

MACKENZIE NEVER CAME out and said she was Micah's girlfriend because he had never said it himself. But she sure felt like one. If she wasn't his girlfriend, why did she have to get up so early to go with him to see his father? Usually neither one of them rolled out of bed until noon or later. That was a reason why they worked. Common interests. Late nights and late mornings. She told him if she had to go, she had to have coffee. He wanted a can of Monster Energy anyway. They stopped at the Speedway gas station just up the road from his house.

They were having a particularly warm spell in Kentucky, and it was already getting hot. "Look at this fucking guy." Micah pointed out the front window of his Mustang Shelby at a little old panhandler who was standing by the road with a beleaguered cardboard sign, in long pants, a hoodie, gloves, and a Covid mask. His gray hair spilled out of the hood, and his beard bushed out from under the mask. "Eighty fucking degrees and not only is this fucking bum bundled up, he thinks he's going to get 'rona standing on the side of the road. Goddamn."

Mackenzie opened her door. "Maybe you should ask him to borrow his mask?"

"I think I'll be all right. Besides, I bet that thing stinks."

She put on a light blue mask heading into the gas station, but Micah walked barefaced through the door that said masks were mandatory for entry, shaking his head at her. He made his way to the back to the big cooler of energy drinks while she went to the self-serve coffee. They reconvened at the counter, where an older man in a tan suit was checking out in front of them at the plexiglassed register. Mackenzie stood back, but Micah stood right on the man's heels, talking loudly to her and paying no heed to the decals on the floor denoting where to stand. The man, who had on a dark cloth mask, turned halfway and looked at Micah, to no effect. Micah kept talking.

The man turned further and said, "If you're not going to wear a mask, could you at least give me a little space?" He held up his hand between them and gestured pushing away.

Micah crossed his arms but didn't move otherwise. Mackenzie reached for his elbow and tried to pull him back to her. "Come on, Micah." He didn't budge.

The man shook his head and finished charging his card and got his small bag of items. As he tried to walk away in a wide arc, Micah leaned his way, got his face close and said, "Baaaaaaaaaaaaaa," long and loud. Mackenzie punched the back of his shoulder.

Micah spun toward her. "Don't fucking hit me."

She stuck a hand right in front of his face. The clerk glared at Micah as she rang him up from the other side of the plexiglass, but didn't say anything. On the way back across the parking lot Micah cracked his Monster and hammered down about half of it.

Once they were back in the car, Mackenzie peeled off her mask. "If you aren't going to wear a mask, you at least don't have to be such an asshole about it."

"Don't even start with that. This whole thing's ridiculous. I'm not going to sit here and act like it isn't."

"That guy was old. He could die if he got it."

"He's not going to fucking die."

Mackenzie looked straight ahead. "You don't know that."

While they were arguing, the vagrant had come from the roadside to their window with his sign, crouched down, and held it so they could see it. The sign read: "Anything Helps. God Bless."

"Oh Christ, what now?"

The man knocked on the window, but he wasn't really making eye contact. He had the sign mostly blocking his face, but his long beard moved up and down below where the mask ended, like he was talking.

Micah tried ignoring him, but the guy didn't go away. He finally rolled down his window a crack. "Get the fuck out of here, you fucking bum. I don't have any money for you."

The man pulled closer, like he couldn't hear.

Micah rolled his window down farther. "I said fuck off. I'm not giving you any money, you goddamn beggar. Now get out of here."

The words were barely out of Micah's mouth when the man leaned his head and shoulders almost into the window, with a pistol pointed up from underneath the bottom of Micah's cheek. "Naw. I don't want no money, Micah," the man said. "I just been waiting on you so I could send your daddy a message."

Micah had gone rigid. Mackenzie breathed, "Oh my god. Oh my god."

The grizzly little man locked his eyes on Micah. "Rot, boy." His hand fanned the hammer spraying the contents of Micah's skull all over the car's cab and Mackenzie, with six shots.

She was shrieking before the blasts of the firing stopped and had flung her coffee everywhere. The man's demeanor remained unchanged as he regarded her. "Hush now. I just done you a favor." He reached into his jacket, withdrew something silver from it, and flipped it across the cab into her lap. "Go on and give that to his daddy." Then the man dropped a half dozen tiny plastic packets of white powder on the front seat and on the ground beside the driver-side window as a car lurched to a stop beside him. He got into the car's passenger side, and it peeled away before Mackenzie could see what he'd tossed at her. It had fallen to the floorboard. People from the gas pumps and inside the store, who had ducked for cover, were starting to show themselves and come closer to see what had happened. Mackenzie reached between her feet, sobbing violently, and picked up what the man had thrown her way.

CHAPTER

43

WHITNEY SPED OUT Four Mile Road, taking the curves with the acumen of someone who'd learned to drive in Jackson County, just like Burl knew she would. Her gloved hands deftly handled the steering wheel of the beige Nissan Altima—a car they'd chosen because of just how extraordinary it wasn't. He had taken off his mask and kneaded his mouth where it had been over his wild gray beard all morning. She reached over and squeezed his arm a couple times but didn't speak a word until they had exchanged vehicles at the recycling center and got on their way back to Harlan. Burl rolled down his window and flicked his beggar's sign deep into roadside brush that was already specked with trash.

In fourteen months their appearances had gone in opposite directions. Burl, who had always kept his sculpted pompadour dyed dark, had let it go gray and long, much like the beard he had grown for the first time in his life. Whitney had dyed her long blonde hair back to its natural brown, cut it to her shoulders, and fashioned herself some bangs. She'd also taken to dabbing concealer on her birth mark any time she went anywhere, and she'd shed the little hoop ring she used to wear in her nose. Just like Burl, she looked a way she hadn't before, and it was so far so good for both of them.

They'd been living out of an Oldsmobile and sleeping in a tent at a campground on Miller's Creek in Estill County since the beginning of August. Each morning they drove into Richmond, and Burl posted up in his beggar's outfit at one of the three gas stations near Micah's house and waited for an opportunity while Whitney stood by. Their patience had finally paid off.

The two most important things Burl was able to take with him when he fled Jackson County were three hundred thousand dollars in cash from a safe at the check cashing store, and Whitney. That money had bought him resources and secrecy, which was what he needed to bide his time until he could resurface to extract his due. Whitney had offered a less identifiable face to go out in the world for him, and a companion to see him through his banishment.

As hardened a man as he might have been, Burl Spoon wasn't one who could get by without a companion. Especially after what he'd been through. The year had been far from harmonious. Burl could be harsh, and Whitney didn't always take it. She'd left more than once, threatening to stay gone. He tried not to let on how bad it shook him each time she did it, but he always softened for a time after she came back. He was in a reduced state, and not only did he know it, he knew she did too.

He'd grabbed her up quick from her apartment, barely giving her time to throw things into a bag before the Feds came. The hardest part was convincing Whitney to leave her iPhone. She was still negotiating to keep it when he'd said, "I pay for the fucking thing—now give it to me," and taken it from her, powered it down, smashed it in his hands, and threw it across the parking lot. He wasn't wrong to rush. He later found out that FBI agents got to Whitney's door less than an hour after they'd entered his farm.

Burl hadn't been able to do half of what he wanted before leaving his own home. He'd left Johnny and Waylon baying

at him in the yard and sent Clarence and Toby to burn everything incriminating on the farm. He knew that was a tall job
for anyone, and especially Clarence and Toby. The thing was,
there was nobody else left.

The man Burl hoped would hide them for just a spell
wound up being the man who had put them up the entire last
year and some change before they had come back to Estill
County in August. After Burl's mother had gotten sent away
when he was fifteen, a judge had shipped him off to his father
in Whitesburg. Burl had landed in Letcher County sad,
bored, and pissed off. A string of juvenile offenses ended with
a break-in at the Alene Theater that netted him a grand total
of forty-two dollars, a case of Goobers, and thirty days in
detention.

Burl didn't even mind going to juvenile detention. He
liked it better than his dad's house. Unlike at home, the fights
he got into in detention he at least stood a chance of winning.
After that first stretch, Burl had made it a point to get back
there as often as possible.

It was in detention that Burl befriended an older boy
named Jewell, whose family was from Harlan. They bonded
over a certain like-mindedness. After they'd aged out of the
juvenile system, Jewell wound up back in Harlan, and Burl
back in Jackson County. They led similar lives and had done
some business over the years that couldn't be done out in the
open. Jewell was one of the few people Burl could think of
who he absolutely knew wouldn't give him up for anything.
It just wasn't in him.

Burl's initial intent was to see if Jewell would let him stay
a few days until his ruptured eardrums, burns, and wounds
had healed up, then figure out his next move. As it turned
out, Jewell had longer-term accommodations to offer. There'd
been an indie movie shot in Harlan a few years earlier, and
lodging there was scarce. Jewell had cut a deal to house a few
of the crew in makeshift cabins he'd built on his property,

tucked away from town. The movie was long done, and the cabins weren't in any demand—one had nearly fallen in— but Jewell had run electric and water to the nicest of them and even put in a composting toilet.

Burl had cash and that was Jewell's language. For two thousand a month, Jewell ran a satellite cable up the hill from his house, kept the electric and water on, and made sure Burl had what he needed to get by.

It was there that Burl and Whitney dug in. They watched TV and sat up nights together while he weathered PTSD and panic attacks caused by seeing Greek and his men go up in flames. Over time he got better, bit by bit. While he did that, he and Whitney smoked cigarettes and talked and hunted and fought and celebrated her thirtieth birthday over a Swiss Roll with a candle in it. They bided time and waited for the world to lose track of the little man from Jackson County who may or may not have blown up a sod farm. The world obliged their needs in one way: it went all to hell. Burl quickly became a small footnote to all that was wrong out there.

CLOVIS STOOD ON the front porch of his unfinished house, with his bare arms crossed, wearing his customary tan overalls. His builder walked the perimeter, inspecting the half-finished brickwork behind scaffolds that surrounded much of the structure. Clovis's phone vibrated in his front pocket, and he answered it.

It was Kendall. Clovis had been trying to get him or Cargo for the last twenty minutes. Clovis asked, "Have you heard from Micah? He's supposed to meet me here at the house a half hour ago, and he ain't answering his phone."

Kendall said, "Naw. I ain't heard from him."

"When's the last time you talked to him?"

"He texted me yesterday something about making a run to Tennessee, but he wasn't planning on doing that until next week."

"You got the number of that girl he's been seeing?"

"Who, Kenzie? I don't think I got it, but I can check. I think Tiffany might have it if I don't. He's probably still sleeping."

"Naw. He knew how important it was that he get here on time."

"Maybe he's sick. Maybe he's got him a yeast infection or something." Kendall chuckled as he said it.

Clovis withdrew the phone from his ear as a local number he didn't have stored in it appeared on the screen. He was stern. "Get me that number." Then he tapped the phone and answered the other call.

A man's voice said, "Is this Clovis?"

"Who's calling?"

"This is Lieutenant Reed with RPD."

Clovis and Reed knew each other a little bit. Reed was in his forties and had been around the department a long time. Clovis had been through a few things at the courthouse that had caused the two of them to become acquainted. All the Begleys were known to the local police, many of whom hoped to bust them for something big, but often had to settle for petty victories like DUIs and misdemeanor assaults. Reed had been involved in a few such shortfalls himself. "I was wondering if you were somewhere that I could meet you."

"What's this about?"

"I'd rather not get into it until we're face to face. Are you in town?"

"I'm at my farm. Do I need to have my lawyer here?"

"No sir. I just need to speak with you. Not as a suspect or anything like that."

"I need to know what you want to talk about."

The line was quiet. Reed eventually said, "Clovis, it'd be better for me to come out there, I promise you. I'm not ten minutes away."

Clovis's lips hung slightly open. He swallowed hard as sickness rolled from his chest down to the base of his stomach. "I'll be here."

45

WHITNEY WAS STILL at the wheel as they made their way south on Route 11, headed back to Harlan. Burl had told her to stay off the interstate and to swing wide around McKee. He didn't get out of the Oldsmobile when she stopped in Beattyville to pee, because he didn't want to take any chance of being seen. They'd both stayed pretty quiet during the drive to that point, but after she'd made some water, it felt like everything that she'd stoppered up was turned loose, and she started talking.

"You always said Micah had to be the first to go. He was kind of all I thought about. With him gone, what do we do now?"

Burl looked at the road ahead with a cigarette between his lips. "I got to sit with it a bit. More importantly, Clovis's got to."

"You ain't going after Clovis?"

"I ain't said that." Burl withdrew the cigarette and blew smoke hard out the cracked window. "What I said was, I ain't doing it *yet*. Hell, I wouldn't have killed him today if I'd had the chance. I want him to have to live with what I done to Micah the same way I've had to live with what all he done. He ain't suffered like I suffered. Not nearly. He needs time to do that."

"So you're going to wait, but he's next? Or you ain't decided on that either?"

"I don't know yet. Maybe he is and maybe he ain't." He scratched the side of his beardy face. "Maybe I'll take another one of his boys or his cousin, or one of his nephews. Make no mistake, I'm going to kill that motherfucker if it's the last thing I do in this goddamn world, but I ain't in a rush like I was. That's what I learned here this last year. I always thought what hurt was getting hurt, but that ain't what really hurts. What really hurts is seeing what you love get taken away and having to live with it. They ain't no pain worse."

Whitney made her lips into a sort of pucker and rotated it around while she was thinking. "I know Micah deserved what he got. I know he did. That's why I don't feel a bit bad about helping you do what you done, but who else deserves it besides Clovis? I mean, I ain't saying I don't understand why you want to do what you want to do. I'm just saying, is it because they deserve it, or is it because Clovis deserves it?"

Burl flicked his butt out the window and looked at her. "Are you trying to say all them motherfuckers don't deserve to die for what they done? The people they killed? Goddamn. They've took everything from me. I ain't got no fucking family no more. I ain't got no fucking house. I ain't got no life. I can't even see my grandbaby. I lost every goddamn thing I ever had. I'm living in a fucking cabin, staring at the walls all day and night, with goddamn nothing. Fuck those motherfuckers. There ain't a one of them that don't deserve to die. Don't come at me with that bullshit."

Miles rolled by and the road began to twist and rise and drop, then rise again. Trees surrounded them in green, then slacked away. Kudzu clung to hillsides, and the rock walls carved through the hills, dominating them and everything affixed to them. Whitney drove on as tears pooled under her eyes and slid down her cheeks. The car radio was off. Road noise was all there was to listen to. Burl just looked out the window, shifting now and again. He almost seemed to be having some sort of conversation internally. Every so often the two lanes would add an extra lane to pass, going up a hill, but Whitney mostly stayed right, going at best a mile or two over the speed limit, doing everything she could not to attract any attention.

Whitney'd given her whole life over to Burl, had stayed up nights with him while he suffered, and still he treated her like nothing more than an appendage. It wounded her, but she was loath to say anything because it only made it worse. Burl felt aggrieved—aggrieved at everything—and any hurt Whitney expressed he only compared to his own suffering and branded her pain trivial and lashed out. It hadn't been that way at the start. Back before everything had happened with DeeDee and the Begleys. Their relationship was unseemly, but she had always felt a measure of joy in it.

Burl said he didn't remember the first time he met her, but Whitney always remembered meeting him. She'd gone to his house when she was a junior in high school. He came into the den, where she was sprawled belly-down on the carpet with another girl, watching Darron and two of his buddies from the basketball team play video games.

Burl had said, "Y'all can have anything in this house you want to eat or drink except my booze. You don't got to ask nobody—just don't go getting into the liquor." Then he walked off.

Whitney could recall that moment vividly, and how none of them had talked about getting into his booze until he mentioned it. She also remembered his house and everything she saw in it, and how different it was from the little three-room siding house where she grew up with her mother, out Sandgap, and how his fancy bourbon burned her throat going down.

After that she didn't see him again up close for over ten years. Not until she served him his dinner at Opal's her first week working there. She knew him on sight because nobody else in the county looked anything like him. She knew his reputation, and she knew just what she intended. He wasn't seated in her section, but she paid his server ten dollars to switch with her.

The woman Whitney paid was called Honeybee. She was in her sixties and had been working at Opal's for as long as anyone could remember. When she stuck the money in her apron, she told Whitney, "I hate to take your money, honey. He don't even tip that good."

That ten dollars proved to be the best investment Whitney had ever made. She went to the bathroom, freshened up her face, plumped up her chest, and fixed her hair as best she could. Walking to his table, she still wasn't real sure how she was going to make her play, but Burl took the play from her. He commented on the beauty mark on her cheek after giving her his order. He tapped the spot on his own face. "You kind of favor Marilyn Monroe. Anybody ever tell you that?"

She grinned and reddened just a bit. All she could think to say was "Well."

He bantered with her each time she came to the table after that. When it came time to pay, he handed her a business card that read "Spoon Convenience, LLC," with the money for the check plus fifty dollars, and said, "Why don't you put your number on there." The three boys who were with him acted like they didn't hear or make anything of it, just side-eyed her.

She stood right there and wrote her number down in big numerals. The first thing she did with that fifty dollars was buy more minutes for her phone and a new box of hair dye. Whatever she did, she didn't want to miss his call, and she wanted to look her best when it came.

Now she was driving him away from a murder scene, and he didn't even seem to register what that meant for her, only himself. She stared at Burl, hardly watching the road when she spoke again. "I ain't nothing, Burl. I know what all they took from you, but I ain't nothing."

"I never said that."

"Do you even listen to yourself? Because I do. Seems like it's all I ever do. Them words came right out of your mouth. You said you got nothing."

"That's not what I meant."

"There ain't no other way to take it. You know something else I heard you say before that you don't remember? You said Cargo tried to save DeeDee's life. I know he's a Begley, and I know what all Clovis and Micah done, but Cargo went against his daddy to try and save her life, and that ought to count for something?"

"All he done is dump her on his mama," Burl said.

"He took her to his mama to try to save her. You told me that yourself. It seems like he's the only one who done anything decent in all this. And you said he's got a daughter. If you hurt him, you hurt that little girl too. I mean"—she reached out and took him by the forearm—"I just helped you kill a man, and I don't feel the least bit bad about it. But killing Cargo just don't seem right to me, Burl."

"So you've got in the business of telling me what's right and wrong?"

Whitney drew her hand back and slapped the steering wheel. "Goddamn, Burl. I gave up everything I had for you. I'm a fucking dumbass for it, but I love you for some reason. I know you don't love me and you won't even touch me no more. I probably threw my life away for nothing, but I'm all you got right now, and I'm telling you, if you aim to kill Cargo, I ain't helping. I'm not."

Burl made a face like he was fixing to spit, but didn't. "I see how it is. A pack of fucking killers and you done picked out one as the good guy and now you going to turn on me for him?"

"I ain't turned on you, Burl. I just don't want no part of making a little girl an orphan. I don't want no part of killing a man who tried to save your daughter's life. I got to live with myself, and I know my choices might not make sense to nobody else, but they make sense to me. If I'm going to go to prison for you, I ain't going to lay there thinking about a little girl crying over her daddy every fucking night." Whitney wiped under one of her eyes with the back of her hand. "I ain't doing it. If that's what you plan on doing, tell me now, and when we get back, I'll go on. I ain't going to tell nobody nothing. You know that. But I ain't staying if you aim to kill that boy that was tenderhearted."

When they turned onto 66 near Oneida, the road really started to twist. Whitney slowed way down and focused on her driving more. Burl had his arms crossed on his chest, and his mouth and lips twitched a bit inside his nest of whiskers. Things stayed that way until they reached the Hal Rogers Parkway, which had been called the Daniel Boone Parkway not long before but had been renamed for a still-living politi-cian who was nothing special but brought home a lot of pork.

Burl seemed to be staring at the road behind them in the sideview mirror. "I won't touch that one so long as he don't get between me and Clovis. If that happens, I can't make no promises. But if he don't, I won't touch him."

Whitney looked at Burl but kept the corner of her eye on the road. He didn't look back at her. She put her right hand on his thigh and squeezed it. "Okay."

He said, "Okay."

CHAPTER

46

CARGO, CLOVIS, RONNIE, and Ephraim all sat in Cargo's living room, red-eyed, talking in bursts before falling quiet and staring at the floor or out the window before opening up again. Cargo broke in after a long period of mostly silence that was marked by the sound of grown men sniffling hard, trying to stifle themselves from outright crying.

"Don't none of it make no sense. None of it. Micah ain't gonna be out there doing some penny ante shit like that in broad daylight. They want to make out like he's some street dealer, but nobody's trying to cop before ten in the fucking morning. He ain't going to be out there selling like that."

"You think it was a robbery?" Ephraim asked.

Clovis's elbows were on his knees, his head was in his hands, and he didn't look up. "I told you all what I told Reed. This wasn't no drug deal. This wasn't no robbery. This was a goddamn execution. This was Burl Spoon."

"But it was point blank," Cargo said. "How's Micah gonna let him get that close without firing back? This guy was in his goddamn car window. How would he let Burl Spoon get that close? It sounds to me like it was someone he knew."

"Could it've been one of the Detroit boys?" Ephraim asked.

"Goddamn, Eph!" Clovis stomped his boot so hard the floor boards vibrated. "I've told you no less than ten times it was a white man, and I'm telling you one more time that it was fucking Burl Spoon. Micah didn't have no beef with the Detroit boys."

Cargo's dog, Dempsey, started barking outside. He was a rescue Cargo'd gotten from a shelter. He was a boxer mix and had a brindle coat that reminded Cargo of Kong. The sound of a car engine approached, and Cargo got up from one of the couches and headed for the door to look out and see who was coming. Every man's hand in the room, including his, rested on a gun.

He stepped out on the porch but left the door open behind him. The dog continued his barking. The engine went off. A minute later Cargo led Kendall and Mackenzie into the front room. She had a mask on, but even so her face was visibly stricken, and her hair was out of shape. She stood by the door as Kendall went and sat on one of the couches.

Before he sat back down, Cargo said, "You ain't gotta wear that mask if you don't want to."

Mackenzie stood there not saying anything, shuddering the least little bit now and again. She looked at the still open door behind her and didn't close it. She took her mask off and held it in her right hand. Her mouth was drawn in. Tiny. The men all waited for her to speak, and it seemed like she might several times but didn't.

Eventually, in a voice Cargo had seldom heard him use, Clovis said, "Mackenzie, honey, I know it ain't easy, but you got to tell us what happened out there. We need to know. We need to know who it was that done this to Micah."

She shook her head but didn't look up at anyone. "I don't know."

Clovis took a deep breath. Everyone else in the room seemed to understand that this was not the time to speak. "Tell us what you do know, then. What'd this man look like? Was he a big man or a little man?"

"I guess he was little. He looked like he was homeless."

"Why do you think he was homeless?"

Each time before Mackenzie spoke, it was like she had to work up the strength to do it. She gathered and said, "He had a sign. He was begging for money. His hair was long and dirty, and so was his beard."

"Did Micah know who he was?" Clovis asked.

"I don't know. I don't think so. But the man knew Micah. He called him by his name."

"What'd he say?"

"He said he had a message for you."

"A message for me?"

"He said, 'Micah, I got a message for your daddy.' Or something—something like that." Mackenzie opened her mouth and sobbed in a way that was just audible. "And then he shot him." After that she broke out crying for real. All anyone could do was watch her as she hunched over and drew her hands to her face, shaking.

Clovis gritted his teeth, and his gaze went from Mackenzie to the other men in the room. Cargo wiped at his eyes with the back of his hand as he got up and went into his hallway bathroom. He came back with a wad of toilet paper that he handed to Mackenzie.

Once Mackenzie had somewhat composed herself, Clovis spoke again. "Where did the heroin come from?"

"I don't know. That man, I guess. I don't think Micah had anything on him. We was just coming out here."

"Did he say anything else? The man?"

Mackenzie looked up. Her blonde hair was in her face, and she compacted her lips to one side. "He said he did me a favor. And then he . . ." She drew her lips in and didn't finish. Couldn't finish.

"What else did he say?"

She nodded her head just the littlest bit, trying to get herself talking again. "He said he had something to give you."

"Give me?"

"It was a spoon. He threw it in the car at me, but the police kept it. Said they had to test it, it might have residue. It was a little silver spoon."

Clovis stilled almost entirely. All the men did. With the door open, the room had gotten hot, which belied the chill that had washed over it.

"How'd he get away?"

"A car came."

"Who was driving?"

"I didn't see. I didn't see anything else. People were everywhere, and the police came. I don't remember anything else."

"It's okay, honey," Clovis said. "You done your best. If you'll go wait at the car, Kendall'll be out to take you on back home. If you think of anything else, you let us know."

Mackenzie bobbed her head and backed out the door. Kendall got up.

"Hold on, Kendall. Close the door." He did as he was told. Only then did Clovis begin speaking again, his fat fists clenched tight and his eyes now in flames. "I told you all it was goddamned Burl Spoon that done this. That son of a bitch ain't going to stop. We're right back where we was last year. That motherfucker'll kill every last one of us if he gets the chance. We only got the better of him last time because we knowed he was coming, and he was reckless. Now he's done waited over a year." Clovis shook his head slow. "That means the next one could be today or tomorrow or in another year. Boys, I'm too old to live that way. I ain't looking over my shoulder every minute of every day for the rest of my life. And I ain't letting him get by with what he done to Micah."

"If he goes back into hiding," Ephraim said, "what are we supposed to do?"

"We're going to smoke him out, and we're going to kill him."

"But every lawman in Kentucky's been trying to find him the last year. How are we supposed to do it?"

Clovis pointed at his cousin, and his voice rose. "He ain't murdered none of your boys, has he? Has he? So we're going to do what the law can't. We're going to hurt what he loves. There ain't nobody off limits."

Ephraim cocked his head. "Are you talking about his son?"

Clovis's nostrils flared wide as his brow descended. "I said *nobody*."

47

Burl and Jewell had spent some time together developing plans for what they'd do if the law ever turned up looking. Jewell was winding down now, but he'd run a variety of illicit operations over the course of his life in Harlan and still had access to many of the resources he'd used to that end.

He'd given Burl use of an abandoned home on family land elsewhere in the county, to stash the bulk of his money and other supplies. Burl could access it easily if he ever had to make a hasty run out of Harlan. They had arranged a system of signals whereby Jewell could alert Burl to flee out the back if law enforcement ever came poking.

The plan was for Whitney to stay put no matter what and claim she was living alone, if it came down to it. They'd been over the plan so many times now that when Burl quizzed her on it, Whitney would say something like, "I fucking know the plan, Burl." Or, "I'm not doing this again. I'm not an idiot." Even so, he would wear her down and make her go over it again anyway.

Burl was small enough that his clothes could pass for Whitney's hunting clothes. He'd taken to wearing the same pair of underwear every day, washing them at night and hanging them to dry while he slept, thinking underwear was the one thing that, if he left it behind, would be a dead giveaway.

Whitney washed her clothes and Burl's down at Jewell's house. He didn't shave, he didn't wear any deodorant, and the two of them shared one toothbrush. It all helped contribute well to his homeless disguise, that much was for sure.

On the rare occasions Burl left Jewell's place with Whitney, they had a procedure to make sure nobody unexpected waited for them when they got back. She'd use a burner phone to call Jewell. When he answered, she'd tell him it was his last chance to extend his car's warranty. If Jewell said, "Yes," that meant the coast was clear.

They'd been gone nearly a month, but a couple miles out from Jewell's place, she made the call, and he picked up. "Hello," she said. "This is your last chance to extend your car warranty."

She'd hardly gotten it out before Jewell said, "No, I don't want no fucking car warranty," and hung up.

Whitney looked at Burl, big-eyed. "He said, 'No.'"

Burl snatched the flip phone from Whitney, powered it off, broke it in two, and tossed it over his shoulder into the back seat. "You know what to do, then. Just how we talked about."

Whitney drove to the far side of the mountain, opposite Jewell's house and his cabins. She pulled off onto a trail they'd gone and scouted a half dozen times in the past. Both got out and stretched their stiff bodies. She stripped down to her underclothes and threw what she'd been wearing into the trunk alongside Burl's arsenal of guns and supplies. She changed into long pants, a long shirt, and boots suitable for a place as snaky as the woods she was fixing to traverse.

"Get you a walking stick from the woods, now," Burl said.

She drew close to Burl and laid her hand on his chest. "I know what I'm supposed to do, Burl."

"Don't hurt nothing to go over it again."

"Hurts my ears."

"Just remember, what they suspect and what they know ain't the same thing. Let them suspect all they want, but don't tell them nothing, and they don't got nothing but their suspicions."

"I heard that somewhere before."

Burl pointed to the open trunk. "You best get your sack and go on now."

Whitney looked into his eyes and shook her head.

"What?" he said.

"So that's it. 'Get your sack and go'? That's all you got to say to me?"

"Goddamn. What am I supposed to say? You want me to say some fucking poetry?"

Whitney took her hand from his chest and shoved the side of his head. "Everything I done the last year was for nobody else but you and you ain't got nothing more to say to me?" She pushed him hard in the chest with both hands. She was crying now. "Fuck you, Burl."

He grabbed her wrists while she struggled to get away. "Goddamn, girl. Calm the fuck down."

She jerked away from him. "No, I ain't going to calm down. I ain't just some slave here to do whatever you need done, Burl. I don't even know what we are anymore, but I've loved you, and you ain't never said nothing about loving me back. Not one time. It's like I ain't nothing to you."

He reached for her. "Now that ain't true."

She slapped his hands away. "It is true." She turned her back on him and went around the other side of the Oldsmobile.

Burl stared at Whitney's back. He dug his fingers into his thick beard and scratched hard at what was becoming scaly skin beneath it. They were in the shade of leafy trees, but the day was only getting hotter. He finally went around the car and stood beside her, waiting for her to turn. He reached for her upper arm. She turned her head just a fraction, revealing rheumy eyes framed by her brown bangs. He pulled her to him and hugged her, side to side. "Goddamn. I love you and that's the truth. You done a lot for me. Don't go over that mountain thinking I don't."

She pulled away a bit, but he pulled her back.

"I mean it," he said. "I know what I said, but it wadn't right. You mean a whole lot to me and I ain't have made it without you. I can't lie. You been there for me when I didn't have a single other thing. I do love you, Whitney. I promise I do."

When he said that, she turned all the way and merged with him. As she did, a pair of chickadees in the tree above them took flight and were quickly gone into the deep woods. She squeezed him hard, and he gave her a squeeze back. He kissed her on the side of the head.

Burl looked up to where the birds had just been, to where a squirrel was tiptoeing small branches. He pictured picking it off with a .22 round. He and Whitney'd eaten dozens of them over the last year, not because they had to, but because they liked to. They'd hunted them just to pass the time at the cabin, and made a game of seeing who could get the most in a week. It was quite possible he'd be eating more soon out of necessity and all by himself, and he knew when it came to that, he'd wish she was there. She laid her head into his chest, and he cradled it.

CHAPTER

48

THE JOB OF going out to the Jewell property fell to Harlan County Deputy Sheriff Robbie Snelling after the FBI called KSP Post 10 in Harlan, requesting a state trooper make the run. The Feds were hunting Burl Spoon. They'd identified some old connection between him and Jewell that apparently nobody thought was all that urgent until that day. But then some drug dealer got killed execution-style in Richmond, and the family and the facts were all screaming Spoon's name, and the abandoned getaway car came back as last registered in Harlan County. Signs were pointing toward the wisdom of paying Jewell's place a visit sooner rather than later.

KSP didn't have anyone in that part of the county, but Deputy Snelling was in the vicinity. That was how he got tasked with holding down the scene until more bodies could be thrown over there. Snelling was outside Jewell's house, making small talk. He lived alone not far from there and had been home, getting a bite to eat, when the call came in. He'd known *of* Jewell just about all his life and had actually gotten to know him the last six years.

Jewell explained he'd had a little girl renting out one of his cabins for a bit, but he'd not seen Burl Spoon in an age.

Snelling was hoping KSP would turn up soon because he was wanting to hand things off and get back to the food he'd left on the table before it spoiled, but it wasn't looking good.

When Snelling had initially arrived, he was on high alert as this Spoon fellow was said to be armed and dangerous. Having spent some time talking with Jewell and looking around the cabins, his guard had come down a good bit. Snelling had worn a mask when he first arrived, as was the protocol, but after being there a few minutes, he'd pulled it off, and it now hung from just one ear. Jewell said he believed the girl was home because she didn't have a car, and nobody'd been up the drive all day. She was probably out in the woods. She spent a lot of her time there, Jewell said. Snelling had already rummaged through the cabin where she was staying, and from what he could tell, it looked like there was indeed nothing but a feral sort of gal staying there, but there were some questions raised by some of what he'd found.

He heard the girl coming down the mountain before he actually saw her. She must've crunched just about every branch on her way out of a thicket, spooking a grouse out of the underbrush as she came. Once she was in sight, he could see that she was in long clothes, using a crude walking stick, and had a sack slung over her shoulder. As she neared, he called to her. "Missy, I need you to come on down here if you don't care to."

She looked at him, seeming apprehensive. "Okay."

Before she reached them, he asked her. "What you got in the sack?"

She shook her head.

"I know you ain't hunting morels this time of year, and you ain't got no gun, so I'm afraid of what I'm going to find in that bag. Hand it over."

She swung it off her shoulder and held it out his way.

"It ain't snakes, is it?"

"It's 'seng."

He pulled a long breath in through his nose. "That's what I thought. You know it ain't ginseng season yet, don't you?"

She sighed. "Yeah."

He looked down into the bag at a collection of dirt-clinging roots and a spade. "Well, it ain't the crime of the century."

"You gonna take 'em?" Her eyes were downcast.

He popped his lips and looked thoughtful. "Naw. Just don't dig no more, and put up what you got until after the season starts. It's just a few weeks off now."

She brightened. "Thank you."

He brightened too. "It's all right." Snelling patted the gun on his hip. She was an awful cute girl, even disheveled and sweaty. She looked to be about his age too. "I suppose I got to ask you if you know a feller called Burl Spoon."

She peered at him. "I know that name. I heard he died."

Snelling chuckled. "You mean he ain't living up there with you?"

"Naw."

"Well, we got to wait for them gray gods to get here so you can tell them the same damn thing. They sure are taking their time today considering how worked up they was for me to get out here."

The girl shrugged.

"Reckon they stopped off and got 'em some Colonel Crispy?" Jewell said.

Snelling was looking the girl over again, thinking she looked better and better and that he was only a couple miles up the road. Maybe she'd take his call sometime if he played his cards well enough. "I wouldn't doubt it," he said, and smiled. The gal with the ginseng sack smiled back. He grinned a little bigger.

49

CLOVIS'S INTENTION TO return to Florida was quashed by Micah's death. Micah was put to rest quickly and quietly by necessity of Covid, but also to avoid exposing anyone to Burl Spoon. Kendall moved back from his girlfriend's, and every Begley who left the location did so only with deliberation and specified intent. Construction continued on the main house, but each vehicle and person who came and went was subject to a new level of armed scrutiny.

The other Begley homes and families out Greens Crossing were also on high alert. As far as anyone knew, Burl was liable to strike any one of them at any time, and the fact that the entire world was suddenly wearing masks only made trips to town more ominous. How do you spot menace when all you can see of someone is his eyes? Clovis vowed that they would do what was necessary to put an end to the situation through any means necessary. Those means were Burl's family.

It didn't take much effort for the Begleys to turn up leads on the whereabouts of their targets. Kendall ran a Google search for Colleen Spoon that returned only the outdated Jackson County address. The farm was a frozen and deserted asset. They knew that much. However, a similar search for

"Darron Spoon Louisville KY" produced an address and phone number in a matter of seconds.

Rather than send either of his sons, Clovis sent his nephew Ronnie to Louisville to watch Darron Spoon's home and see who came and went. For the first day and a half, there was very little action. A Black man went to a police car in the driveway in the evening and left. He returned the next morning, parked in the same place, and went inside. Not until that afternoon did anyone else stir. A white man Ronnie knew to be Darron Spoon went to the mailbox, collected the material inside, and went back in. The home's backyard was surrounded by a privacy fence, so if anyone came or went from there, Ronnie couldn't tell.

Around seven in the evening, the garage door went up, and a sedan backed out. Ronnie expected to see Darron at the wheel, but it was a woman. A mature woman. Maybe in her fifties. He considered what to do and ultimately followed the car.

He kept a distance, but he managed to stay behind it as is it traveled just a couple miles to Seneca Park. When it pulled in and parked near a playground, Ronnie went on past but watched the woman and a little girl get out. He didn't come back that way. He didn't need to. He was certain he had located exactly what his uncle had hoped he'd find: Colleen and Chelsea Spoon. He dialed Clovis before he left the park grounds.

CHAPTER

50

Not knowing what happened back at Jewell's cabin, and having no way to find out, Burl was left to believe the law was closing in. He was agitated and flying blind. Driving felt strange, as he hadn't done it in over a year. On the few occasions he'd been out, Whitney was at the wheel, so if they were pulled over, the attention would be on her, not him. It had cost a good bit of money, as arrangements with Jewell tended to, but he had supplied her with a driver's license belonging to a woman from Knott County who resembled Whitney, and an Oldsmobile that he said should "check out" if she was ever pulled over.

Even though Jewell had assured him the old house where he'd taken him to stash his money and belongings was safe from the world and the law, Burl was wary as he drove up the overgrown, tire-rutted path and a little on edge as he got out of the car and went inside. The only sound on the wind was the flowing of a nearby stream, bird calls, and a bug that made a rapid ticking noise. The air was full of the smell of pollen.

If the law had somehow tracked him to Jewell's place in Harlan, who was to say they weren't lying in wait at every property that had ever been owned by his line? The house looked like it'd been built a room at a time, and the last never finished, still clad in white Tyvek wrap that was only just hanging on. Any fear Burl had that someone lay in wait inside was allayed when he shouldered open the sticking wooden door and a possum hissed at him before scuttling from the main room down the back hallway. Though it quickened his heart rate, it was reassuring. If anyone had been inside, that possum would have been long gone.

As hot as it was outside, it was even warmer in the house. Burl and Jewell had bruted the old refrigerator out of the way together the last time they were in that kitchen. On this day Burl had to walk it slowly across the torn linoleum himself, and gouged the floor even more getting it out of the way. He was dripping wet with sweat by the time he had it clear. The wall behind it had a panel of unfinished, unaffixed drywall that he popped out with the toe of his boot. He knelt down and reached inside the hatch. His carry-on-style plastic suitcase full of cash and clothes was right where he'd left it.

Unless things had gone terribly wrong, the remnants of the fifty thousand Burl and Whitney had been living on were still jammed up inside a mossy hollow tree near a lichen-covered rock in the woods behind Jewell's house. Burl hoped whatever happened, Whitney'd have the chance to retrieve it and use it for herself. They'd tucked a phone up there as well, so if either of them ever got displaced from Jewell's cabin, there'd be a way to communicate that the law was unlikely to find.

He carried the little suitcase, even though it had wheels. Going out the door, he said, "You can come out now, possum. It's all yours."

He popped the trunk open with the key fob as he approached, and set the suitcase inside along with his guns and ammunition and the clothes Whitney had tossed in before she'd gone off into the woods.

As much as he maintained an air of callousness, he already knew how badly he'd miss her presence. Of all the shoes she'd had to fill, it was Greek's that were the most difficult. Better than half the words Burl spoke in any given day had been to Greek. Burl wasn't one to talk about having a "best friend," but if he had been forced to name one, Greek would have been the only choice. For weeks after Greek died, Burl thought to call him or ask him something, only to be reminded of what had become of him and his own role in it.

Jewell and Burl spoke some, but Jewell mostly kept his distance. That meant Whitney was tasked with replacing Burl's best friend, his wife, and all his associates, in addition to being his therapist. She stayed up nights talking him through panic attacks so intense he sometimes wished he'd just go on and die. At first he'd tried to drink his way through them, but it seemed only to make things worse. Whitney talked him into drying out, and it helped, but he was still wretched.

Add to all that, as nasty as he felt like he'd gotten, she occasionally still wanted him. For reasons he couldn't bring himself to say, he couldn't. She seemed to take his lack of physical interest as a sign he didn't care about her, when in fact the more she came to mean to him, the less he desired her in that way.

The torment of grief and terror he endured while awake in the night was rivaled by what waited in his sparse and fitful sleep. His rest was marred by unwelcome dreams of the dead and the distant. His subconscious continually brought back Greek and Pot Roast and the other boys, only to kill them again. Then DeeDee would appear before being displaced by Whitney or Colleen or Chelsea, such that he lost his sense of where one ended and the others began. And when he woke, there was only Whitney to proxy for all of them. He'd wake her and coax her to talk about something, anything, just to hold the demons at bay. As their cloistered time wore on, the dead receded from his dreams, and sleep found him more often, but those old dreams affected him in a way that was difficult to beat back even after they'd gone, and changed who she was to him in a way that couldn't be undone.

In truth, his need for Whitney now had everything to do with her companionship and less to do with anything else. He already knew he'd miss having her nearby just to pass a cigarette, let alone every other need she'd expanded to fill. In fact, there was only one person whose presence he craved more and whose existence soothed his wretched soul, and something about parting from Whitney made his longing for Chelsea even more acute.

He'd left the engine running while he went in the abandoned house, but he spent a moment ciphering a paper map, trying to determine which way he thought police were likely to approach. Trying to avoid them and traffic in general, Burl decided to head out of Harlan, north on 421.

51

B URL HAD BURNED a half dozen Marlboros before 421 bore west and took him through a long quarry where he was surrounded by nothing but raw gray rock on either side. He only had one smoke left in his pack by the time he reached tiny Bledsoe on the opposite end. He was tempted to stop at the Dollar General for more smokes but talked himself out of it. He picked up 221 to Pineville and willed himself not to light the last one. He finally caved and lit it on the far side of the little city, tossing the empty hard pack over his shoulder into the back seat. Burl swore to himself he wouldn't stop for another pack until after he'd crossed the state line. He got on 190 west and took it through the Kentucky Ridge State Forest and on south into Tennessee.

After crossing the line, the question became where he could stop with the lowest risk of being recognized. He didn't really know how much heat was on him. Jewell said the sod farm explosion had made the news in Harlan and his picture was everywhere for a few days, but that'd been over a year ago, and he looked a whole lot different then. He had no clue what was being said about him now, if anything.

The way he figured it, the best way to minimize his risk was to get gas and cigarettes and something to eat and drink and take a piss all at the same place. If he was lucky, he might even find a new burner phone. He was looking for a place that had every item on his list, but not a crowd of people. With everything that had gone wrong for Burl in the last year, the one stroke of good fortune that had come about since he had gone on the run was the mask phenomena. Everyone was covering their faces.

Tennessee was quick to provide what he sought. The first little community he came to was Clairfield, just south of the state line. It was tiny, but there was a little brick store with a deli in it right on the main road. It had a single analog gas pump literally on the front porch. The pump was protected by a bright yellow guard rail and marked "Unleaded." Aside from the store, the only other things around were a few houses and an auto parts store. Burl raised his mask before turning in, pulled up to the pump, and killed his engine. There was only one other car in the lot.

He got out, looked over the pump, then peered inside the store. He couldn't see anything telling him to prepay, so he went ahead and pumped his gas. Deep gray clouds had begun to gather to the west, and the type of wind that foretold of coming rain cut through the late afternoon heat. Once his tank was full, he headed in the single front door. It had a sign taped to it that was ripped in a corner that read, "Please wear a mask."

Inside he found largely what he was hoping for. The place was similar to his stores in Jackson County, with a wall of groceries, some spread-out racks of chips and snacks, and a deli counter. A man behind the register, in a light blue medical-looking mask, jeans, and T-shirt with one of those cancer ribbons on it, said to him, "Just the gas?"

Burl looked at him without making good eye contact. "Naw. I need me a cheeseburger and some groceries. Where's the toilet?"

The man raised his chin. "In back. Let me get that burger started for you. You want a single or double?"

Burl paused in the middle of the place. "Double."

"Alrighty. You want bacon?"

"Naw."

"What else can I put on it for you?"

Burl pursed his unseen lips. "Lettuce, tomato, pickles, ketchup, and mayonnaise."

"You want fries?"

"Why not."

"Alrighty. I'll get that on for you."

"Okay." Burl made his way to the back of the place.

The bathroom was a one-header. He had himself a piss and flushed, then washed his hands before he took off his mask and looked himself over in the mirror. He had to wonder: Would the father DeeDee knew even recognize the man looking back in the mirror right now? Every hair on his head and face was overgrown, but it was more than that. Under his eyes were deep half circles, and the other lines in his face were similarly pronounced. Next to his nose, to one side, was angry red with a raw sore in the middle of it. Add all that to the graying beard and hair that shed dandruff all over his shirt, and he was someone that he himself would have looked on not so much with pity but disdain not long ago.

Burl smacked his face with one hand and then the other, snapping himself out of his contemplation. Introspection led to inaction, and his best bet was to keep moving. He wet a paper towel, wiped his forehead and upper cheeks, put his mask on, and left the bathroom.

The smell of his burger frying on the flat top made his stomach draw in out of sudden realized hunger. Burl began walking the store, taking items from shelves and setting them on the counter. He had no way to keep perishables cold, so he stuck to chips, and bread, and Spam, and a few other items.

The fellow at the deli counter had a Styrofoam container laid out with a dressed bun in it. He was pressing down on one of the sizzling patties on the flattop.

Burl asked his back, "You got any TracFones?"

"No," the fellow said without turning. "I sold our last one Wednesday. We have more coming Monday if you want to stop by then."

Burl didn't respond, just kept looking around. He picked up a twelve pack of Coca-Cola cans and also got a plastic twenty-ounce bottle from the cooler and took them to the counter.

The man making the food had turned over the fryer basket and was pouring Burl's French fries in beside his burger. "You need any ketchup packets?"

"Yeah."

"What about utensils?"

"Yeah." Burl wasn't too sure he was going to use either right away but figured both would be worth having if he wound up out on the road very long. The fact was, he'd planned what to do if he had to leave Harlan, but hadn't really planned for what he would do after. Burl wasn't the least bit sorry for what he'd done to Micah. In fact, he was still feeling pretty good about it. Being separated from Whitney and pushed out of Harlan were what had thrown him off-kilter. He was again visited by the unwelcome feeling that he wasn't in control of anything anymore, and he had to push away the fear. He'd overcome the panic attacks, but at one time the fear of them was what had brought them on, and he couldn't return to that cycle. It'd ruin him and he knew it.

The shopkeeper brought his food to the counter in a white plastic bag with red lettering. He had the handles tied up and the ketchup, utensil packet, and napkins on top of the container inside. "You just passing through, then?"

"Yeah."

"Where you headed?"

Burl's eyes tightened a hair over the top of his mask, trying to discern whether this was a pointed question. He concluded it wasn't. "Chattanooga." He shifted his weight from one leg to the other and studied the man. "Going to see my grandbaby."

The guy scanned Burl's items and bagged them without even looking up. "Oh, well that's great. Can I get you anything else?"

"Let me get a carton of Reds."

"Hard or soft?"

"Hard."

Burl paid with twenties. The man marked each one with a marker before putting them in his drawer and giving Burl his change. When it was all said and done, Burl had bought more than he could carry. The man followed him out to his car with his twelve pack and one of his bags.

Rain had begun to come down, and the air smelled of wet asphalt. Drops pattered Burl as he left the porch. He started to pop the trunk out of hurry and habit before stopping himself. The grocer had no need of seeing the contents. He went to the passenger side door and put his food and one bag of groceries in before he went back to the porch to get the rest of his stuff from the shopkeeper.

"Be safe getting to that grandbaby," the man said.

Burl was about to respond when he spotted the white police cruiser pulling in the lot. A Dodge Charger that had a blue and gold ribbon the length of it, with the word "Sheriff" embedded in it and under that "Campbell County." He took his bag and his pop from the man without ever saying another word and went around to the driver side, with one eye on the police car as it pulled up to the store and stopped. The man from the store waved at the car and went back inside.

Burl got in and set the stuff in the front foot well. The cruiser parked in front of him nosed to the porch of the store. Burl sat parallel to the porch beside the gas pump. Between the rain and the tint of the cruiser's windows, he couldn't see what the driver was doing.

Studying the situation, Burl didn't want the police officer to get a look at anything more of him or his car than had already been seen. If he pulled away, he would show not only more of his face, but also his license plate, so Burl decided to wait it out, and let the officer go in the store before pulling away.

The problem was the officer didn't get out. Burl sat in the idling car and nothing happened. Several minutes in, it occurred to him that if he'd been made, the officer had probably called for backup and was just waiting on it. The longer he sat there, the likelier it was that more law would get there. He started to put the car in gear and pull away, but then reality spread over him. He was in a fucking Oldsmobile. Not a bad car for being nondescript, but a terrible choice for outrunning a patrol car.

Burl had to remind himself he had a mask on coming out of the store, and unless the clerk had called while he was in the john, he'd never picked up a phone. The car from the shooting was a Nissan, not an Oldsmobile, so he couldn't see how they were on his current car unless Jewell or Whitney had given him up, which he couldn't imagine. Oddly, this real-time danger didn't threaten to cause the kind of panic attacks he had suffered before. This threat was tangible. The traumas that brought on those attacks were in his past and in his head. Still, his heart was hammering.

He thought about what would seem the most natural. Maybe go ahead and eat his cheeseburger, but that'd mean taking off the mask, so even with the rain on his windshield, that was a no-go. He was in a staredown in which he didn't even know if the other side was staring.

The police car door finally swung open, and Burl said, "Okay now," in a relieved sort of way, because it meant the female sheriff's deputy who was getting out wasn't waiting for backup. He muttered, "Fuck," when he realized she was coming to his driver side window. Her plastic-covered duty hat kept the falling rain from soaking her face and thereby her black mask and also the brown ponytail sprouting from the back of her head.

His right hand sat on the butt of the .38 he had tucked between himself and the center console. Burl had killed a man that very day, but not all killing was the same. Not hardly. Micah'd had it coming, but did this deputy? Could he kill a police officer? A woman? In his life, he'd never done either, and he'd not had either done at his behest. For all his talk of going after families, he'd never had to do it. Saying it had always been enough. These disordered thoughts were flying by when she tapped his glass.

As Burl rolled down the window, he conjured another plan: draw on her quick and hope she doesn't draw back. Lay her flat in the lot at gunpoint, take out her tires, and fucking go before she could get up.

His hand was beginning to twitch upward with the gun, when she said, "Sir, if you're done with the pump, I'd like to get some gas."

Burl released his grip at once, and the gun made an audible thump when it fell to the car's floor at his feet. She didn't seem to hear, perhaps because of the sound of rainfall. "Oh. Yeah, I'm done. I was just—I was just getting ready to pull out."

She nodded. "Appreciate it." She stalked back to her car through the building rainfall.

Burl dropped the Olds into gear and pulled away. He watched the Charger back up and pull to the pump in his rearview. The thought of eating that cheeseburger made him positively sick now, but he slugged down a long drink of that

cold Coca-Cola. Soon he was streaking down the road and
into the Tennessee mountains on the winding two-lane, the
water on his back window obscuring what had felt for a
moment like a reckoning behind him. Now that reckoning
once again lay ahead.

CHAPTER

52

WHITNEY SAW THE state troopers down the hill at Jewell's place, milling around in their gray costumes. She'd let that deputy hit on her for a good ten minutes earlier before he had finally relented and let her go back in her cabin by herself. She hadn't been in it in nearly a month since they'd gone to the campground in Estill County, and she could hardly remember how she and Burl had left it. If anything was out of place, she couldn't tell, but everything there that she thought Burl could've possibly touched she dropped down the composting toilet. Then she'd gone to the bathroom on it. Looking down the hole, she didn't figure there was anyone the police could want bad enough to fool with going down in there.

It was a half hour after she went inside that the state boys had showed up. There were three troopers that she could see, and they came in as many cars. Some had spread out into the woods around her cabin, but for whatever reason, they'd not bothered her yet, and at least an hour passed after they got there before anyone came calling on her.

When someone finally came rapping at her door, he wasn't in gray, but black. This one was in a smart-looking suit and glasses, and his haircut didn't seem like one that a man could get around Harlan. He had come to the door all by himself. When she opened up, he said, "Good afternoon, Miss Cope. How're you doing?"

"I'm all right. How are you?"

He shrugged. "It's a little hot out for this suit, but other than that, not too bad. The cold'll be on us, and I'll be missing the warm before you know it."

"Yeah."

The man looked at her like he was thinking she might say more. When she didn't, he said, "I'm Agent Carlson with the Federal Bureau of Investigation. The deputy down there tells me he saw you come in from the woods a little earlier, and you were all alone. Is there anyone else in there with you now?"

"Naw." Her voice was a little quivery. Whitney's pulse had jumped at the knock on her door and hadn't slowed down yet. She'd taken the measure of Deputy Snelling pretty quickly, and he didn't concern her much. The troopers arriving had concerned her more, but then they'd left her alone. Even though Burl had been through this with her a good hundred times, Agent Carlson put the fear in her in a way she'd never felt.

"I need to talk to you about a few things. Let's step inside and have us a talk."

She swallowed hard and called on her memory. Burl had told her to ask questions and see what she could learn, but not to answer anything and not to give any ground that she wasn't forced to give. That whoever came for her might answer a few things just to loosen her up. "Ain't no reason not to talk to them just so long as they's the ones doing the talking," Burl had said. "Soon as they want to know something from you, that's when you shut the fuck up. You got to remember, if it's a federal agent, you can go to prison just for telling them one thing that ain't true."

The FBI agent looked Whitney over. His eyes lingered on her bare and grimy feet. She looked down at what he was looking at. She had taken her boots off once she was back in the cabin, because it helped her relax. She leveled her eyes up and met his. "What was you wanting to talk about?"

He took half a step forward. "Let's go inside."

"Why do we need to go in?" Whitney didn't budge.

The agent almost smiled. "Seems like a better place to have a conversation."

"I'd like to stay out here?"

"We can, but it's awful hot. Aren't you hot?"

"I'm okay."

Agent Carlson seemed to consider the impasse they'd reached, and weigh whether he wanted to keep pushing. He could badger Whitney all day, but until someone told her she had to let him in the cabin, nobody was going in but her.

He retreated back that half step, sighed, and cut to the chase. "I need to talk to you about Burl Spoon. Specifically, I need you to tell me where he's at. If you do that, I may be able to keep you out of some trouble."

"Oh." She pushed her lips together, making a sort of round pucker. Burl had implored her to think about each question. To not ask anything that would give anything away. Especially not knowing what anyone else had said, including Jewell. She came up with the shortest question she could possibly think of. "Ain't Burl Spoon dead?"

"No, Miss Cope, he's not dead. He's your boyfriend. Or at least he was. Last seen leaving your apartment in McKee with you. If you're intent on pretending you don't know him, this may not go very well for you."

He already knew that much. She'd not given it away. She was relieved and just a little proud. So far, it felt like she was playing the game right. She teed up another question just as vague as the last one. "What's not going to go well?"

"Uh, this interview. Your future. *His* future. If you want to improve any of that, you'll tell me where to find him, and you'll help me bring him in. If you care about him anything at all, that's what you'll do." He paused. He studied her. "If we find him, that's going to go real bad. We know he's armed. We know he's dangerous. And we're looking real hard right now. You can imagine what'll happen if we find him." He locked his stern eyes on her, waiting for her to react. He tilted his head slowly but noticeably, like he was doing it for dramatic effect.

She decided to ignore everything he'd just said. "Why are you looking for him?"

The agent took his glasses off, tilted his head back, and let out a huff. "Am I interviewing you or are you interviewing me?"

Whitney tried to figure out if he wanted her to answer. He paused so long she decided he was waiting on her reply. "I don't know."

"I guess that makes two of us, then. I was hoping you might do what's best for everyone and help me bring him in safe. If you were to do that, that'd go a long way to mitigate what all you've been into with him, but the way you're acting now's starting to give me some serious concerns that your loyalty to Mr. Spoon is going to make you do some things that aren't in your own best interest."

Whitney squinted at his mouth. "What's in my best interest?"

Agent Carlson closed his eyes and shook his head. "Okay. Let's just forget it. If you want to get interrogated like a murder perp, let's just have at it. I need to know where you were this morning between nine and ten AM."

Whitney threaded her fingers under her dark hair and scratched her scalp. "So, do I need a lawyer?"

Agent Carlson tapped his foot. "Perfect."

"I do, don't I?"

He looked off into the trees over the top of her head and let out a long quiet groan. Down the hill a redbird alighted on the powerline that ran from the power company pole in Jewell's yard and the side of his house. It began cleaning its feathers.

CHAPTER

53

A GENT CARLSON HAD let Whitney alone for a bit, so she went back inside the cabin and sat on the edge of the bed to think. She rubbed her toes against the rough wood planks, and it comforted her. She used to like to do the same thing on her mother's little wooden porch back in Sandgap. She missed it. Her mom had spent almost three years dying of lung cancer. She'd gotten sick when Whitney was seventeen and was gone before she turned twenty. When her mother finally gave out, her house had gone to master commissioner's sale. The bank bought it back. Then they sold it again. Whitney had to find her own way after that, and she'd not been on that porch since, but she'd driven by it a hundred times.

The knock on the door the first time Agent Carlson came up had seemed sort of nice. The second time, there was aggression to it. When she opened up, she found that Carlson had not only Deputy Snelling but also Jewell with him. A few state troopers still lurked around down at Jewell's house, but there were more cars parked down there now than men. She looked at the three men at her door and then down at the troopers, but she didn't say anything.

The federal agent leaned one elbow against her door-frame, seeming like he wanted to look casual. "I know you asked me about an attorney, and you have a right to one, but you've not to this point outright invoked the Sixth Amendment. Before you do that, I just want to make sure you understand your situation."

"What's my situation?"

Agent Carlson winced like what he had to say pained him. "Before you got here, Deputy Snelling performed a search of your cabin. What he found makes it pretty clear that you haven't been staying here in quite some time. It shows, in fact, that you just arrived back after a lengthy absence. Your milk was bad, all your food was spoilt, and there were a lot of store receipts in your trash, but none was recent. They were all from a month ago or longer." Deputy Snelling cringed as the agent said it.

"Why was he in my cabin?"

"Because the owner here, Mr. Jewell, gave him permission to search it, and you don't have a lease." Carlson gestured with his head at Snelling. "Isn't that right, Deputy?"

"Yeah, I'm afraid so," the deputy said.

"Under those circumstances, he has the right to enter and search. So maybe, just maybe, you want to change your tune about wanting a lawyer while you still can."

Whitney fidgeted with her hands and looked at Snelling with pleading eyes. Then at Carlson. Carlson's expression struck her as smug. Like he'd just called a checkmate.

Jewell spoke up. "Now, I don't think you got that quite right, mister agent, sir."

Carlson's nose stacked with wrinkles, and his eyes drew thin. "How's that not right?"

"Well, for one thing, what Snelling asked me was did she have a written lease, and she don't, so I said, 'No, she don't got one.' That was what he asked me, and that was what I said. But she does got a lease—it's just verbal's all. Month to month. And she's paid up. He didn't ask me nothing about that."

The FBI agent's eyes shifted to Snelling, and the deputy gritted his teeth.

Jewell went on. "Now, I don't keep track of her comings and goings, so I couldn't say when she was here last, but the other thing Snelling asked me was did I have a key. I told him I don't because she's got the only one, but the lock is broke. I told him that when I need to get in, I can force it open, even when it's locked."

Snelling's head had popped straight up. He looked from Agent Carlson to Jewell rapidly. His hands went into the air. "But you said I could go in. You flat out said that."

"I never said no such thing. What you asked me was did I have a key, and I said I didn't. Then you asked me how I got in, and I said I broke in, and then you went and broke in yourself. I was wondering why you done it, but you're a lawman, so who was I to tell you not to do it? I don't reckon none of what you took out of there could you use in a court because you done it all wrong. You didn't get none of it the right way."

Snelling's eyes smoldered a hole into Jewell. Agent Carlson's head was pitched Snelling's way, and his right hand hung open at his side in a way that looked like he had it cocked to smack Snelling upside the head. Jewell looked at Whitney and raised his eyebrows. Whitney pointed over her shoulder with her thumb and said, "Can I go back inside now?"

54

The Pigeon Roost Campground was tucked inland on a bend of the Cumberland River in rural Jackson County, Tennessee. It seemed every state had a Jackson County. The office was in a gray single-wide trailer at the head of a long driveway leading in. Burl paid twenty-five dollars cash for the night plus a little more for a shrink-wrapped bundle of firewood. The owner who ran the place didn't have any mask on, and he didn't ask any questions. Burl had his mask in place but didn't ask questions either.

The camping area wasn't much more than a bottom between wooded hills, but that suited Burl just fine. He picked a spot away from the smattering of other campers, got his two-man tent set up, spread out in it, and closed his eyes. He smoked a cigarette with it sticking straight up out of his mouth like a fence post. It was the first time he'd stopped moving all day. It was too warm for Burl to fall asleep, and he had an errand to run as darkness fell.

He went back to the office to ask directions to the nearest store before everything closed. The owner told him to follow the road south along the river to Gainesboro, where he'd find a Dollar General that stayed open until ten.

Burl knew Dollar General had started out in Scottsville, Kentucky, before sweeping across the south with their yellow and black signs. They spread like some kind of invasive species, outcompeting native stores and killing them off. The one in McKee was something of a thorn in Burl's side, but the company was a reliable source for TracFones, Burl had to hand them that. They were equally reliable for having plenty of video cameras, so he parked beside a building next door that housed some sort of state-run human resources agency and an insurance outfit that were both closed for the night. If Burl himself got caught on camera, so be it, but he hoped at least to not give away the details of his vehicle.

Most of the people in Dollar General didn't have masks on, including one of the two clerks. Burl kept his big black one snugged tight, and the trip in and out was uneventful. He'd gotten the cheapest unit they sold, a flip phone that came pre-charged.

The status of cell signal back at Pigeon Roost was doubtful, as tucked away as it was—the reason Burl had chosen it—so he dialed the number of the hollow tree phone while he sat idling in the lot where he had parked, hoping Whitney had found a chance to retrieve it. He had left his mask on just in case. The ring of the flip phone was tinny, but the call got picked up on the first ring. The connection between the two burners was consummated.

Whitney said, "Hello," in a hushed tone.

Burl said, "You home?"

"Yeah."

"You have any company over?"

"Not right now."

"So, you alone?"

"I think so, but maybe not."

Burl took a moment to absorb that. "You got ghosts?"

"I might. This place might be haunted."

"Did you have any company over earlier."

"I did."

"How many people came over."

"A lot."

"How many families."

Whitney paused, seeming to consider her answer. "Three."

"Anyone from out of town?"

"Yeah."

"But they all went home?"

"I don't know. I don't think so."

"Anyone over down the hill?" he asked.

"Earlier, but I think they left there now."

"What would you think if I was to come over?"

"I think that'd be a bad idea. I'm pretty tired."

"Well, that's a shame. I'd've liked to have seen you."

"I sure wish you could be here."

A car approached from Burl's left, and its headlights shone on him. He turned his head away, and it went on by. "It ain't in the cards, I don't guess."

"Do you have someplace to sleep?"

"Oh yeah. Right cozy."

"Good. Give my love to the driver."

"Will do. I'm sure he'd send it back." The line went so quiet Burl took the phone away from his face to make sure they'd not gotten disconnected. He put it back to his cheek after seeing they hadn't. "Good night, now."

"Good night."

Burl punched the red button before he wiped the sweat off the open phone on the upper sleeve of his shirt, powered it off, and closed it. He spun it into the seat beside him before looking over his shoulder to see if he could back out.

Just a little way up the road on the route back to the campground, he passed a Giovanni's Pizza, and it called to him so hard that he nearly pulled in. The three other cars parked outside kept him away, but was it really that great a risk just to get a pizza? He felt like it wasn't, but still, he made himself keep going north. He finally lowered his mask and lit a smoke to take his mind off his pizza craving. As much as he wanted to sit by the fire with some nice greasy slices and drink some Cokes, he'd settle for Spam and toast cooked over the camp stove. If he was going to take a risk he didn't have to, he'd make sure it was worth it first.

55

HOLT WAS ASLEEP when he heard the banging. His uncle's dogs started barking. Holt was the only one home. He was inclined to just let the dogs keep barking and ignore it, but whoever was doing the banging was relentless.

His Uncle Goldie worked for the City of Mount Vernon Water Works, which meant he left early every morning and came home early every afternoon. Holt hadn't worked since he first got indicted and went to jail. He'd been staying in Rockcastle County ever since he'd stabbed that boy in Jackson County and Clovis Begley made him leave Greens Crossing. His paid lawyer in Richmond had set the old case Clovis bonded him out on for a jury trial, and now that there was a pandemic, the court system was about halfway shut down. Lane Spicer said they couldn't even set a trial date, which suited Holt just fine. He had to keep up with pretrial and piss clean, but other than that, he was marking time. His mother sent Goldie money every month to house and feed him.

Holt swung his bare feet to the ground and groaned his way out of bed. Goldie's dogs were a couple of mutts that had shown up at his house after someone had dumped them. Goldie liked them because they kept him company after his wife left, but Holt thought they were a pain in the ass. The little one was turning circles and barking into the air as Holt approached the front door. He kicked it, and it yipped before running away. The bigger dog kept right on barking, even though Holt told him to shut the fuck up and threatened to backhand him.

Holt peeked through a broken place in the vinyl blinds in the window beside the front door. Clovis stood on the front porch, looking about like he always did—pissed off. Holt cussed quiet enough that Clovis couldn't hear from the other side. He leaned his entire body, including his face, against the backside of the painted metal door and weighed not answering it.

"Open the door, Holt." Clovis beat on it again, and the vibrations ran the length of Holt's body. "You don't answer, and the next person at this door's going to take you back to jail after I pull your bond, you understand? I know you're listening."

Holt lolled his head back and stared at the water-stained popcorn ceiling. He had kept his word and stayed away. Clovis had left him alone for over a year. Why couldn't it just stay that way? Clovis hammered the door one more time.

Holt finally unlocked the bolt and swung the door open. He rubbed his eye with his palm, exaggerating his sleepiness. "Hey, Clovis. What's going on?"

Clovis walked straight in with the dogs still going berserk around him. He drove his knee into the side of the big one to get it away from him. It hardly seemed to faze it, but it kept a little more distance. Clovis tracked to the middle of the room with his boots on, but that scarcely mattered. The carpet in Goldie's house was kind of a tan color, but there were dark patches all over it. It looked like the skin of a potato. "It's time for you to pay on your account."

"I don't have any money, Clovis. I'm waiting to go to trial."

Clovis grimaced. "I'm not talking about money. I'm talking about work. I need you to go with me to do a job."

"What kind of job?"

"The kind of job we ain't going to talk about. That kind
of job."

Holt was shirtless, and his dark tattoos were popping off
his gray-looking skin. He had his hands stuck down in the
waistband of his gray sweatpants as if they were in pockets.
"When do we go?"

"Get dressed."

"Now?"

Clovis's jaw muscles flexed visibly. "I'm not here to play
fifty questions. I'm here to collect on your debt. I'll tell you
what you need to know when you need to know it. Now get
dressed. We're going."

Holt stared at Clovis with his mouth sagged open. He
shook his head like he was trying to clear the cobwebs.
"Okay."

"Where's your phone?"

Holt pointed to it lying on an end table in the main
room, plugged in, charging.

"Don't touch it. Leave it there."

"For real?"

"I mean it. Now get dressed and grab a change of clothes."

Holt scratched his head and scowled. Ultimately, though,
he did as he was told.

CHAPTER

56

CLOVIS AND HOLT went directly from Goldie's house in Livingston to the hotel in Louisville where Clovis's nephew Ronnie was staying. Holt was to stay in Ronnie's room, and Clovis had his own. There was no checking in. Ronnie already had the rooms when they got there.

The ride to Louisville in the well-tinted Jeep Grand Cherokee Clovis was driving had been a quiet one. When Holt started asking questions again, Clovis said, "You'll find out when we get there."

The radio was tuned to conservative talk radio. Holt wasn't much for dissecting politics aside from being partial to anything with a Confederate flag and whatever that stood for, so he was pretty bored.

Somewhere around Frankfort, Holt asked, "Could we stop off so I can get something to drink?"

Clovis drove with his thick right arm extended, his hand at twelve o'clock on the steering wheel. "No, sir."

Holt started looking around the cab of the vehicle. "You got anything in here I can use for a spitter? That's what I'm really wanting?"

"Shut the fuck up and sit there. You can have you a dip when we get there."

Holt twisted in his seat, putting his back more to the door and glaring at Clovis. "You ain't gotta talk to me like that."

Clovis turned his head only a shade and eyed him "Well, I don't want to talk to you at all. If you'd just be quiet, that'd solve both our problems."

Now Holt thought of a hundred more things he'd have liked to have said, but he also remembered what happened to him the last time he'd said too much to Clovis sitting in a vehicle.

At the hotel, in the room he was sharing with Ronnie, Holt finally got to have his dip, and he finally got let in on the job he was there to do. He and Ronnie sat on the ends of their beds, and Clovis was in the lone chair beside a small round table. The blankets on the beds were quilted and garish. Holt had unwrapped one of the disposable coffee cups and was drizzling Grizzly spit into it.

"Ronnie's been on the house, and Spoon's wife and granddaughter are both there. That's who we're after," Clovis said.

"What're you wanting to do?" Holt asked. "Take 'em out? The lady and the kid?"

"No. I want the kid. If we can get her without hurting Spoon's wife, okay. It ain't a deal-breaker if we got to hurt her, though."

Holt put his lips to the rim of the cup and let brown liquid leak out. "Why do you need me for?"

"Because it can't be none of us. Spoon'll know who done it, and we want him to come looking. But we don't need nobody else to know."

"You want me to break in the house and take a little girl?"

"Naw," Clovis said. "Ronnie says they're staying with a police, but they go out some. Just the woman and the kid."

Ronnie was nodding. "She takes the little girl to the park. Both times they went right before dark. She just sits there and reads a book. The girl's all over the place. There was hardly anyone there, and there's no cameras in the park. Like, at all."

"We got you a mask," Clovis said.

"Right," Ronnie said. "Nobody even notices people in a mask right now. It's not a big deal. What I'm thinking is, I go up to the lady like nothing's up, while she's reading, and pepper-spray her before she even knows I'm there, and I take off running. If there's anyone else there, all the attention will be on me and her. That's when you grab the kid. She's not that old. She won't be that hard to get. Uncle Clovis is sitting there, waiting. You throw her in, and you're gone. The whole thing might take thirty seconds."

Holt's eyes were slits looking at Ronnie. "What if there's a lot of people there?"

"Then we wait," Clovis said. "If they's too many people, you don't even get out. We'll only do it if the conditions is right. It might take a few days. Ronnie's seen her go to the park twice, so we think she'll go back, but we might figure out we can get her somewhere else."

"Hell," Ronnie said, "it's possible we could snatch her up out of the yard if the cop ain't there. I don't know. It don't gotta be the park. I just know the park would work."

"Why you want to kidnap this kid? What's that get you?"

"Burl Spoon," Clovis said.

"I mean, I'll do it, but it seems kind of crazy doing all this because of that guy."

Clovis stood, his knuckles practically popping, his fists were clenched so tight.

"He killed my cousin," Ronnie said. "Murdered him. Two days ago."

Holt shrank a little. "Oh. Shit."

"Yeah." Ronnie eyed his uncle. Clovis's eyes were blazing, and he was kind of stooped, his hands clasped, wringing. Like he was stifling himself. Ronnie looked away from him. "Holt, you think you can do that? Snatch up that little girl?"

Holt's elbows were on his thighs. He was measuring Clovis, and he was uneasy. "Yeah. If it means staying out of jail, I can do it. When're y'all planning on doing it?"

"Tonight, if possible," Clovis said.

Ronnie bobbed his head. "If the opportunity presents itself, we'll do it tonight."

57

THE PROTESTS IN Louisville went on for months. Michael's nights off were rare. He'd piled up overtime and the checks that went with it, but the money was no balm. As a police officer, he was eyed with disdain by many of the protesters. As a Black officer, as a gay officer, he was held at arm's length by many of his "brothers" on the force. He knew why people were angry because he was angry too.

Still, Michael believed in the need for law and order. For people to feel like their city wasn't in chaos. Black people. White people. All people. The fact was, in spite of what was broadcast to the country and the world, the protest area was relatively small. It covered a few blocks of Louisville for a few hours each night. At the heart of them, the protests felt big and intense. For ninety percent of the city, they existed only as unease that came through their televisions and the internet. Most people who lived in Jefferson County had never even seen a protest with their own eyes.

Michael wanted and needed a night at home with family. His family now included Darron, and that meant Colleen and Chelsea were family too. The only other family member he saw regularly during the pandemic was his mother—from her yard, with her on the porch. With his father passed on, he hated thinking of her all alone, but he also knew her house was the last place he or anyone else should stay. A couple times he saw his sister, her husband, and their kids, meeting them at his mom's. They all stayed distant, and none went anywhere near his mother, who was terrified of the virus because she knew what it could do to people. Especially knew what it was doing to Black people.

Michael had come down with a sore throat back in April, and a splitting headache soon followed. Then his breath got short, and he couldn't taste or smell anything. He moved out of the house and into an apartment with another officer while he waited for his Covid test to come back. It was no shock when it was positive. Darron and his mother and Chelsea were a little panicky, but each got tested twice, and none got it. It took more than three weeks before Michael's symptoms let up and he felt comfortable going back home. The only good thing about it was the antibodies he'd produced. They made him feel better about going to work each day, still seeing his mother, and going back home after shifts.

Besides work and the visits to his mom's, it was just his and Darron's family. And they were spending his night off together. Darron picked up a family meal, and when he got home with it, they unbagged it and sat down together and tried to feel some shade of normal. In spite of everything.

"Well," Michael said, eyeing Chelsea, "what'd you do today?"

Chelsea had a noodle and a piece of chicken, from the chicken alfredo they were eating, speared on her fork and pointed up beside her head. "We watched *Emily's Wonder Lab*."

Michael looked to Darron, who shrugged. Colleen put her hand to her forehead. "Oh my gosh, that was our whole day. It's a show on Netflix that all the kids in her class are watching. As soon as she got done with class, that was all she wanted to do."

"She's a girl scientist," Chelsea bubbled up. "She does experiments. Kids can do 'em."

"Oh lord," Colleen said, "she had kids walking on eggs, and Chelsea wanted to try it. I told her we don't have enough for that to work, so she was trying to get me to buy five dozen on the Kroger Click List."

"If you have enough, you can do it," Chelsea said. "They don't break unless you mess it up."

Michael flexed the corners of his mouth, impressed. "I'd like to see that, but what would we do with all those eggs after you walked on them?"

"Scramble 'em," Chelsea said.

"She must've watched every episode three times. They're short, but there are a lot of them."

"There's ten," Chelsea said. "The egg one's my favorite. And the tornado one. Oh, and there's this one where they cook food with the sun. I want to do that. Nana says we can do it in the yard."

Darron was smiling. "I'm surprised you didn't try it today."

"She would've if you weren't getting dinner," Colleen said. "I had to talk her out of it."

"Did you guys go anywhere?" Michael asked.

"She didn't want to," Colleen said. "She was too eat up with Emily. I tried to get her to go to the park, and she cut the biggest shine ever was. I just said forget it."

Michael's demeanor shifted. He glanced at Chelsea, who had finally put the bite she'd been waving around into her mouth, and was now chewing. He laid a hand flat on the table and caught Colleen's eyes. "Did you hear any more about what happened in Madison County."

She shook her head. "No. They called me with more questions, and I told them again that they know more than I do."

All any of them knew was that the boy in Richmond who gave DeeDee that fatal dose had gotten shot to death at a gas station. Michael had told Colleen to expect a phone call. She had told him she was certain Burl was behind it and that she couldn't believe he'd waited as long as he did. None of that changed the fact that she didn't have any concrete information.

Michael shook his head. "Well, they don't loop me in on it, but it wouldn't surprise me if they asked for some extra patrols. Whether we have the manpower to do it, I have my doubts, but you might see something."

"That man has never been here in his life," Darron said. "Has avoided it completely. Why would he do it now?"

"They might not have any new leads," Michael said. "Sometimes when you don't have much, you fixate on what little you do have."

Chelsea looked from Michael to Colleen, and back. "Is this about Papaw?"

Darron put his finger to his lips as Michael looked to Colleen and winced. Colleen said, "No, it's not about your papaw. This is about something else."

Chelsea laid her fork on her plate and crossed her arms. "Well, I know it is. You all are talking about Papaw."

Colleen reached for Chelsea's arm and patted it. "No, honey. That's not it."

"Yes, it is. Whenever you all talk about Papaw, you talk the same way. You say everything quiet, like I can't hear it, even though I'm right here."

Darron slashed his finger across his throat, signaling his mom to hush. The three adults all looked from one to another and to Chelsea, but nobody said anything else. Michael and Colleen turned their attention to the food, which had become quite interesting.

Darron said, "Chelsea, what other experiment could we do that Kim did besides cooking with the sun?"

"I told you all, I want to walk on eggs."

58

THE GIOVANNI'S BOX didn't burn as well as Burl thought it would, but it was nearly gone. He fed it to the fire one piece at a time while he smoked cigarettes and drank a Coke. They had a deal where you could call in your order and they'd bring it out to your car and lay it in the back seat. Burl had stuck his money out the window as the lady walked up, and they had never so much as made eye contact. He'd eaten the whole thing and was burning the box only so he didn't have to bother throwing it away.

He'd risked getting the pizza as a way of trying to shake off the night before. For the first time in months, lying in the dark in his tent, he'd had a panic attack. Like before, the tumult was internal and nearly unbearable. Unlike before, he was alone. Burl still feared no man. But he feared his own thoughts, and that fear triggered the panic. Back when they were in the cabin, Whitney had sat through the nights with him. She'd held his hand and spoken to him while he repeated a mantra, "It's only my mind. It's only my mind. It's only my mind." Somehow that helped. And he'd try to think of things to reset his thoughts. Usually Chelsea. Or his dogs. Simple things that brought him joy. And eventually the two of them would talk him through it, and he'd get to the other side.

The whole thing humiliated and exhausted him. Whitney being there was sometimes all that stemmed his urge to put a .38 to his head. It connected him to her in a different way than he'd ever connected to anyone. She never judged him for it. Never suggested that he was weak. Colleen would have. He knew that much about her. He was the same way as her. If it had been someone around him dealing with it, he'd have had nothing but contempt for their frailty. Whitney wasn't like that. She said he was strong.

"Most people couldn't get through what you been through, Burl. They'd be in the hospital or in the ground. I'm amazed at you." He didn't really believe what she said—that he was strong—because he felt pathetic, but she said it. That was what mattered.

When they were in Harlan, before the pandemic, he had sent her to Knoxville to mail packages to Chelsea more than once. There came a point when she started dressing better when she left, staying gone longer, and coming back in the predawn hours to Burl waiting. She smelled of perfume and a barroom. Neither spoke of it, and they fell off to sleep lying side by side. Her coming back was all he cared to ask of her anymore.

He hadn't been able to reach her in two days. Whether that's what had caused him to bottom out the night before, he didn't know, but a thousand scenarios had played out in his mind and put him in a bad state. If he talked to Whitney, he hoped it'd set him somewhere closer to right. When he went into town to get the pizza, calling her was half the point.

She answered after several fizzy rings. He exhaled hard, but she was short with him. "This ain't a good time."

"No?"

"I still got company. I think they're listening."

"You want to come visit?"

"I wish I could."

"Hell, I'd like it."

"Yeah. Well. I have a feeling I wouldn't be coming alone."

"Shit. Then you're probably right."

"I'm sure of it." She fell quiet for just a beat. "I should get off this phone."

"Go on then. We'll get it worked out."

"Okay."

"Okay."

She was gone. No lingering on the line. No coded affection.

After that call, Burl understood there was no going back safe to Harlan and no bringing her to him. Not anytime soon. And he also knew he shouldn't let grass grow too long under his feet at Pigeon's Roost. He had no help, and he wasn't protected. His first night it had rained and soaked him and his camp before he could get it all stowed. He'd had to sleep in the back seat of the Olds. It'd taken a day to dry things out. He needed something more permanent.

After a month camping out in Estill County, he'd been looking forward to getting back to the cabin in Harlan just so he could sleep in a real bed. Instead, he was right back in the tent. Worse, he was alone. What he needed was another roof and a way to get Whitney back to him. Neither of those outcomes was in the offing if he stayed put.

Problem was, he hadn't identified where to go next. Outlaws from Kentucky always fled to Florida, and they were always getting extradited back. If he was to get caught, it wouldn't be down there. He thought about heading north because who would expect that? Problem with Burl in the north was the way he talked would stand out like a busted thumb, and he didn't know a damn soul up there. The way folks talked in Lexington and Louisville was a little out of place up north, but they paled up next to his mountain accent. Burl wouldn't even be able to get himself a pack of cigarettes without someone saying, "Where you from?"

With no idea where to hole up next, and knowing he couldn't link up with Whitney just yet, something else gnawed at him that'd worked on him not for a day or a week or a month, but over a year. And it did lie north of him, but not in *the North*. And even though he knew he might never be able to have what he really wanted ever again, if he could have it just for a little bit, it'd be worth the risk. Burl didn't linger too long on calculating it. He didn't really want to know. No matter how it tallied up, he'd resolved it was a chance he'd take. Come morning, he'd pack up his campsite and make his way to Louisville.

59

CLOVIS CALLED IT off once the sun went down. He and Ronnie had alternated sitting on the house on Meadow Drive with the other parked nearby and ready to move. They'd decided to have Holt ride with Ronnie so Clovis didn't strangle him before he could serve his purpose. Ronnie and Holt both grew up out Greens Crossing and had known each other their whole lives.

Not only did Burl's wife not go anywhere with the little girl, but the Louisville Metro cruiser also never left the driveway. The only person who went anywhere was Burl's son, Darron, and he was by himself and he came back twenty minutes later. Clovis was tempted to follow him wherever he went and kill him on the spot. But as bad as he wanted to take him from Burl, it would only stoke Burl's ferocity in coming for another of Clovis's kin. Killing Burl's boy served no purpose other than vengeance. The satisfaction of it wouldn't be worth the price. They'd just continue trading grief back and forth. Whereas if he could get the little girl, he could hold onto her and use her to draw Burl out.

As long as Burl walked free and drew breath, he was a threat to Clovis's family. If Clovis could get Burl to show himself, one of two things might happen. Ideally, he could kill him. Failing killing him, he could try to bait him into exposing himself to the law. The question then became what to do with the girl once she'd served her purpose. Clovis didn't relish what he might have to do, but Burl had killed his son, and the consequences of that were on Burl's ledger, not his.

When the streetlights fuzzed on, it was clear that Burl's family was hunkered down. Clovis was the one on the house at the time. He called Ronnie, who was parked in a lot a few blocks away. "Why don't you head on back to the hotel. Ain't nothing going to pan out here tonight."

"Okay, Uncle Clovis. We was just wondering how long you was wanting to stay out."

"They ain't going nowhere."

"We was thinking about stopping at the Burger King near the hotel for some supper. You want us to get you anything?"

"Naw. I don't want no Burger King."

"We can get something else. What do you want?"

"Y'all go on and get what you want. I'll be back directly. I'm just going to set here a little bit longer and see what happens after dark."

Clovis was parked in front of a house down the block with a "For Sale" sign out front, in the space between the street and the sidewalk. All the way along Meadow Drive, the sidewalks sat about a third of the way from the street to the front stoops. A lot of big trees occupied that wide space, so it wasn't always easy to see the houses. Clovis had his seat reclined a bit, but not so much that he couldn't see most of the Spoon boy's house down the block. His windows were tinted deep. For all anyone passing by knew, there was nobody in the vehicle.

Ronnie'd seemed so confident that Colleen Spoon and the girl would go to the park that Clovis had accepted it, but now he was questioning. It was just one night, but maybe Ronnie'd declared a pattern where one didn't exist. Watching the lights in the house, Clovis weighed whether they'd need to get a little more flexible in their planning. How long could they sit on this house before someone in the neighborhood began questioning the strange vehicles? Ronnie'd been hanging around a few days already. If the pattern didn't hold like they'd anticipated, they'd have to improvise. Improvisation brought with it increased risks.

Clovis gripped the base of his steering wheel. He thought about Micah. The permanence of his loss afflicted his heart in a way he'd not felt since stomach cancer had taken Micah's mother from him. Cancer had done its evil, slow and deliberate, to his wife, and he couldn't put any face to it. Burl Spoon had ripped Micah from him like his guts were being torn out, and he knew the face of that demon. He'd give anything to see the light go out of those eyes.

CHAPTER

60

BURL ROSE, BROKE camp, and was on the road to Louisville by seven in the AM, taking 56 North, looking to link up with I-65 in Cave City, Kentucky. He stopped only once all the way there, at a little gas, grocery, and deli in Gamaliel, Kentucky, for cigarettes, fuel, a new TracFone, and a foil-wrapped tenderloin biscuit.

When he reached Louisville, Burl headed for the West End, believing that was his best bet at finding what he sought. It was an hour of roaming before he spotted a motel, on Dixie Highway in Shively, that looked like it could suit his needs. He drove around back and found that every room had a back window. He parked deep in the U-shaped parking lot and walked to the office with his hood and mask both up. A thick little woman who looked to be about his age met him at a glass partition that had been installed at the doorway to the lobby. Her name tag said "Joy," and she came to the window in a pink gingham mask, opened a small sliding glass hatch, and asked Burl how she could help him.

"Need a room."

"You want a single or a double?"

"Either's fine, but I'd like it at the back."

"How many nights?"

Burl looked skyward. "Hmm. Three nights."

"It's seventy-five a night plus tax."

"You take cash?"

"Sure do, but I'll need to see an ID."

"That's the thing. I done lost my wallet, but I got plenty of money. How much is a room that don't take ID?"

The woman looked Burl over, her head tipping ever so slightly to one side. "Those rooms are seventy-five plus tax."

"Okay."

"But there's another fee." She looked at him dispassionately.

"How much is that?"

"Fifty a night."

Burl nodded. She wrote up a paper receipt for three nights at seventy-five plus taxes, which he paid with cash out of his wallet, to which she said nothing. When that was done, she held her hand out for another one-fifty in cash that she slipped beneath the neck of her shirt and into her bra. "I thank you," she said.

Burl nodded and took his key. Before going to his room, he hotboxed a cigarette. Then he got the little suitcase from his trunk. The curtains in the room were pulled shut, and it was dark as a coal seam when he went in. He flipped on the light switch. It lit a hanging lamp with a big round shade that hung over nothing but air in a location that seemed to suggest a missing table. The room was otherwise as expected: shabby, dated, smelling of mildew with a hint of insecticide. He locked the bolt, pulled the chain, rolled the suitcase to the closet and put it inside, had him a piss in the bathroom, came out, pulled back the blanket, sat on the edge of the bed and pulled off his boots, then lay face down in his clothes and was dead to the world in two minutes.

Burl slept like a day-old corpse. Going down, he reckoned he'd be up by late afternoon and go looking for Darron's house. He had the address, but he'd never been there, so he'd have to get a paper map. He'd not been to Louisville at all since the late nineties for a UK ball game. He woke with a start to the sound of an approaching police siren. He was up and reaching for the suitcase in the closet, planning to head out the back window, when the sound Dopplered on by.

Burl went to the front window and looked out. The sun wasn't all the way down, but it was close. Business signs and streetlights around were already lit. A few more cars were in the lot, but still little more than half the spaces were filled. Two men and a woman were outside one of the rooms on the left side of the U. One man was smoking and the other was crouched down, drinking from a big can in a paper bag.

Looking out, Burl decided he'd have to wait another day before going to Darron's. He might have liked to go under cover of night, but he knew there'd be more anxiety for him to turn up at the door after dark. Darron and Colleen wouldn't welcome him, but he hoped he could break through that. He didn't have much feeling for Colleen one way or the other. They'd been more like colleagues than anything for years. Even that partnership had come apart. He was past mourning it.

About Darron, something had begun to shift in him. Some of that shift may have come from his losses, but there was something else. Between negotiations over whether they should watch the History Channel or Bravo, a ball game or CMT, or whether they'd hunt squirrels or morels, Burl and Whitney had parsed through anything and everything in their lives. One topic she always came back to was Darron. She couldn't countenance why Burl would throw away the only son he ever had over something she saw as trivial.

"What difference does it make to you?"

"It ain't right."

"Who says that?"

"I don't know. The Bible."

"The Bible? Give me a break, Burl. The only time I ever hear you mention God's name's when you say 'Goddamn it.' Did you ever even read the Bible?"

He cocked his head. "You saying it ain't in there?"

"There's a whole lot in there, and you don't follow hardly none of it. Why would you want to pick out the one thing that makes you not like your own son?"

"It's an embarrassment."

"So it ain't about him. It's about you?"

"That's not what I said."

"If he ain't embarrassed, then who is?" Whitney tossed her hands.

"He oughta be."

"Why, though? Darron's a good boy, Burl. He was good to everyone. I think you're the only one I ever met who don't like him, and you're his daddy. That don't make sense."

They'd go on like that. She'd never budge. Burl never let on that he'd budged, but the consistency of her saying he was wrong nibbled at his edges.

He called Whitney but got no answer. He was a little disappointed, but not surprised. He was feeling off, and that didn't help. One thing that seemed to bring on his dark spells was hunger. He'd not eaten since that tenderloin biscuit in the morning, so he was ready for something. He'd passed a Popeye's Chicken earlier, and that sounded real good. The prospect of eating something and getting himself ready to see Chelsea brought him around a little bit. He decided to head out and get his mind busy.

He'd driven by a Walmart earlier. He figured Walmart would have a big crowd to get lost in, and looking the way he did, he'd fit in okay. Besides a map, he planned to get some scissors, clippers, a razor, a box of Just for Men hair coloring, and a tub of pomade. If he was going to go see Chelsea, he wasn't going as some ragamuffin. He was coming as the papaw she'd always known.

CHAPTER

61

For the second night in a row, Colleen and Chelsea Spoon didn't go to the park. They did leave together in a car, and Clovis tailed them, with Ronnie and Holt hanging back. Instead of the park, they went to a Kroger store but never went inside. They parked in a lane and had groceries brought out and loaded into the trunk. After that they went through a Wendy's drive-through. Those were the only two stops. The car pulled straight back into the garage, and the door closed behind it. Clovis's impatience and frustration simmered watching the garage door go down. The police cruiser hadn't been there all night. That started playing on his mind.

Back at the hotel, in Clovis's room, they ate pizzas that Ronnie and Holt had picked up at Bearno's. Ronnie dusted off his hands after finishing his fourth slice. "It ain't Porthos, but it's all right."

"I tell you," Holt said, "that's one thing I miss about living in Richmond. Only place in Livingston's got pizza is Bingham's. It ain't bad, but I'm tired of it. If you want anything else, you got to go to Mount Vernon." Holt took a bite of crust and kept talking with his mouth full. "How long do I got to stay down there anyway? I mean, if I beat them charges, does that mean I get to come back to Greens Crossing?"

Cable news was on the television. Clovis never took his eyes off it. "We'll see."

"Seems like if we do this thing, and then I get walked, there ain't no reason I shouldn't be able to come home. How's it fair to keep me down there after I done my part?"

"I said we'll see."

Holt got up and headed for the bathroom. "It's getting ridiculous if you want to know the truth."

Clovis's head turned quick. "Where you going?"

Holt stopped. "To take a piss."

"Not in my bathroom you ain't. Use your own goddamn bathroom. As a matter of fact, why don't you go on back to your own room. I got to talk to Ronnie."

Holt turned his hands palms up. "So now you're throwing me out?"

Clovis's chin was drawn into his chest, and when he spoke, he hardly opened his mouth. "I ain't throwing you out, I'm telling you I need to talk to my nephew alone, but if you want me to throw you out, I will."

Holt crossed his arms and stared at Clovis like he might say something else. Ronnie looked from his uncle to Holt. He stood up and put a hand on Holt's shoulder. "Go on back and I'll be over in a minute. *Fast Five*'s coming on HBO tonight. Uncle Clovis ain't going to want to watch it in here anyway."

Holt went out without saying anything else, and Ronnie exhaled. Clovis watched him go and shook his head. "Goddamn waste of oxygen."

Ronnie sat in a chair on wheels and rolled back where he and Clovis could look each other in the eye. "He never was too smart. Meaner than hell, but dumb as hell too."

"That's where I miscalculated," Clovis said, shaking his head. "My own fault. Whether it would've changed anything, I don't know, but I should've known better than to involve him."

"Why do you trust him on this?"

"I don't, really, but we'll be there, and it's simple enough. I don't want neither of us seen taking that girl. Whoever does that's going to be a target. We gonna put that on him. After it's done, we'll be rid of him."

"*Rid* of him?"

"You see any other way?"

Ronnie screwed up his lips and closed one eye, like he was thinking. "No. I don't guess."

"Tomorrow'll be our last day here."

"Really? Because I think if we just wait long enough, they'll go back to that park."

"You may be right, but we can't keep sitting on that street. Sooner or later people's going to start asking questions."

"So, we're going to give up?"

"No. We ain't giving up. We're going to send Holt in. If that police car ain't there tomorrow night, and they don't go to the park, once it's dark Holt's going to the door, and if they don't open it, he's going to kick it in. We'll see if he can come out with the girl."

"You really think that'll work?"

"Maybe. I don't know. Maybe not. But we got the element of surprise. The only ones in that house besides the kid are Spoon's wife and his boy. His wife's getting old and his boy's a queer. And like you was just talking about, Holt's mean as hell. We ain't going to give him no gun, but if we let him take a knife, I still like his chances."

"We don't go in?"

"Hell no. If it don't go right, we just get out of there. If he comes out with the girl, we done what we set out to."

"What do you think he'll do in there if they fight him?"

"I don't care. Do you care what happens to Spoon's people?"

Ronnie frowned. "No."

"Do you care what happens to Holt?"

"Not really."

"Then all we really got to worry about is us. No matter what happens, we'll meet where we planned, ditch the Cherokee, and get out of town."

"Man, I hope they just go to the park."

"I do too. Be a lot cleaner. But we can't wait forever. For all we know, Spoon's still in Richmond. Sooner or later, we got to bait the trap. You understand?"

"Yeah."

"Good. Now don't tell that dipshit nothing. If he ends up having to kick down the door, I don't want him to know nothing about it until it's time. I don't want him to think about it or decide why he won't. We just tell him he's going in, and he goes."

"Yeah."

"Okay." Clovis rose and went to the sink to wash his hands. "Now you go watch your movie, and don't worry about tomorrow. We can't control everything. We just got to control what we can and take whatever opportunity presents itself."

Ronnie stood and started to leave.

"One other thing," Clovis said.

Ronnie stopped with his hand on the door handle.

"You put them extra zip ties in your trunk like I told you?"

"Yeah, but I thought you was going to have him zip-tie her in the Cherokee."

"I am." Clovis came closer to Ronnie, drying his hands with a white towel. "Them zip ties in your trunk ain't for the girl. I got two cans of gas in the back of the Cherokee.

How much attention you think they'll pay to your car once they got a vehicle fire? And how fast will their investigation go after they figure out they got a body inside? While they're fooling with that, we're getting on home with the girl."

62

T HE LOUISVILLE METRO cruiser was gone before three in the afternoon. Darron Spoon went to the mailbox about an hour later. He stopped and studied what he'd gotten out of it. Then he looked up and down the street and seemed to stare at the car where Ronnie and Holt watched him from up the block. Clovis was parked blocks away in the Cherokee, waiting to hear something. Darron headed back in but paused on the porch, and it seemed like he was scrutinizing the car again.

Once he was inside, Ronnie got on the phone to his uncle. "Spoon's kid was staring at us. I think he's suspicious about something."

"What'd you all do?"

"Sat here like nothing's up. He looked a long time. He looked again before he went in the house."

"Shit. Give it a minute and pull out of there. I'll pull back up in a different spot. You're going to need to go over the plan with Holt, because if they ain't on the move soon, we're sending him in."

"Okay. How long you want us to wait?"

"Give it two minutes. I'll head that way."

"Okay."

Ronnie'd barely ended the call before Holt asked him, "What's he saying?"

"He says we ain't going to wait much longer. He wants to go in and get her."

"Damn."

"Well, the thing is, he's wanting you to do it."

Holt put his hand to his chest and swiveled his head hard away and then right back. "Me? Why do I got to do it?"

"I guess he thinks you'd be able to do it fast. I mean, they ain't expecting it. You go in with a knife, you snatch her up, and get out of there."

"I don't get a goddamn gun?"

"He don't want you shooting. If you was to start shooting, we'll have police all over us. You won't need a gun for them two in there. It's nothing but an old lady and a fag. What're they gonna do?"

"Easy for you to say. You ain't the one going in."

Ronnie picked up a half-eaten bowl of mashed potatoes and gravy from Lee's Famous Recipe that he'd left on the dash, and took a bite before talking with his mouth full. "So, you're saying you can't do it? You can't handle them two?"

"I didn't say that."

"Then what're you saying?"

"What I'm saying is why am I the only one going in?"

"Uncle Clovis is guarding the door. If anything goes wrong, he'll go in."

"Where you going to be?"

"Somebody's got to drive. I'll be waiting on you all."

Holt sat there making and unmaking fists. "God. I don't know. Why I got to be the one doing all this shit?"

"Seriously? You don't know? Maybe because my Uncle Clovis got you outta jail over a year ago, and you ain't had to go back. He got you a lawyer. You think all that shit was free?"

"I know it ain't free, but I already done a job for him."

"Yeah, and you fucked it up. You made shit worse."

"I'd like to see what anyone else would've done. I—"

Ronnie threw an arm across Holt's chest, the plastic mashed potato spoon still in his hand. "Hold on. Shut up."

"What?"

"Shhhhh." Ronnie spoke through his teeth and pointed out the windshield. "Shut the fuck up."

Up the block, coming down the sidewalk, then cutting through Darron Spoon's front yard was a little man in a big black mask. He had shining dark hair and was headed for the front door. Ronnie dropped what he was eating to the floorboard before he raised his phone so fast he almost dropped it, placed a call, and pressed it hard to his cheek. Clovis answered, but before he could say anything, Ronnie said, "It's Burl Spoon! He's at the house!"

CHAPTER

63

BURL HADN'T PARKED too close to Darron's house. He'd pulled in up the block, folded the couple of map panels back that he had open, laid the map on the passenger seat, and got out. He'd not gotten his hair perfect, but he'd cut it as close to how he used to keep it as he could, then dyed it back to black. He'd wished the whole time he had Whitney there to help him. He'd made a mess of things and gotten the hair dye all over. The empty bottle, the box, his hair, his beard, and everything else related to his transformation he'd bagged up and thrown in a garbage can at a gas station on his way to Darron's. He didn't want to leave anything behind at the motel that would reveal that he'd shed his disguise. Not even to the maid.

Burl kept looking at his hands coming up the sidewalk. The hair dye had stained them like a coalminer's, and no matter how many times he'd washed them, he couldn't get it to lighten much. Normally he'd not have thought much of it, but having not seen Chelsea in so long, he didn't want anything to seem off. His hair wasn't looking its best, and he had that sore on his face. His grubbed-up hands were just one more thing throwing things off. He cussed it as he crossed the lawn and ascended the porch.

Burl punched the doorbell twice in rapid succession with a darkened finger, and he could hear the quick rings sound inside from out on the porch. It took a moment for the door to open. Darron was there in a maroon cloth mask. He said, "Hello," not seeming to recognize his father for just an instant; then realization spread across what showed of his face. He pushed the storm door open, forcing Burl to step back. "What the hell are you doing here?"

Burl raised both his hands. "I ain't going to stay. I just want to see Chelsea. Just for a minute."

Darron's voice went up. "You can't be here. I have to call the cops. Even if you leave, I have to call 'em. If they find out you were here, we're all screwed."

"My baby girl. Just for a minute. I ain't seen her in over a year. I come all this way."

"Have you lost your mind? The FBI talks to Mom all the time. They've hounded her. They've hounded me. Do you know how much trouble we'll be in?"

"I'm sorry for what I done to you, okay?" Burl grabbed Darron by one wrist. "Just get her."

As he said it, Colleen and Chelsea appeared up the hall from the front door.

She was so much bigger than when he'd last seen her. It pushed the wind out of his chest. Burl said, "Hey, baby girl."

Chelsea stopped in her tracks. "Papaw?"

Burl reached to try to move Darron out of the way when a shoulder hammered into his side, driving him into the open storm door, tearing it nearly off its hinges. Burl and the man who'd tackled him flew over the railing and into the shrubs alongside the porch. Disoriented while tumbling in, he could hear Chelsea and Colleen screaming.

Buried in the bushes, a man Burl didn't recognize—a young man—drew back his fist and hit him twice in the face before he could react, rattling his skull and further disorienting him. Then, as fast as he was on him, the man was yanked off.

Burl reeled a moment—his head was so scattered he nearly went out. Light flashed in his vision, but he was still cognizant that the branches that surrounded him jabbed into his body. The flashing cleared, and he was able to raise himself up. Gasping for air, Burl tore his mask away from his face.

On the lawn, Darron straddled the man at his waist, his legs twined under the man's thighs. Darron cocked his elbow back, then hammered the point into the man's eye socket, not once but over and over. The man's hands flailed in front of him, but he seemed powerless to block the onslaught. Burl rested on his haunches, reeling, and watched the pounding.

Just as the man beneath Darron seemed to go almost entirely limp, another man streaked into Burl's line of sight and latched onto Darron's back. In that man's right hand there was a glint of metal that Burl recognized as a knife blade. Before Burl could even move, the man drew it back, then drove it into Darron's side just below the ribcage. The man withdrew it, pulled it back wide as the length of his arm, and drove it in again. He had drawn it back once more and was coiled to plunge it in a third time when Burl reached him.

Burl had fumbled for the .38 he kept in his waistband, but he'd lost it in the bushes. Desperate, he kicked the man with everything he had, and although the knife swing threw him off balance, he managed to connect his boot into the man's teeth, and they gave. The knife blade glanced off Burl's hip. The man he'd kicked tumbled backward while both his hands flew to his mouth. Burl's follow-through spun him around, and he landed belly down in the grass beside his son, who had slumped off the man he'd been beating.

When Burl raised his head, he found the three other men sprawled in differing fashions, all bleeding. The first man's head lolled side to side, his right eyebrow split wide, and deep red pooled in the socket. Darron was motionless on his side, his abdomen in tatters. Burl looked at his own hip, but it was only grazed, his wound shallow. The man with the knife had lost his grip on it. That man's fingers clutched his face, the thick blood that poured from his mouth escaping despite his best efforts to hold it in.

Burl pushed up on his elbows and knees and reached for his son. "Darron," he pled. He laid his hands on Darron's two deep wounds trying to stem the rapid flow of blood from them. "*No*, Darron." In spite of all that had happened, Darron's mask was still over his mouth, and it pulsed in and out as he gasped for air. Burl could hear his wife's voice but didn't register anything. "Nine-one-one," Burl said to her. "Nine-one-one! Nine-one-one!" he repeated, hoping she could hear him. He was so lost, he couldn't comprehend his own voice.

Burl pressed his son's side with everything he had, trying to slow the outflow of blood. He took one hand from the wounds just long enough to get the mask off his son's mouth so he could breathe more freely. Darron's face had gone pale. For the first time in years, he saw the boy he raised in the man who lay in the grass. And he anguished at what had been done to him on his account.

A hand the size of a lunch pail closed around Burl's throat and cleaved him from Darron. Another hand gripped around the back of Burl's neck and lifted him off the ground, squeezing his neck from either side like a pipe clamp. Burl groped for Darron for another moment. Clovis turned Burl so he could look into his wild, dilated eyes. Sweat from the top of his bald head leaked down to his fat brow. Burl clutched at Clovis's wrists, clawed them with his darkened and bloody hands, to no effect. His vision began to spot. The man with the bleeding eye appeared beside Clovis, gun drawn, trained on Burl as well, but he was battered and seemed content to let the big man end Burl with his hands.

Burl's toes scarcely touched the ground. He kicked at Clovis, connecting several times, but nothing changed. His blood and breath had stopped flowing between his head and body so quickly that in the matter of seconds Clovis had his hands on him, Burl was nearly gone. He couldn't see the man anymore. Couldn't see anything. Then he heard the first blast and came back to.

CHAPTER

64

Burl hit the ground hard. Air flowed into his lungs so urgently that they felt seared. A second blast sounded. Then a third. The dark lenses over Burl's eyes cleared, and he raised himself. The man with the wrecked eye who had held a gun was laid out on his back in the grass. The one who'd had the knife was at a car in the street, getting in, and just as quickly speeding away, smoking the tires. Clovis's big body thundered down the sidewalk with one hand clutching at the opposite shoulder.

Burl looked for Darron. He hadn't moved. He was bleeding out. Burl heard a clatter of metal on concrete. Colleen had dropped her Sig Sauer to the porch—it tumbled off and into the grass. She ran past Burl to Darron, where she pressed against him as Burl had, straining to keep the life in him. Burl's eyes went from her to Clovis receding, to her handgun in the grass. He lunged for the gun.

By the time Burl was up with the weapon in hand, Clovis had reached a Jeep Cherokee and was in it. He ripped the wheel and U-turned away from the direction of Burl's approach. As hard as Burl tried to run, he was beaten, and he was aging, and he was losing ground.

He raised the gun and fired at where he thought Clovis's head might be inside the tinted passenger compartment. He emptied the magazine. Bullets struck metal, they struck glass, but the vehicle kept going. Then it swerved hard, and it clipped a parked car, then careened back the other way, across the opposite lane of travel, and hit another. The momentum of the vehicle now caused it to travel sideways, skidding on its tires before flipping onto its roof, then rolling violently two full rotations. It returned to its roof and scraped down the asphalt on its top, throwing sparks, before it came to rest against another parked vehicle.

Burl dropped the weapon as he watched the SUV destroy itself. He lit out after it before it had stopped careening. He felt nothing. Inside and out, he was so numbed by adrenaline. He didn't break stride until he got to the wreck. Every window was shattered. He crouched down and drew the .38 from his ankle holster, with his smudged hand shaking, then put a knee on the blacktop just before the driver's window. He had the gun trained in, ready to empty it into Clovis.

He found Clovis contorted, his head sideways against the roof, cocked at an odd angle from his huge shoulders. Blood ran from his crooked nostrils down his cheek toward one of his mangled ears, and also from lacerations on his head. His gray beard looked pink in places that had soaked. Clovis muttered to himself, "I can't feel nothing. I can't feel nothing."

Burl kept the barrel on him but didn't fire. He watched Clovis's lips move as he kept saying the same thing.

"Clovis," Burl said, "you hear me?"

That finally broke the repetition. Clovis paused and his eyes sought out Burl. His head seemed fixed in place. "I hear you, Burl."

"Now listen to me. This is going to be your one and only chance to save Kendall's life. I ain't killing Cargo. I promised I wouldn't, and I ain't going back on my word. But I'll kill

Kendall. I promise you that. The only way to stop it is to tell me true."

Clovis was still. Wordless.

"Who was it blew up my men?"

Clovis wet his lips with his tongue. "I done it. That was me."

"You ain't lying?"

"I ain't lying."

"And who was it that done Pot Roast that way?"

Clovis blinked his eyes in quick succession as he spoke. "Holt Peters done that. He wasn't supposed to. He's the one—" His speech cut off, and he gasped for breath three times in succession. It took him some time to gather after that, but he spoke again. "He's the one that stabbed your boy. He stays with Goldie Owens in Rockcastle." He gasped again.

Burl lowered the gun. "All right."

"Kill me, Burl." Clovis remained still except for the features of his face. His eyes sought out Burl's. "You got to. Your daughter. Your men. Your boy. I was part of all that. This's your chance." Their eyes came together. Clovis's sagged, but they were on Burl's.

Burl raised the gun. Sighted it on Clovis's forehead. Clovis closed his eyes. "Naw," Burl said. "I hope you live. I hope you live a long time." Burl withdrew from the window. Clovis's eyes flew open, and he was begging. Burl stood up and listened to him plead to be killed. Burl didn't say another thing before he took off running.

This was his window to flee. The Oldsmobile sat at the opposite end of the block, past Darron's house. He'd parked it such that he could make a quick getaway. The keys were still in his front pocket. As fast as he could go wasn't as fast as he wanted, and his balance was off.

In Darron's yard, Colleen was lying across him with both hands pressing against his wounds. Chelsea stood on the porch, impossibly big, her face contorted, sobbing. Colleen was talking to her, trying to comfort her. The man Colleen had shot lay there. There was no mistaking that he was dead.

Burl grabbed the neck of his shirt as he ran and pulled it off over his head. He barreled into Darron's yard with it in his hand. After crossing the sidewalk, he slowed and stopped. He knelt beside Colleen in the grass.

"Did you call nine-one-one?"

"Yes."

"Let me put the pressure on. You take Chelsea in the house."

Colleen didn't move. She looked at him. "They're going to know who you are, Burl. We'll all suffer for you being here."

"I never set foot in that house. I ain't talked to or seen none of you in a year, and that's the truth. They can have me. I ain't leaving my boy."

Colleen held her place.

"Baby girl don't need to see this. She needs you," Burl said. "She don't need me. Let me do it. When they get here, they can take him, and they can have me."

Colleen repositioned her hands on Darron, but blood still flowed. She said, "Get right here so you can keep the pressure on him."

He came in close, shirt in hand.

"On three," Colleen said. Burl rested shoulder to shoulder with her. "One, two, three."

Colleen withdrew her hands fast, and Burl's replaced them with the shirt bunched tight. Sirens called out in the distance. Colleen fell back on her haunches.

"I need one thing," Burl said. "Go in my pocket and get my phone. Turn it on and dial the last number."

"You can't hold your phone, Burl."

"Just dial it and lay it by my face. That's all I need. Then you take Chelsea in. Tell her Papaw loves her and he's sorry."

Colleen retrieved the phone from his pocket, placed the call, and laid it down. With the phone in place, she went to the porch, gathered Chelsea, and in spite of her pulling toward her uncle and her papaw, Colleen got her in the house.

Burl leaned close to the phone, trying to hear it, pressing into Darron's wounds so hard his stained hands were becoming numb. He could barely hear the phone as it was. The coming sirens made it even harder. When he thought the faint ringing had stopped, he began talking, not knowing what was being said on the other end of the line or if he could even be heard.

August 29, 2020, Louisville, Kentucky

E MERGENCY PERSONNEL RESPONDED to Meadow Drive and found one (1) man dead on arrival and three (3) others injured. The deceased was identified as Ronnie Begley, of Madison County, who suffered two (2) gunshot wounds to the chest.

Begley's paternal uncle, Clovis Begley, also of Madison County, was extracted from an overturned vehicle at the scene. He had suffered a gunshot wound to the right shoulder and a spinal cord injury in an ensuing multiple-vehicle rollover accident in which he was an unrestrained driver. He was transported to the University of Louisville Hospital, where he underwent emergency surgery.

Darron Spoon, of Jefferson County, was located outside his residence with multiple stab wounds. He was also transported to the University of Louisville Hospital, where he underwent emergency surgery.

Burl Spoon, of Jackson County, father of Darron Spoon, was located at the scene, rendering first aid to his son. His injuries included contusions and superficial lacerations. Upon contact with law enforcement, Burl Spoon surrendered himself to custody on multiple outstanding warrants. He was treated for non-life-threatening injuries and released from University of Louisville Hospital, then transported to the Louisville Metro Police Department for questioning. He invoked his Sixth Amendment right to counsel and was subsequently lodged in the Jefferson County Detention Center to await further proceedings.

Burl Spoon's estranged wife, Colleen Spoon, of Jefferson County, resides at the home of Darron Spoon and LMPD Sergeant Michael Branham. Upon questioning, she alleged that Burl Spoon arrived at the residence after more than a year without contact but was denied entry. An additional statement obtained from Sergeant Branham was also consistent with her statement, as well as security footage obtained from other residences in the area that do not indicate that Burl Spoon entered the residence on the day of the incident.

On the date in question, Burl Spoon was apparently pursued to the location by Ronnie and Clovis Begley as well as a third unknown assailant. Ronnie Begley allegedly assaulted Burl Spoon, and thereafter Darron Spoon acted in defense of his father, in the course of which he was allegedly stabbed by the unknown third assailant. Colleen Spoon stated that she retrieved her personal firearm and returned to find Burl Spoon being held at gunpoint by Ronnie Begley as Clovis Begley strangled him.

Colleen Spoon alleges that she discharged her firearm twice in defense of Burl Spoon, striking and killing Ronnie Begley, after which Clovis Begley released his grasp on Burl Spoon. Colleen Spoon further alleges that she believed Clovis Begley to be reaching for a firearm, and she discharged her weapon a third time in self-defense, striking him in the right shoulder, at which point he fled. She proceeded to render aid to her son.

Burl Spoon allegedly retrieved the firearm that had been discarded by Colleen Spoon and pursued Clovis Begley on foot as he fled by motor vehicle. He appears to have discharged the weapon nine (9) times, striking the vehicle, and Clovis Begley subsequently lost control of the motor vehicle, which overturned and rolled, striking three (3) parked vehicles in the process. Consistent with Colleen Spoon's account, Clovis Begley was found with one (1) holstered handgun on his person, and a second was discovered in the passenger area of his vehicle, as well as zip-tie restraints, duct tape, and two (2) cans of gasoline.

At the time of this report, both Darron Spoon and Clovis Begley remain admitted at the University of Louisville Hospital. Clovis Begley is not considered a flight risk due to his apparent condition as a quadriplegic.

65

THE HARD PLASTIC chairs were the softest things in the small room. The walls were beige-painted block; the floor was concrete; the table was steel. Michael wiped the light sheen of sweat from the midday September heat off his forehead, then rested his hand flat on the table. When he moved it, his fingertips left liquid prints behind on the silver tabletop.

He'd spoken to inmates in the Jefferson County Detention Center countless times over the course of years, so on the surface there was nothing extraordinary about this trip. In reality it was anything but routine. For starters, it was likely his last entry into the facility as a member of Louisville Metro PD. Besides that, he was there to see Darron's father, who had requested his presence specifically.

Colleen was apprehensive about Michael going in to speak to Burl. She hadn't visited lest it rekindle the Feds' earlier suspicions that they were somehow colluding. She was a little worried they'd view Michael's visit the same way. He had assured her they wouldn't. From LMPD's perspective, Burl's case was more or less closed with one exception. That loose end was the identity of the man who had stabbed

Darron. Colleen could only vaguely describe him, and Clovis thus far had provided nothing. If Burl had anything to offer, Michael seemed the most likely officer he would trust. Especially since he was asking to speak to him. Locating the man with the knife was what tipped the scales in favor of Michael going inside. He was intent on finding that man before he left the force.

Like everything in the system, jail visits were "hurry up and wait," even for officers. Like always, Michael sat and listened to loud voices, buzzes, clicks, and bangs while his heels lost heat. The sound of feet shuffling down the hall outside was followed by the click-buzz of the door as a deputy jailer opened it and stepped aside so Burl could pad in, his orange jumpsuit rolled up at the wrists and ankles.

Burl sat in the chair across from Michael with his hands on his hips. He looked expectant, but Michael said nothing. Eventually Burl said, "Well, what do you know?"

Michael's palms went up. "What I know is that you asked to speak to me, so here I am. Before we go any further, I want to confirm that you don't have a lawyer."

"Yes and no." Burl shifted in his chair as he spoke, stifling a nervous energy that Michael had never noted in any of their previous encounters. "I got one. I just ain't brought her in on this just yet."

"So you are currently unrepresented by counsel. Is that correct?"

"Yeah. That's correct. Not yet."

"Then I suppose we could talk about whatever it is you were wanting to discuss." Michael had learned years back never to go directly after what he wanted most. Not to seem too eager. You had to sidle up to it. With Burl and Darron's past, and the ever-shifting code outlaws followed, he wasn't too sure where he stood. Would Burl withhold what he knew over some perverse sense of honor? Michael couldn't be sure.

Burl leaned in. His eyes were big as boiled eggs. "I want to know about Darron."

They may not have been on the same page, but they were in the same chapter. Still, Michael wouldn't go straight at his objective. "Well, Mr. Spoon. He's hurt. He's hurt badly and he nearly died. But I'm certain you know they were able to save his life."

"I know they saved him, but what I want to know is will he be all right?"

"Eventually they think he will be. They had to do surgery, as I'm sure you know. His liver and kidney were both cut up pretty bad, but from what the doctors tell me, he should be okay. He still has a drain. He's on antibiotics, but we brought him home. I don't know what the long-term effects will be yet, but the doctors don't act overly worried, so we're trying not to be either. Obviously, he's got a lot of scars. He'll look different as far as that goes, but if that's the worst of it, I guess we're lucky." Michael dropped off there. He hoped he'd left Burl at a point where he'd take him where he wanted to go next.

"Good. That's good." Burl nodded perceptibly and chewed his lip as he spoke. "That's what I was hoping you'd say. It ain't good that it happened. I hate it. But he's going to be all right." Burl seemed to go slack. The air leaked out of him like a dying balloon. He settled back in his chair and gazed around the edges of the room at the ceiling. It looked like he was done. Like he'd heard what he wanted and checked out.

Michael waited for Burl to reengage, but he didn't. He weighed his approach before finally deciding he had to go in before the topic slipped away. He was done sidling. "I don't guess you know who it was that did that to him? That's the one thing we haven't been able to put to bed. Whoever that was, he ought to be brought to justice. Someone like that shouldn't just be out there."

Burl sat upright, brought his hands together in front of him, and kneaded them together. He looked Michael over, seeming to contemplate his answer. "I wouldn't worry about that."

"Mr. Spoon, with all due respect, I *am* worried about that. I'm very worried about that. And you should be too." Michael's state of calm was gone just like that. His back teeth didn't part as he spoke. "That man very nearly killed your son. I believe that's something very much worth worrying about."

Burl glued his eyes onto Michael's. "No. You miss my meaning, son." His words came out slow. "I ain't said it's not something *worth* worrying about. I'm telling you that *you* don't got to. Understand me?"

As it washed over him, Michael's muscles untensed. He maintained his gaze on Burl, who was unflinching. "Okay," Michael said. Then a silence passed between them. As if information still flowed in spite of the fact neither spoke. It felt to Michael like several minutes passed before the quiet was broken.

"How's my Chelsea doing?" Burl said. "Has she asked about her papaw?"

"She has. She's worried about you. We've explained to her what comes next as best we can."

"You tell her don't worry." Burl smiled a genuine smile. "Tell her that her old papaw will be just fine."

"I will." Michael padded his index finger lightly on the table. He'd more or less resolved the matter he'd shown up to resolve. There was no reason to withhold the unwelcome news he also carried. He unpacked it. "She's also nervous because we're moving. She wants to stay to be near you. We've explained that just because you're close doesn't mean she can pop in and visit whenever she wants. That it doesn't work that way. Anymore, most prison visits are virtual, so it won't matter where we live. I don't know if she gets it."

Burl slumped back in his chair again. "Moving?"

"I took a new job, Mr. Spoon. In the private sector." A light above them began to flicker. Michael glanced at it, but it didn't stop. "I'm getting out of policing. Our house already sold. It didn't take two days. I'm headed for Maryland in three weeks. The rest of them will be coming along right after the closing."

"Everyone? Colleen and Chelsea too?"

"The whole family."

Burl fell forward and bowed his head. He stared straight down at the steel surface of the table. He wasn't six inches from it. Michael drew back and tried to read his posture, his breathing, to see if Burl was gathering for aggression. Michael's hands gripped the edge of the table, ready to shove back further if Burl lunged. Burl didn't move, though. His small body expanded and contracted ever so slightly as he took in air. His breathing wasn't labored, but it was audible. He finally stood. He extended his hand to Michael but averted his eyes.

"I want you to promise me that you'll take good care of them."

Michael was slow to loosen his grip on the tabletop. He gathered his feet beneath him, pushed up from the table, and took the little man's hand.

"I'll do that. You have my word. I love them."

Burl nodded ever so subtly. "I believe you do." He released Michael's hand, went to the door without looking back, and gave it a hard metallic rap. He shouted, "We're done in here."

EPILOGUE

Holt's head was already pounding when the dogs started going off. His mouth felt like it was full of murder hornets. Fucking Burl Spoon had knocked three of his teeth out at the roots, and it wasn't like he had any way of seeing a dentist. He'd driven Ronnie's car all the way back to Mount Vernon and ditched it before walking to Uncle Goldie's work and getting a ride home. When Goldie asked him what happened to his face, he said, "You don't want to know," and the subject dropped.

He'd just had a bowl of cereal, avoiding hitting the raw spots in his mouth with the spoon by pouring the Great Value Honey Nut O's to the back and chewing with his molars. Then he'd taken the last four ibuprofen in the house and lain down on the couch before a knock came at the door. Of course he was nervous it was the cops. He'd been tracking the news, and it looked like Ronnie was dead, but they weren't saying much about Clovis or the guy he'd stabbed.

He shoved the dogs out of the way so he could peek out. He did a double take when he saw a pretty little brown-headed woman standing at the base of the porch, looking around. He held the dogs back as he opened the door a crack and spoke to her. "Can I help you with something?" He was self-conscious of how bad his mouth looked.

She didn't seem to notice or mind. She smiled. "My car's broke down out on the main road. It shouldn't be out of gas or nothing, so I don't know what it is. Looks like there's isn't anything else around here. Could you help me?" She held up her cell phone. "There ain't no signal."

Holt wasn't much of a car person, but she was acting nice, and she was awful cute. Most women who looked like her weren't too interested in talking to him, but she needed something. He doubted he could do anything with her vehicle, but Goldie was out in a work truck, so his car was there. Holt could offer her a ride to town. If he did that, maybe he could get her to come in the house. "Let me get some shoes on. You want to come in while you wait?"

She ran the palm of her hand up the back of her neck. "That's okay. It's pretty out."

The dogs were still in hysterics. He tried to ignore them and get his shoes on. He managed to get out the door without them slipping out, and she seemed pleased to see him come her way. He took the steps down the porch to the drive.

The sound of the two dogs carrying on inside was loud and clear, even with the door closed. One of them was scratching at it. Songbirds sang, but it was hard to hear them over the racket. A light breeze rolled across the bottom. The ends of the woman's brown hair swayed with it, and a piece went in her mouth. She brushed it out with the tip of her finger. She was in a long summer skirt, a T-shirt, and sandals. She made Holt feel something.

She said, "What was your name?"

He said, "I'm Holt," trying not to show his missing teeth. "Would you want to come in and get something to drink? This might take a minute."

"Naw," she said, "I ain't thirsty."

He pulled in a little closer. "You sure?"

"Hold on." She held up her hand. "We ain't got no masks on. Could you give me six feet?"

He stopped but didn't step back. "I ain't got no 'rona. I ain't been around nobody."

"Whether you got it or not, I still want my six feet." She backpedaled a couple steps. "I'm Whitney, by the way." She pointed to her left, beyond the side of the house. "And that's Clarence and Toby over there."

At the edge of the woods, an overweight man knelt down in a Realtree camo hat with a rifle sighted in on Holt. Another guy in a Cummins diesel shirt, carrying a sack of something, stood behind him. Before Holt could do or say anything, a gut shot seared through him. He stumbled backward, then landed on his ass. He lay there, clutching the entry wound and looking at the woman, trying to make sense of what was happening.

"Good shot," she said. "You got him, Clarence."

The two men approached, one with the rifle and the other with the sack. They both seemed calm, and so did the woman. The heavy one said, "I put it a little off center. I's aiming for a liver shot."

Holt rolled to his belly and tried to stand.

"Looks like he's fixing to run off, Clarence," the woman said.

"He ain't going nowhere."

Holt heard but didn't see the man eject the first cartridge. Just as he had almost managed to will himself to his feet, the second shot hit the back of his knee, and he went down like a busted chair. He rolled over and over around the gravels, clutching at his thigh above the shot, spilling blood as he went, keening like dog.

"That oughta do it," the man with the sack said.

"You gonna get that pig out?" the woman asked him.

"I am."

Holt rolled to his back, gnashing his teeth, his still good leg kicking at the air. The man in the Cummins diesel shirt lifted his sack and turned it over. A small dead hog spilled out and flopped on the ground a few feet from Holt. The hog's eyes were blank and open. Its pink tongue stuck slightly out of its mouth, and it smelled ripe.

The two men and the woman looked at the scene in front of them. The pig carcass and Holt lying in the driveway. Blood all over. The big one bent over, picked up the shell casing, and put it in his pocket. Once he had, they seemed satisfied and started to walk away. About thirty yards out they stopped and turned to look. The sun was high in the sky, but it wasn't as warm as it had been lately. Holt's vision was beginning to get a little spotty, but he could see them. He shouted at them, his voice breaking, "Why you doing this to me? I ain't hurt you."

The Cummins diesel boy said, "No, but you done Pot Roast something awful. And you hurt Darron. And you need killing."

Holt howled and carried on, swearing on his mother that it wasn't him, but the three were unmoved. They didn't respond to anything. He pled and he begged all to no end. Blood continued to pool around him and the inert little pig.

Listless, whimpering, barely able to lift his head, he finally landed on a question that provoked a reply. "Y'all just gonna stand there and watch me die?" Shadows had begun to pass across Holt's form.

The woman gazed into the sky. "Naw," she said. "We was just waiting on the birds to come."

ACKNOWLEDGMENTS

F IRST, AS ALWAYS, Valetta, Barrett, and Grady. Without you all, what's the point?

My agent, Alice Speilburg, is quite simply, the greatest. Thank you for believing in me and advising me so well at every turn. Sara J. Henry, my editor—the exact same status. Thanks to the whole team at Crooked Lane Books: Dulce Botello, Mikaela Bender, Mia Bertrand, Megan Matti, Stephanie Manova, Rebecca Nelson, Thaisheemarie Fantauzzi Pérez, Doug White, and Matthew Martz. What a pleasure to work with you all. Also thank you to my copyeditor, Jill Pellarin, who worked so hard.

I owe an immense debt to a whole lot of people who read drafts at various stages. I hope I don't forget anyone. Robert Gipe and Leah Hampton persuaded me this book was worth keeping at a time when I was faltering. Denton Loving, Elizabeth Glass, and Mark Westmoreland offered endless counsel and support. Jake Reed and Nate Coppage once again helped me with technical questions and solutions. Felecia Johnson, Kara Fairfield, and Noah Alvarez also provided invaluable feedback. The last person who helped me tune it up before publication was SA Cosby. That meant a lot. Scott Blackburn also chipped in with frequent guidance about the process.

My big sister and big brother, Dr. April Gago and Dr. Shannon Browne, answered my many medical questions. I love you guys regardless of your help, but also thanks.

Thank you to Walter M. Robinson and EastOverArt. I wrote a big chunk of this book there in a short time. Your generosity and hospitality were amazing.

While I was writing and revising this book, two people passed who meant a lot to me. Ed McClanahan and Tony Pham were both great friends and also wonderful human beings. I think of you often, and I miss you both.

We also lost John Prine. Even in absence, a role model, an inspiration, a light in the world.

And thank you for reading this book. It means more than you know.